MURMUR IN THE MUD CAVES

CHAPARRAL HEARTS ~ BOOK 4

KATHLEEN DENLY

WILD HEART
BOOKS

For my two eldest sons, Quintin and Ethan,
who sacrificed their own desires to help me in my hour of need.

Greater love hath no man than this, that a man lay down his life for his friends.

John 15:13 KJV

ACKNOWLEDGMENTS

In the middle of drafting this novel, I suffered injuries that prevented my use of the computer. I spent seven weeks essentially bedridden and as of this writing (more than two months since the pain began) I am still severely limited in my ability to use a computer. I would not have been able to complete this story in anything resembling a timely manner, were it not for the selfless assistance of my two eldest sons. They sacrificed hours and days of their summer vacation to transcribe my dictation and manage my urgent emails. This allowed me to communicate my situation with my publisher and complete this manuscript. In fact, my fourteen-year-old, Quintin, is typing this for me. I will be forever grateful for their kindness.

I am also grateful for and humbled by the understanding and encouragement of Misty Beller, owner of Wild Heart Books, my publisher.

You are most likely holding this book due, at least in part, to the beautiful cover designed by Carpe Librum Book Design. Working with Carpe Librum after submitting each new manuscript is something I look forward to.

I am grateful for the editing skills of Denise Weimer which helped put the polishing touches on this story.

As always, I could not include the historical details woven throughout my stories without the kind and dedicated efforts of local historians such as Larry and Arvilla Johnson, Ella McCain, and Cherry S. Diefenbach.

I would be unforgivably remiss if I did not mention the

heroic efforts of Karen Bousselot, Denise Colby, Holly Bleggi, Cara Grandle, and my mother, Lori Carlson to beta read this manuscript in an incredibly short time. You are all rock stars!

Last, (but so far from least) I must express my eternal gratitude for the patience, love, and sacrifice of both my husband and Jesus Christ my Lord.

CHAPTER 1

*B*ridget "Biddie" Davidson's future might hinge on this next bite. The tick-tock of the mantel clock in Mr. Green's office seemed loud in the near silence of his elegant home. She held her breath as he took his first taste of her *mille-feuille.* The ingredients for the complicated pastry had cost her two weeks of pin money, and preparing it had taken the majority of her day after a week filled with the frenetic baking of each of her best dishes. Yet it would all be worth it if Mr. Green agreed to invest in her bakery. Well, not *her* bakery, exactly. Not at first.

If, after sampling the half-dozen baked dishes Biddie had prepared for him, Mr. Green believed her talent worthy of investment, he would purchase and remodel the newly vacant building on the corner of Eastwood and Bradbury. He'd even provide funds to purchase the supplies she would need to get started. She would then run the bakery in exchange for twenty

1

percent of its profits until she'd saved enough to purchase the business from him.

Mr. Green took another bite, his expression inscrutable.

Biddie swallowed down the urge to jump with excitement. *This is it, Mama. I can feel it.* Mama would be so proud of her. So would Mother and Father.

From the first, her adoptive parents had encouraged Biddie to follow in Mama's footsteps as a baker. They'd even offered to purchase the building she needed to start her bakery, but Biddie had declined their generous offer.

Any money spent on her would take away from the good works they did through the Davidson Home for Women and Children, which desperately needed expansion to accommodate more of the city's vulnerable citizens. After nearly a year of fundraising and saving, her parents almost had enough to move forward with the project. In three months, they were due to receive the remainder of the needed funds, thanks to an investment they'd made in Mr. Green's latest venture. Purchasing the building for Biddie's bakery would have meant delaying The Home's expansion. She was determined to find a better way.

Her parents had sacrificed enough for her. This bakery was her only hope of beginning to repay them.

Mr. Green set his fork on the plate and reached for his tea. Sipping, he eyed her over the rim of his cup.

She returned his calm, dark gaze. What was he thinking? Golden afternoon sunlight added an almost angelic glow to the thick brown curls crowning his head. The clock on the mantel of his study ticked loudly in the silence. She held her spine straight, chin level, ignoring the urge to fidget.

With his free hand, he gestured to the half-eaten desserts littering his desk. "You made all this yourself?"

"Yes, sir."

"Tell me again how you gained such skill."

"Mama was a baker."

"Mrs. Davidson? I was unaware—"

"No." Realizing a moment too late that she'd interrupted him, she cringed but plowed ahead. "My, um, first mother. The woman who gave me life. The Davidsons are my adopted parents. I call them Mother and Father. We refer to my first mother as Mama." Biddie was careful to keep her smile in place though her stomach quavered. She had thought he knew of her family status. Most people who knew her family seemed to be aware that Henry and Cecilia had adopted her. She nibbled her lower lip. It was always complicated and awkward explaining why she had two mothers. And she never knew how a person might react to such news. Most seemed accepting, but a few...

"I see." Mr. Green nodded and set aside his tea. "That explains the lack of resemblance between you and the Davidsons."

Biddie nodded, unsure what else to say. With her pale blond hair and blue eyes, Biddie had Mother's coloring but not her striking beauty, nor her inherent grace. Biddie could, perhaps, claim some of Father's intelligence and entrepreneurial instincts, thanks to his careful tutelage. Though that was not something that could be seen with the eyes.

Mr. Green appraised her from head to toe, his eyes narrowed. "Who *were* your parents?"

Oh no. Perhaps she ought to have kept her adoption to herself. What if he were among those who still believed children shared in the shame for the sins of their parents? People like Mrs. Prichard who'd called her a wastrel. Suppressing a shiver, she shut the memory away and firmed her chin. Even if Mr. Green held such beliefs, he'd have found out the truth eventually. Better to know now where he stood.

Please, God, don't let him turn me down over something I can't change.

3

Mr. Green's brow lifted. Oh dear, she'd been silent too long. But how could she answer his question without revealing the full truth of her past? *Stick to what matters.* "Well..." She licked her lips. "As I said, Mama was a baker. In fact, my ancestors have been bakers for generations—first in England, then in America. When Mama passed on, our family recipe book was left to me." Biddie withdrew the precious, leather-bound book from the bag at her feet and clutched it to her chest. "I've studied these pages for as long as I can remember."

"May I?" He held his hand out for the heirloom.

Though grateful that her family's legacy seemed to have distracted him from her omission of the man who'd sired her, Biddie still had to force herself to relinquish Mama's dearest treasure.

Mr. Green leafed through the pages, pausing occasionally to examine a recipe more closely.

She cleared her throat. "Before I could walk, Mama gave me a bowl of dough and taught me to knead it. As a child, I sat beneath her work table and learned what it took to be a great baker. I've been improving my skills ever since." She leaned forward, a fire burning in her chest. "If you give me a chance, I will not disappoint you."

He returned her book and reclined in his chair, drumming the tips of his fingers against its leather arm. "There is more to running a successful bakery than creating delicious food. It's a business that requires careful accounting and excellent customer service that makes people eager to return."

"Father is renowned for his business instincts and has taught me well, I assure you."

"Yes, he wrote you quite the glowing letter of recommendation." Mr. Green popped the last of a half-eaten scone into his mouth, chewed, and swallowed before continuing. "It was his letter that convinced me to give you this meeting. There aren't many women truly prepared to run their own business, but when Henry Davidson says he'll stake his reputation on something, wise people listen."

Biddie smiled, recalling the contents of the letter Mr. Green referred to. Father had been hesitant to write the endorsement, not understanding her desire to do this on her own. Only after she remained adamant that she wished to accomplish this dream without his financial aid did he finally write the letter. When he'd shown her the words expressing his unhesitating confidence in her abilities, tears of joy had leaked from her eyes.

She held Mr. Green's gaze. "Then you know I have the knowledge, the skills, and the talent to make this bakery an incredible success that will soon repay your investment many times over."

"That may be true, but you are still rather young to be running your own business—still of a marriageable age. What happens when some young man comes along and sweeps you off your feet? Most men want their wife at home, not gone at all hours, running her own business."

Biddie resisted the urge to huff. At least Mr. Green hadn't told her that women ought not tax their delicate minds on business matters. Father had been right in his assessment of Mr. Green's progressive views. "I am twenty-three, sir. Well old enough to know my own mind. What's more, there have been men who declared their interest in me, yet here I am." She waved her hand to encompass the study. "As you see, none have deterred me from my goal." It did not matter that those would-be suitors had given up their pursuit upon learning that Father—with her blessing—intended to leave the bulk of his wealth to his charity home rather than bestow it upon his two children. "Any man who loves me will encourage my dreams, not prevent me from fulfilling them. I assure you, married or single, I will forever be committed to this endeavor."

"You say that now, but you may change your mind if the right man comes along."

She gritted her teeth. "I assure you, I will not." She lifted the recipe book. "Baking is in my blood, in my soul. It's who I am. I cannot—will not—forsake my dreams for any man."

A smile parted Mr. Green's lips, and he stood, offering her his hand. "Very well. I will invest in your bakery."

She surged to her feet and accepted his shake with a grin. "Thank you, sir. You'll not regret it."

"Good." He stepped around the desk, coming to stand before her. "However, you will need to be patient. I've made several investments recently that tied up my ready cash. It may take some time to free up the funds necessary to get started."

"I understand but..." She hesitated to press him when he'd just agreed to help her, but couldn't withhold her concern. "What if the building sells before—"

He patted her shoulder. "Oh, don't worry about that." He stooped to retrieve her bag, then offered it to her. "I've already spoken with the owner, and he's agreed to sell only to me."

Relief flooded her as she slid the bag onto her shoulder and he steered her toward the door. "That was wise." She stepped through the threshold and turned in the hall to face him. "When should I expect to hear from you?"

"Hmm?" Studying the watch in his hand, Mr. Green appeared to have already dismissed her.

The butler appeared at her side, handing his employer an envelope. "Pardon me, sir. This came for you by courier." The servant turned, obviously prepared to escort her to the door.

She held her ground and rephrased her question. "Do you have some idea of when the funds should be available? Or how long the renovations will take?" She'd estimated they'd take about six weeks, but perhaps he had connections that could accomplish the work sooner. Imagine—two months from now, she could be standing in her own bakery. "I'll want to time my orders for the necessary equipment and ingredients so that they're delivered as soon as the renovations are completed."

Mr. Green opened the letter, his eyes on the missive as he spoke. "Oh, of course. Well, never mind about that for now. There's still plenty of time to figure that out." He reached for the knob, clearly intending to close the study door.

She smothered a niggle of irritation. "Yes, but how much time?"

"Not long, I assure you. Two, three..." He swung the door closed, his last words barely reaching her as the latch clicked shut. "Four months, at most."

∼

JUNE 11, 1873
ARIZONA TERRITORY

*G*ideon Swift reined his horse to a stop at the crest of the hill and squinted against the heat waves rippling across the wide, dusty desert below. Was that a stagecoach stopped on the road ahead? He angled his hat to shade his eyes from the bright June sun and made out two men standing beside the idle coach—one pudgy, the other skinny as a string bean. A third man knelt in front of them. Luggage lay open on the ground.

Gideon stiffened. A holdup? He reached for the Henry repeating rifle in his saddle holster. A blurry line, curled like the letter *C*, appeared in the right side of Gideon's vision. He paused, clenching his jaw. *Not now.* He almost asked God to hold off the episode. Then he remembered God wasn't listening to him anymore.

Sweat dripped from Gideon's brow, blurring his vision further. He dipped his head and wiped his eyelids across his dusty shoulder. Another hard blink restored his sight. Except for that *C*.

The man who'd been on his knees now stood, gesturing wildly to the nearest wheel.

Gideon followed his motion. Sand. The coach's front wheel was stuck in deep sand.

He took one more survey of the desert spread out before him. Several Joshua trees dotted a landscape littered with mesquite, yucca plants, desert grasses, and a variety of cacti. Bandits or Indians could be hiding behind a trunk or thick clump of bush, but Gideon saw no sign of them. He left the rifle in its holster and nudged his horse down the slope.

When he was near enough for the men to hear the clatter of his many canteens dangling from both sides of the saddle', they spun, guns in hand.

Gideon reined to a stop once more, careful to keep his motions slow and his hands far from the Remington army revolver at his waist. A glance through the windows confirmed his hunch that the coach was empty. He focused on the three-armed men. "I mean no harm. Noticed your coach was stuck. Thought you could use some help."

The men holstered their weapons, and the one who'd been kneeling in the sand turned to the others. "You see?" He jerked his thumb toward Gideon. "That there's a real man who ain't afraid of a bit of hard work."

"Now see here. You're the driver. Digging us out is your job." The large-bellied man twisted the ends of a long blond mustache. "Seems to me, you're the one shy of hard work."

The skinny older man nodded his head vigorously. "Just like when you made us roll them rocks from the road. It ain't right. We're paying customers."

The driver whipped the hat off his head and beat it against his thigh. "Them felled rocks was blockin' the road. If'n I'd done it all myself, we'd of been a whole day behind schedule."

"You call this a road?" Pudgy scoffed. "Like those hovels you've called stations? If the next one isn't better—"

"You got a shovel?" Gideon slid from his horse. He could see the tool lying in the sand near the wheel, but these men needed a distraction before they pulled their weapons again. This time on each other.

The driver's mouth worked and his face turned several shades of red as his gaze bounced between Gideon and the two passengers. Finally, he clamped his mouth shut and plopped his hat back on his head. He retrieved the short shovel and tossed it at Gideon.

Gideon caught the tool and set to work.

A moment later, the driver joined him with a second shovel. Together, they dug a good-sized hole around the wheel and tamped down the sand in front as best they could. All while the passengers sipped water from canteens and lounged in the shade of a nearby scrub oak.

The driver took four boards from the coach and handed them to Gideon.

String Bean turned his canteen upside down, letting what appeared to be his last drops of water trickle into the parched earth. "You almost finished?" His nasally voice stretched each word like worn out strings on a fiddle.

Gideon's pulse beat against his right temple. He ignored the warning along with the whining passenger and set the wood in front of the wheels.

The driver climbed onto his seat and urged the mules gently forward.

As soon as the wheels were on the planks, Pudgy strode toward the door. "About time."

"Not yet." Gideon reached for the man's wrist and missed. He silently cursed his worsening vision and tried again, this time catching Pudgy's upper arm.

The man flushed. "Who do you think you are? Unhand

me." He jerked his arm free.

Gideon moved to stand between the man and the stage. "If you board now, it'll sink again as soon as it comes off the boards."

Pudgy glared at Gideon. "Are you insinuating it's *my* fault the stage was stuck?"

Gideon suspected the man's added weight *had* been a contributing factor but chose to voice a kinder truth. "*Any* extra weight in the coach while it crossed this stretch of deep sand was liable to sink it. It's safest if we all walk until the ground is firm." Gideon had no plans to board the stage at all but knew from previous experience that including himself in the suggestion somehow made it more palatable for men like these.

"How long is that?" String Bean crossed his arms.

The driver looked down from his perch. "Ain't but another quarter mile or so. Just past there." He pointed to a large shrub in the distance.

Well, Gideon assumed the vaguely round object was a bush. He'd reached the stage where he could no longer make out details. He took a long, deep breath in a vain attempt to settle his stomach.

The driver clicked his team into motion, and the coach eased off the wood, continuing on through the deep sand.

Every sound was like the clang of church bells in Gideon's ears, but he kept his expression calm.

The two complainers hefted their personal belongings with an abundance of grumbling and set off after the departing stage.

Gideon let his eyes fall shut, savoring the growing quiet. Only for a few seconds. Then he forced his eyes open again and gathered the planks. His stomach churned with each bend to retrieve a board, slowing his efforts. The throbbing at his temple spread across his skull, beating like a blacksmith's hammer. By the time he'd secured the awkward load to his horse, the two men had almost reached the coach which waited beside the large shrub.

It took Gideon two tries to place a foot in the stirrup. Then a surge of pain in his head stopped him from mounting. His eyes slammed shut. Balanced on one foot, he leaned his forehead against the saddle. The searing heat of leather baked by the sun made him jerk back, losing his balance. He fell hard on his backside.

A shout came from the direction of the stage.

Just great. Gideon couldn't make out the words but could tell from the tone that the driver had seen him fall and was worried. With his eyes still pressed closed against the pain and nausea, Gideon lifted his hand in a gesture meant to reassure the man.

Gideon took another breath. Then he pried one eye open to peer at the coach. Still there. He let his eye close again and summoned his last bit of energy to force himself back onto his feet. With his eyes still closed—something he fervently hoped the driver couldn't discern from this distance—he clutched at his horse's saddle and waved as vigorously as he dared for the coach to continue. He'd deliver the boards to the next stage stop. When he could ride again.

Another surge of his stomach broke Gideon's control. The little he'd eaten as he rode that afternoon came spilling back out to cover the sand beside him. When his stomach was empty, he took another peek at where the coach had been.

It was gone.

Good. Gideon let his legs collapse and fell back against the sand. He shoved his hat over the top part of his face and tugged his bandanna up to cover his neck and chin but left his mouth clear to breathe. Just a little nap. That was all he needed. Then he'd continue on to California and the job waiting for him.

~

*B*iddie climbed the stairs to the front door of the Davidson Home for Women and Children and let herself inside. The chatter of children and motherly voices merged with the clatter of running shoes and the scrape of chair legs across a wooden floor. Despite the cacophony, no one else occupied the entry and hallway. For the moment, she was alone, and she took the opportunity to lean back against the door, close her eyes, and just breathe. Despite Mr. Green's apparent lack of urgency to complete her bakery, he *had* agreed to complete it. She would not allow the sin of impatience to steal the joy of that triumph from her.

Thank you, Lord.

She opened her eyes with a grin. Now to share the wonderful news with Mother and Father. She pushed off the door and started down the hall, toward the stairs.

Mother was in her upstairs sitting room. She sat in one of the four chairs flanking the embroidered fireplace screen that hid the empty fireplace. The furniture in this private room—reserved only for their family and personal guests—was finer and more ornate than the pieces chosen for most other rooms of the large charity home. When Biddie was young, Mother had decorated the shared downstairs sitting room with equally fine furniture, but the delicate pieces didn't last long. Since then, sturdier furniture had been chosen for the rooms where the charity's many children would spend their time.

Afternoon sunlight streamed through the two windows that filled the wall opposite the fireplace, adding a soft glow to Mother's golden hair. She looked up from her needlework at Biddie's entrance. "Oh, you're back. I was just praying about your meeting. How did it go?"

Biddie hesitated. "Where's Father? I'd like to tell you both together, if I may."

"Of course. He's gone to meet Lucy, but they should be home soon."

Biddie took a seat across from Mother, her shoulders sagging. Then she straightened. If she had to wait, at least she'd be able to share the good news with her best friend at the same time. "Wait, today is Friday." Biddie frowned at Mother. "Is something wrong? Why isn't Lucy working?"

When she was young, Lucy had lived in the charity home with her mother. Back then, Biddie and Lucy shared secrets every night after classes. But after Lucy's mother fell back into her opium addiction and was evicted from the charity home, Lucy chose to find room and board with her employers. She worked six and a half days as a maid in Mr. Green's hotel, sending most of her earnings to her mother's landlord. Every Sunday, Lucy spent the first part of her half day off trying to convince her mother to give up the opium. The rest she spent at the charity home with Biddie.

Mother shrugged. "I don't know what happened, just that a note arrived an hour ago and your father left to meet Lucy at her mother's apartment. I made him promise to bring Lucy back here unless she was needed by her employer."

"Then she may not return with him." In that case, Biddie would have to wait two more days to share her big news with her friend.

What had happened that Lucy wasn't at work today? Hopefully, she hadn't lost her position. Although, Biddie couldn't imagine the prim and proper Lucy doing anything to warrant a dismissal. No one who knew the quiet brunette would ever guess her mother was an opium-addicted prostitute. No, it was more likely that something had happened to Lucy's mother.

Biddie closed her eyes and said a quick prayer for the health and safety of Father, Lucy, and her mother.

A shout outside drew Biddie's attention to the window. In

the busy street, a pair of brown horses shook their heads as the driver stood in his wagon yelling at someone she couldn't see.

Behind her, Mother muttered. "Ah, here is our invitation to Dianna's Summer's End Ball. Yet still, we have not received an invitation to The Society's afternoon tea fundraiser."

Biddie faced Mother and found her sorting the day's mail. Biddie's throat thickened. The Ladies' Protection and Relief Society was a charity run by the wealthiest and most influential women of San Francisco. Before meeting Biddie and Mama, Mother had been the second most influential woman in the city and in line to take over running the organization. Adopting Biddie had ruined all of that.

But she had a plan.

Before her death, Mama'd been winning the hearts of this city's elite through her baking. Mr. Green's investment and Mama's recipe book would give Biddie a chance to do the same and restore Mother's standing. "Isn't that event next week?"

"Yes, and I begin to fear we will not receive one at all. There was a time such a notion was inconceivable. However, that was many years ago, and I've been much too busy of late to be as involved in the Society's affairs as perhaps I should be. The new president is rather close with Irene Prichard, or so I've heard. No doubt, if we do not receive an invitation, it will be due to that woman's influence."

Biddie clasped her hands together. "Surely, the other ladies won't allow you to be excluded."

"Hmm." Mother's lips pressed together. "We shall see, won't we?"

Biddie didn't like the lack of confidence in Mother's tone, and there was a sorrow in her eyes. The same sorrow Biddie had seen there all her life whenever San Francisco's elite were discussed.

"Oh! I almost forgot." Mother's voice interrupted Biddie's

melancholy thoughts. "You received two letters today." She lifted a stack of envelopes from the small table beside her chair.

"Two?" Biddie accepted the letters, moved to a seat across from Mother, and checked the handwriting on the cover. One she recognized as being written by her younger brother, Charlie, who'd left last month with her cousin Eliza's family to visit their other cousins in Massachusetts. The other handwriting, she didn't recognize. She opened that one first.

Lupine Valley Ranch
Campo, California
May 19, 1873

Biddie,
There's ben a fire and Oliver is dead. I need supplies and sum money to get the ranch up and runing again. Not a lot. Just enuff for a few breeding cows and the things I need to keep them safe and fed. I aint asking for a handout, just a loan. I will pay back every penny plus whatever intrest you think is fare. I woodnt ask if there wer any other way. Please respond quickly so I can make plans.
Your sister,
Virginia Baker

Biddie reread the name at the bottom, and her fingers began to shake. "Ginny," she whispered.

"Biddie?" Mother's voice sounded as though she stood at the other end of the block. "What is it, dear? You've gone white as a ghost."

Biddie blinked hard, willing her frozen mind to conjure words. "It's Ginny. She says Pa is dead." The thought of his passing left Biddie numb. She read the letter again. "But Ginny's alive and she needs my help." Clutching the paper, she caught Mother's eyes. "We have to help her. Please say we can help her."

A small voice inside shouted that she was being greedy. Any money they loaned Ginny would come from their personal donation to the expansion fund. Hadn't her parents given her enough? But Biddie shoved the voice down. This wasn't for her. This was for Ginny, the big sister who'd protected her on the horrible night that had echoed in her nightmares for years.

Mother moved to the seat beside Biddie and placed a hand to her shoulder. "Calm down, dear. You're not making any sense. Who is this Ginny and what does she need?"

Wonder lifted Biddie's chest as the truth filled her. "She's my sister."

Tears welled up and spilled down her cheeks with the miracle of it. After all these years of wondering what had become of her brother and sister after Pa had stolen them away in the middle of the night when Biddie was just four years old, she finally had an answer. A partial one, at least.

Mother gasped. "You mean, Virginia? She's written to you? But how? What does she say?" She gently tugged at the letter, and Biddie released it. Mother quickly read the brief message. "So Oliver's dead." She lifted her gaze to Biddie's. "I'm so sorry, dear."

Biddie swallowed the sudden lump in her throat. She had only one clear memory of Pa and it wasn't a pleasant one. Adding that he'd taken her siblings and abandoned Biddie and her mother had removed any desire to ever see him again. Or so she'd thought. But now that the possibility no longer existed, she found a small ache in her chest, mourning the loss of what might have been. There would be no healing of their relationship this side of heaven.

More tears spilled, though of a different kind this time.

Mother offered her handkerchief, and Biddie used it to blot her face.

Mother examined the letter again. "This says Virginia's in California. But it doesn't say anything about your brother. Do you suppose he's on this ranch with her?"

She shrugged. "I have no idea."

Mother gave a rueful smile. "No, of course you don't. Silly question."

Lucy entered in her well-worn brown day dress with Father behind her, his curly brown hair mussed by the wind. "My goodness, what's wrong?" She hurried to Biddie's side, concern etched in her expression.

Father looked at Mother. "What's happened?"

Mother passed the letter to him. "Virginia Baker has written."

Lucy gasped and wrapped an arm around Biddie's shoulders. "Your big sister?"

Biddie nodded, immediately soothed by the presence of those dearest to her.

Lucy's brow furrowed. "But that's good news, isn't it? Why are you crying?"

Mother answered for her. "Oliver has passed away."

"Oh." Lucy looked from Mother to Biddie, clearly still confused. And no wonder. As girls, she and Biddie had bonded over their equally horrible pas and their contentedness never to see them again. They'd both agreed Henry Davidson was the only father figure they needed in their lives.

Yet here Biddie was crying over the news of Pa's death. It made no sense. She wiped the tears away and forced herself to calm.

"Campo..." Father adjusted his glasses. "That's that new settlement down by San Diego. The one they're calling Little Texas. Not much of a town yet. The Gaskill brothers have a blacksmith shop and a store that doubles as a post office. Other than a bunch of homesteads, that's about all there is, as I recall."

Mother nodded and returned to her usual *Bergère* chair. "I knew it sounded familiar. Can you believe she's in California? It could have been so much farther."

A meaningful look passed between Mother and Father.

"That will make things easier." He handed the letter back to Biddie, then took the blue wingback chair beside Mother.

Biddie straightened. "Then you'll help her?"

Mother's eyes widened. "Well, of course. She's your sister."

"And beside that,"—Father covered Mother's hand with his —"we promised Poppy."

They'd made a promise to Mama?

"That's right." Mother turned her hand over to twine her fingers with Father's. "We promised your mama that if your siblings ever returned or ever needed anything, we'd do whatever we could to help them."

Biddie sagged against her chair. "Thank you."

Father ran the fingers of his free hand through his gray-speckled brown curls. "Of course, I'll need to verify this letter is actually from your sister before I can send any funds."

Lucy gave Biddie a quick squeeze before moving to the seat beside her. "How will you do that?"

"It's too bad Richard and Daniel are both back east." Father looked at Mother. "They're so well connected in the San Diego region, it would have been easy for them to ask around."

Mother tipped her head. "What about Mr. Thompson? He knows just about everyone in that county, doesn't he?"

Father chuckled. "He'd like to think so, but it's a pretty big county. He can't possibly know everyone. Still, he'd be a good person to ask." He nodded. "I'll send him a letter first thing in the morning."

Biddie shot to her feet. "But sending letters will take weeks! Ginny needs help now."

Mother's expression softened. "Now, I know you're worried,

but it would be irresponsible of your father to send the money without looking into things first."

She lifted the now crumpled paper. "But I know this is Ginny." She could *feel* it, deep inside.

Father cleared his throat. "Even so, I—"

"I want to go." The words were out before she even realized she'd made the decision. Yet they were true. "I want to see her."

Mother smirked at Father. "You see?"

Father sighed. "Yes, you were right."

Biddie clasped her hands together, squeezing her fingers. "Right about what?"

Father turned to smile at her. "Your mother predicted you'd want to visit your brother and sister if they ever contacted you." He patted Mother's hand. "And as usual, she was right."

Mother pressed a quick kiss to Father's cheek.

Biddie studied their expressions. She could sense worry beneath their smiles. But they *were* smiling. "Does that mean I can go?"

Father sighed. "Yes, but I'm coming with you."

Lucy hugged herself. "And me?"

Biddie's mouth fell open at her shy friend's uncharacteristically bold request. "Yes." She bounced on her toes. "Please, may Lucy come?" Seeing her sister for the first time in almost twenty years would be far less daunting with her parents *and* her best friend at her side.

Mother frowned. "What about your position?"

Biddie stilled. In all the excitement, she'd forgotten about Lucy's job as a maid. "Oh, right. What *are* you doing here on a Friday?"

Lucy's cheeks pinked, and her gaze dropped to the floor. "I um...lost my position today."

"What? Why?"

Lucy shook her head, still not meeting anyone's gaze. "I'd

rather not talk about it, if that's all right." She peeked at Biddie. "I just thought but maybe..."

Biddie tipped her head. "What?"

"Maybe there's something of God's hand in the timing?" She shook her head. "But that's silly. I just—"

"No, it isn't silly." Biddie grasped Lucy's hand in a firm squeeze. "That's exactly right. Because now you're free to come with me." She turned back to Mother and Father. "She can come, can't she?"

Mother nodded. "I agree. This does seem to be God's timing, because I'm afraid I can't go with you."

"Why not?" Biddie pressed a hand against her middle, the yo-yo of emotions leaving her unsettled.

"Well, with everyone else gone, who will watch over things here at The Home?"

Of course. Ordinarily, her parents timed their trips so that her cousins Eliza and Daniel Clarke were around to make sure things at The Home ran smoothly. But the Clarkes wouldn't return from the east for another month.

And Father rarely traveled without Mother. Biddie bit her lip and looked at him. "But you'll still come'?"

Father's eyebrows rose. "You think I'd let you go without me?"

She smiled. Of course he wouldn't. Pa may not have cared two bits for her, but Father would sacrifice his last shirt to keep her warm and safe. In fact, once, he'd done just that. Which was why Mr. Green's agreement to invest in her bakery was so important. It was past time she stopped taking from her parents and started repaying everything she owed them.

Should she speak with Mr. Green before departing? How soon would he be ready to order supplies? Would this trip to see her sister cause a delay? Surely not. Hadn't he mentioned it would take a month or longer? That was plenty of time to travel and return again without jeopardizing the plan. Wasn't it?

CHAPTER 2

A coyote's howl stirred Gideon from sleep.

Another howl brought his eyes open. The critter was close.

And he wasn't alone.

Gideon sat up and searched the darkened desert for signs of the pack scuffing the dirt. The near-pitch-black of a moonless night made it almost impossible to see anything. The movement of deeper blotches of black against more black was all he could make out.

He reached for the hat that had fallen off sometime in his sleep and plopped it on his head. Judging by the tightness of the skin on his face, it'd fallen off while the sun was still up. He had a sunburn, for sure. But right now he had bigger problems.

Sensing eyes on him, he drew his revolver. Most likely, the pack had thought him dead before he sat up. Now they were out there, watching. Waiting.

Gideon surged to his feet with a mighty roar and fired into the air above where the sounds had come from.

Pebbles scattered and twigs broke as the frightened pack sprinted away from the unexpected threat.

He holstered his weapon. Behind him, Legend nickered. Thankfully, the bay gelding had been a warhorse. Steady and true, he was unaffected by the sounds of battle.

Unlike Gideon's heart.

Despite the nine years that had passed since his medical discharge from the Union Army, Gideon's heart still pounded against his ribs like a rabbit trying to break free each time he fired his Remington revolver. He sucked in a breath and stroked Legend's neck. The horse nickered again and nudged his big head against Gideon's shoulder. Poor boy was probably thirsty.

How long had Gideon been asleep? He searched the sky for the North Star and then the Big Dipper. A quick calculation told him it was about one in the morning. He was still too close to Apache territory to risk lighting a fire in the dark. Instead, he ran his hand along the gelding's side until he found his saddle-bags. He pulled out a big tin and set it on the ground. Then he untied one of his canteens and filled the bowl.

Legend didn't wait for an invitation and drank greedily.

Gideon watered his own dry throat and munched on a bit of hardtack and jerky. It was far from a pleasant meal, but it filled his belly without need of a fire.

What now? The pain in his head was gone, and he felt rested. So his vision was probably fine, although the stars didn't provide enough light to tell for sure. In any case, it was much too dark to travel safely. He looked over what he could make out of his surroundings and used his memory from the previous afternoon to fill in what he couldn't see. He stood in a clearing roughly ten feet wide and filled with the deep sand of the wash that ran through it. The sand had made for a decent bed, and the coyotes weren't likely to return now that they knew he was alive and not the free meal they'd assumed. Still, he didn't relish the idea of bedding down again where the critters had found him. Besides, he wasn't really that tired.

He touched a hand to his cheek. Tight and hot to the touch,

as he'd expected. He found the jar of burn lotion and applied it over his scorched skin and chapped lips. The cool cream soothed his skin, but the desire to keep moving remained. He'd been on the road for weeks, and the appeal of sleeping beneath beautiful stars had long been outweighed by the discomfort of laying on rocky ground after long, hot days in the saddle. The moment he'd received Oliver Baker's letter agreeing to hire Gideon as a cook for his *vaqueros*, Gideon had packed up and hit the trail. With Pa and Ma both in the grave and the ranch auctioned off, thanks to Gideon, there'd been no reason to stay in Montague, Texas. He only hoped he'd made the right decision and wasn't bringing danger to Lupine Valley Ranch.

June 11, 1873
Eastern San Diego County, California

*B*iddie adjusted her grip on the hard bench as the freight wagon creaked and rattled its way up the steep grade. It seemed to her, the rough dirt road that had been carved into the mountains east of San Diego could have been a bit wider. Her breath caught as the driver guided his four mules around a small pile of fallen rocks, moving them even closer to the sharp descent on their right.

Lucy, who sat between Biddie and the driver, leaned forward and craned her neck to see around Biddie. Her eyes lit with admiration as she took in the view of the valley stretched out below.

Knuckles aching, Biddie didn't dare look down and kept her attention on her pretty friend. "I'm glad you're enjoying the trip."

Lucy offered a small smile and nodded. "Thank you for allowing me to come."

Father spoke from his spot in the wagon bed. "We're glad to have you. You've already been a blessing to Biddie."

It was true. Having Lucy share her stateroom aboard the steamer had given Biddie someone to talk to rather than spend her nights worrying about Ginny's reaction to Biddie's arrival. Would her sister welcome her or—?

The sharp lurch of the wagon's front right wheel slipping off the side of the road jarred Biddie from her thoughts. A scream lodged in her throat as the vehicle tilted toward the sharp drop. She scrambled from the edge, pressing into Lucy's side.

The driver pulled on the reins, and everything came to a halt. "Sorry 'bout that, ladies. Suppose I got a mite distracted." He hopped to the ground. "I'll have her back on the road in a blink." He walked around the front of the wagon and stepped off the road onto the steep slope.

Biddie nudged Lucy's shoulder. "Let's get off until we're back on the road."

Lucy slid across the bench and climbed off the same side the driver had.

Biddie was right behind her, and Father hopped off the back of the wagon.

The driver let loose a few words Mother wouldn't approve of. "Wheel's stuck in the rocks."

Father joined him at the front of the wagon. "I'll help you get it free, but I'd appreciate if you refrained from using that sort of language in the presence of ladies."

The driver's face flushed as his gaze shot to Biddie and Lucy. "My apologies. I'm not used to having womenfolk on these trips."

"You're forgiven," Biddie assured him before moving as close as she dared to Father and lowering her voice. "Are you sure you want to help? That slope's terribly steep and slippery."

"I'll be careful." He patted her shoulder. "You and Lucy wait over there." He pointed to the opposite side of the road where a large manzanita provided a bit of shade.

Biddie tugged two canteens from the wagon before joining Lucy beside the red-barked tree. Father and the driver set to work digging out the nest of rocks the wheel had sunk into. As they moved, trickles of gravel trailed down the precipitous incline. Biddie shivered and looked away.

Lucy's big brown eyes watched her. "Are you nervous?"

"Of course. Didn't you see how many boulders there are on the cliff?"

"It's not a cliff."

"It nearly is."

Lucy rolled her eyes. "In any case, that's not what I meant."

"Then what did you mean?"

"You'll be reunited with your big sister by nightfall. Have you figured out what you're going to say?"

Biddie's stomach flipped. "Honestly, I spent so much time trying to figure out the right words while we were on the ship... I've given up and placed it in the Lord's hands. Hopefully, He'll give me the right words when the time comes."

Father shouted, "Look out!"

Biddie spun in time to see the wagon's wheel roll over the driver's hand.

The man screamed.

Father tried to stop the wagon, but it knocked him backward.

"Father!" Biddie dropped their canteens and rushed toward him, but Lucy grabbed her arm.

The wagon rolled past, careening down the road as the mules galloped away.

"What in the world happened?" Lucy murmured. Then she stared at Biddie. "Where's your Father?"

Biddie dashed to the edge of the road and peered down. Father lay against a large rock just a few feet down the steep slope, groaning and clutching his leg. She said a quick prayer of gratitude that he hadn't slid farther. "Is it broken? Does anything else hurt? How's your head?"

"My head's fine." Father spoke through clenched teeth as sweat poured down his reddened face. "The leg's definitely broken. Not sure about anything else." He huffed a pained breath and tried to sit up but fell back with a strangled cry. "I pulled a muscle in my back, I think."

"Then don't move. I can help. Just give me a minute to think." Biddie looked to where Lucy was checking on the driver, who was still crying and moaning on the edge of the road. Blood dripped from his mangled hand.

Lucy lifted her skirt and began ripping her petticoat. She glanced at Biddie. "We've got to stop the bleeding."

Biddie glanced down at Father.

He nodded and waved her toward them. "Go. He's worse off."

Though she hated to leave Father on that dangerous slope, he was right. She hurried to join Lucy. Two of the man's bones were protruding from his skin.

Biddie gagged and turned away. She closed her eyes and forced herself to get control of her breathing. She couldn't lose her breakfast. The man needed help. In, then out. In, then out. After one more long breath, she turned back to Lucy. "What can I do?"

Rather than answer, Lucy looked at the driver. "Can you hold still while I wrap your fingers? It's going to hurt."

He pressed his lips together and nodded, though his entire body continued to tremble.

Lucy faced Biddie. "You hold his arm steady while I wrap."

Biddie avoided looking at the worst of the man's injury and focused on positioning herself to gain the steadiest grip on his arm that she could manage.

Lucy held the makeshift bandage over his hand. "Are you ready?"

Biddie tightened her grip. "Ready."

The driver's face paled, but his chin held firm. A vein pulsed in his jaw. "Ready."

In minutes, Lucy had stopped the bleeding and immobilized the hand with a tight bandage. To his credit, the man hadn't moved or cried out once while she worked.

Biddie released his arm. "Now we need to help Father."

"There's no point risking your necks on this hill," Father called from where he lay against the boulder. "I'm too heavy for the two of you to haul up."

Biddie gaped. "We can't just leave you here."

"Of course not. I'm no martyr." Father uttered a weak laugh. "But you'll have to go for help."

Biddie scanned the empty landscape surrounding them. The mules and their wagon were long out of sight. Aside from the primitive road that had brought them there, no other signs of human life met her gaze. She looked back the way they'd come. How long had it been since they'd seen a home?

CHAPTER 3

June 11, 1873
Lupine Valley Ranch
Eastern San Diego County, California

*G*ideon urged his horse to the peak and looked into the mountain valley below. Two black-charred boards were all that stood amid scattered piles of ash punctuating the desert chaparral. Large swaths of plants had been burned away, leaving charred sugarbush branches, burned stumps of juniper shrubs, and shriveled limbs of cholla cactus amid the stones encircling the desolate scene. There was no hint of the purple flower that had given the ranch its name.

Where *was* the Lupine Valley Ranch? According to the directions he'd received from the manager of the last stage station, the homestead should be here. The man hadn't mentioned anything about a fire.

With a sinking feeling in his gut, Gideon nudged his horse to continue down the slope into the valley. As he rode, he kept a sharp lookout for any signs of life. Horses, cattle, ranch hands.

Even if the place *had* burned down, shouldn't there be something or someone about? Where was everyone?

A large mound of disturbed dirt lay far off to one side of the burnt remains, almost at the edge of the wide valley. He'd have missed it if it weren't for the lopsided cross made of twined-together mesquite branches. A grave?

The closer he came, the more convinced he was the mound was too large for one person. Could someone have buried their horse? There were no carvings on the branches to indicate who or what lay beneath.

At the foot of the grave, he swung Legend back toward the center of the valley. A desert finch fluttered from the shrubs. Still, there were no signs of people or ranch animals about.

Gideon's shoulders sagged as he guided Legend back to the piles of ash. He'd received the letter accepting his application for the position of ranch cook seven weeks ago. Except for the one migraine that had set him back a full day, he'd made good time. Better than he'd expected. Still, he hadn't been fast enough. He slid from the saddle and kicked one of the two remaining boards. The base shattered and it toppled into the dust.

Gideon covered his face with his hands. Could he succeed at nothing?

The cocking of a rifle echoed off the rocks, bouncing around the valley.

Gideon's head came up, his hand going to his pistol.

"Leave it," a voice warned. Again the sound echoed so that he couldn't determine the location of the source. But had the voice sounded...feminine?

He hesitated, his hand resting on the pistol's handle. If it were a woman, she likely wasn't alone. But if she had a man, why hadn't he been the one to speak? Not daring to move lest the owner of that voice get scared and accidentally pull the trigger, he scanned his surroundings once more. Too many large

29

rocks and shrubs to even guess at where the shooter was taking cover.

"Get your hands in the air." The voice came again, and it was definitely a female's.

Feeling every inch the fool for letting his guard down, Gideon slowly raised his hands. "I mean no harm, ma'am. Perhaps I've come to the wrong place." He didn't think so, but one could hope. "I was told the Lupine Valley Ranch had its homestead in this valley. I'm looking for Oliver Baker"

"Well, he's dead. So you best head on back to wherever you came from."

Gideon winced. Judging by her tone, there'd been no tears shed over the matter. "Going back isn't an option for me. Perhaps I could speak with whoever's in charge now?"

Had he arrived while the new owner was off gathering supplies for rebuilding? Oliver's letter had stated half a dozen men worked here. Yet not so much as a shadow had moved to indicate anyone else about. Did they all abandon this woman after the fire? The no-account varmints. Gideon might be new to the area, but even he knew bandits and hostile Indians roamed these parts. He hadn't seen another homestead for the last ten miles, and the last five had been rough, rocky terrain that'd taken him nearly a full day to traverse.

"*I'm* in charge, and I told you to go. So get. I won't ask again."

She was in charge? Must be Oliver's widow. Still...what had happened to all the men?

He glanced at Legend. He should remount and leave as the lady demanded, but it grated against his honor to leave a woman alone under such circumstances.

He was almost certain she was hiding somewhere to the east of him, though he still couldn't pinpoint where. So he aimed his voice in that direction. "Aren't you at all curious why I've come?" Perhaps if she knew he'd been hired by her husband, she'd lower her guard and they could have a more civilized conversation. If he could convince her to trust him, maybe she'd let him escort her to civilization. Surely, she had family somewhere who'd take her in. "Oliver hired me to—"

A shot flew past his head and left a hole in the only board that remained standing just two feet away.

"That's your last warning."

Had the woman intended to shoot the board? Or was it a lucky shot? Either way, she'd made it clear, sticking around wouldn't end well for him. "Fine." He turned slowly toward Legend. "I'm leaving." The hairs on the back of his neck stood straight as he lifted one foot to the stirrup.

Lord, don't let her shoot me as I mount up.

～

*J*t had been too long since Biddie and Lucy left Father and the driver. Biddie's feet burned in places where blisters had likely formed. Her face felt tight and hot despite the sheltering shade of her bonnet's brim. And her legs ached from nearly three hours of constant walking. Yet she dare not stop as she led Lucy along the narrow trail to the rustic home they'd spotted from the road as they walked back toward San Diego.

Please let the owners be home, Lord. And please let them be kind and willing to help us.

Faded and frayed fabric fluttered in the breeze through glassless windows on the sun-bleached wooden home. A few yards away stood an equally sad-looking barn, and several corrals divided the landscape beside it.

A cow mooed from inside the barn as they entered the well-packed dirt yard. "Hello?" Her voice emerged scratchy from her dry throat.

Lucy tapped her side with their canteen. "Drink it."

31

Biddie opened her mouth to repeat her earlier refusal to take their last swallow of water and insist that Lucy drink it, but another voice spoke first.

"Hello." A tall woman stepped from the home with a welcoming smile. "It's been quite a while since we had visitors, but..." One glance took in Biddie and Lucy's bedraggled appearance and another searched the area behind them. "Oh dear." The kind woman turned her head toward the barn and shouted. "John, you better come quick. Someone's been hurt."

How could she know? Biddie looked at Lucy in surprise. Then her gaze fell to Lucy's bodice front. Dark blood stains splattered what had been a beautiful yellow-check fabric.

A stout man, presumably John, ran from the barn as the woman disappeared into her home. "Who's hurt?" He noticed the strangers in his yard and reached for the holster at his waist.

Biddie said a prayer of gratitude the belt was empty. "My father and the man who was driving our wagon are both hurt. We need your help."

"Billy!" John shouted over his shoulder, and a moment later, a teenage boy exited the barn. "Get my gun." The boy dashed back into the barn, and the older man turned back to Biddie. "Bandits?"

She shook her head. "Our wagon ran off the road and a wheel stuck. Father and the driver were trying to dig it out when something spooked the mules. The wheel ran over the driver's hand, and my father was knocked down the slope. His leg's broken."

"Where abouts did this happen?"

Biddie described the section of road where they'd left Father and the driver.

The teenage boy returned with a pistol. John slid the weapon into his holster. "I think I know the place you mean."

He turned to the boy. "Let's get the wagon hitched and see what we can do to help."

The kind woman returned with her bonnet in place, a small satchel in one hand, and three canteens dangling from the other. "Here." She lifted the canteens. "Take one for each of you. You must be thirsty after such a long walk."

Biddie thanked her and passed a canteen to Lucy.

By the time they'd drunk their fill, the family's wagon was hitched and ready to go.

Biddie hurried to climb in but stumbled over a low-growing weed.

The woman gasped and rushed forward to steady her. "You poor dear. Why don't you stay here and rest while we go get the injured men?"

Biddie wanted to protest, but a wave of dizziness stole her words.

Lucy clasped her arm. "Thank you, ma'am. That's very generous. We're in your debt."

The woman climbed into the wagon beside her husband and son. "Don't be silly. Helping one another is the only way any of us survive out here."

Before Biddie could summon the energy to climb aboard, John shook the reins and the wagon left the yard.

～

*G*ideon dared a glance over his shoulder as he rode Legend away from the mountain valley cradling the ashen remains of Lupine Valley Ranch. What was he going to do now? More importantly, what was that woman going to do? There hadn't even been a roof left to sleep under. Was she camping out among the boulders? How long had she been living like that? How long before someone with less honorable intentions discovered her vulnerable situation?

Like a cactus burr in his boot, Gideon couldn't escape the notion that he shouldn't have left her there. Not that she'd given him much choice. Still. Mama had raised him never to leave a woman unprotected.

He turned Legend around and eyed the sun's position in the sky. If he waited until near dark, he could ride back and sneak onto the valley ridge. Maybe he'd see there was a man with her after all. Her bold claims of being in charge might have been bravado to convince him—a strange man—to leave. The notion didn't have the ring of truth to it. Still, he held on to the idea. If he could just confirm there was at least one man there to protect her, Gideon could ride on with peace of mind. Then maybe he could figure out what he was going to do with the rest of his pointless existence.

If he returned and she truly was alone...? Well, he'd figure out what to do if it came to that.

First, he needed to find a way to approach the ranch's valley without alerting her to his return.

CHAPTER 4

$\mathcal{B}$iddie pulled ten puffs from the Dutch oven and set them on a platter to cool. After she'd rested, she'd grown too anxious to sit and wait. So she'd taken inventory of the family's pantry and found they had at least one jar of preserves and everything she needed to bake the puffs. Hopefully, they wouldn't mind that she'd used their stores and would receive the pastries as the thank-you gift she intended.

For the past hour, Lucy had kept watch through the open window of the kind strangers' home. She glanced back at Biddie. "I think they're coming."

Biddie hurried to the window and looked out. A large plume of dust drew nearer along the road leading to the small homestead. "I think you're right." She turned and began cleaning the dishes she'd used. It was important they leave the home in the state it had been in when they'd entered. Or rather, better than they'd found it, since Lucy had spent the first part of their time in the home tidying, dusting, and sweeping. She'd even ironed the family's linens.

By the time Biddie had dried and returned each dish to its

rightful place, the wagon was pulling into the yard. She grabbed the canteens she'd refilled and rushed out to meet it.

On the wagon bench, John sat beside his wife, whose name Biddie realized she'd forgotten to ask. In the back, the driver sat propped against a large sack of something, and Father lay stretched across the wagon bed, his head cushioned by a smaller sack. The trouser had been cut from his injured leg, and two long pieces of wood were bandaged tightly against either side of his limb.

The moment the wagon stopped, Biddie climbed into the bed and knelt beside Father. "How are you?" She lifted a canteen. "Are you thirsty?"

Though his face was reddened by sunburn and his eyes held pain, he smiled. "They've given me plenty to drink, thank you. Mrs. Leach even set my leg for me."

"She what?" Biddie looked from Father to the woman who'd initially greeted them.

Mrs. Leach climbed down from the wagon. "I'm afraid it isn't the first time I've been called upon to perform such a task, and it likely won't be the last."

Biddie opened her mouth to reply, but John appeared in the wagon beside her.

He spoke to Father. "It's too late to take you to the doc's tonight. We'll have to go in the morning. Do you want me to move you to the house, or would you prefer to sleep here?"

Biddie's mouth fell open. Was he seriously suggesting her injured father sleep outside, in a hard wagon, exposed to the elements?

Father, it seemed, didn't share her concerns. "I'll sleep here, if you don't mind."

John nodded as though it was the answer he'd expected. "I'll have Arvilla bring you a blanket and some supper when it's ready."

Father thanked him, and the man turned to help their driver from the vehicle.

Biddie waited for the others to leave before speaking in a hushed voice. "Father, you don't have to sleep outside. I'm sure I can persuade the Leaches to make a bed for you indoors. I—"

"My leg may be splinted, but moving is still incredibly painful."

Biddie's lips rounded in a silent O. "But won't you be cold?" As soon as the words escaped her, she realized the foolishness of them. As hot as it was, he'd likely be more comfortable outdoors than she would be crammed into the tiny house with the heat she'd created baking those puffs. Oh dear. Why hadn't she considered that their fireplace was in the same room as their bed? No wonder the fire had been cold when she first entered. She might have created a delicious treat for the family to enjoy, but she'd traded it for their sleeping comfort. She winced and explained her mistake to Father. "I think I should go apologize."

Father patted her hand. "Don't worry too much about it. I've known many families who live in this warmer climate to sleep out of doors on nights like these, anyway."

Lucy climbed into the wagon with a blanket and tin plate. One of Biddie's puffs had been split and the fruit spread slathered across the open surface. "Mrs. Leach was worried you'd fall asleep before she finished cooking their evening meal."

Father thanked Lucy and made short work of the pastry. He smiled at Biddie. "Delicious"—a yawn paused his words— "as always."

Lucy reclaimed the plate and scooted toward the foot of the wagon.

Father's eyelids drooped. "I'm sorry about the delay, dear, but we'll get to the ranch and your sister as soon as we can."

Ginny! How had her sister's plight completely escaped Biddie's thoughts these last hours? Of course this situation would cause a delay in their arrival at the ranch. But could her sister continue to survive without the funds she'd requested? How dire was the situation? Ginny's message had been so vague. What if they'd lost their entire pantry and were surviving on what they could hunt or forage until Biddie arrived? She looked out across the deepening twilight shadowing the chaparral around them. There seemed so little greenery in this place, and yet Father said the ranch was located in an even more barren part of this land. Could there truly be enough natural resources to sustain human life?

She turned back to Father and found his face relaxed in slumber. What could she do for him? She knew almost nothing about medical care—certainly nothing about healing a broken bone such as his. When Charlie had fallen off the banister and broken his arm, it had taken weeks to heal. Surely, Father didn't expect her to wait that long to reach Ginny. Did he?

~

*G*ideon woke slowly with the rising of the sun. He stretched stiff limbs across the hardscrabble ground he'd slept on near the ridge of the valley. He'd found a small-game trail leading up from the north and followed it to a large stone near the top. From that position, he'd watched for hours as the lanky blonde had gone about her business below. What that business was, he wasn't certain. But it sure required a lot of rocks. She'd carried enough dinner-plate-sized rocks from one side of the valley to the other to dam the Red River.

With each trip, she'd carry her load between two large boulders that stood near the southeast end of the valley. Where she went from there, he couldn't see. She'd reappear seconds later, empty-handed, and go get more. With the aid of a quarter-moon, this went on well past nightfall.

It was close to midnight when she disappeared between the boulders again but didn't reappear.

He'd watched for another half hour before deciding the odd woman had finally gone to bed. Whatever that bed looked like. Then he'd gone to sleep himself.

Now, he pulled himself onto his knees and peeked around the boulder into the valley. There she was again, hauling those rocks. With a heavy sigh, he leaned back to where she couldn't see him and considered the glowing horizon. What was he supposed to do now? Having watched for so long, Gideon was thoroughly convinced the woman had been telling the truth and lived alone in the valley. If he left, Mama would be appalled. Yet the spitfire below had made it plain his assistance was unwelcome.

He searched his mind but could find no solution.

Perhaps it would come to him after a bit of breakfast. He rose and half slid, half scrambled down the outer slope to where he'd left Legend the night before. After watering him from the canteen, Gideon had tied the gelding to the trunk of a scrub oak surrounded by a patch of desert grasses.

Legend greeted him with a soft nicker. His bowl was empty, and the grasses beneath the tree were considerably shorter than they'd been the night before. Gideon patted the horse's neck, refilled the bowl, and retrieved his last bit of oats from the saddlebag. "Here you go, boy." Once the horse had finished his treat, Gideon rinsed his hands and set about preparing his own breakfast.

As he chewed a bit of dried beef, he recalled the woman grinding some sort of pod with a rock the night before, just like the Indians did. She'd added water from a tin bucket to create a mush that she ate with a knife. Did she have no cutlery? It made sense the fire had stolen her food stores, but why hadn't she purchased more? And where were the ranch's cattle?

At least she appeared to have a source of water. He'd

noticed a rabbit hopping down the slope yesterday. Perhaps he could do something about her food situation before he moved on.

Decision made, Gideon checked that the woman was still hauling rocks. She was. So he set off in search of game.

A few hours later, he returned with two rabbits slung over his shoulder. He'd almost shot a third, but a sneeze caught him unaware and startled the creature who'd dashed from view. Two would have to do. If the woman knew enough to forage whatever those beans were she'd ground last night, she likely knew how to cook and preserve the meat from his catch. If not, he'd teach her.

Assuming she'd let him.

But if the gift of free food didn't earn her trust, he didn't know what would. And he needed her to trust him. At least enough to let him escort her back to civilization.

He checked that Legend was still doing well, then started up the hill toward his lookout spot. Just before he reached the ridge, he glanced south and paused. A cloud of dust drew nearer along the trail leading toward the ranch's mountain valley. No doubt it was being kicked up by a beast of burden. More than one, from the looks of it.

Gideon set down the rabbits and checked his guns. If the riders were looking for trouble, he'd be ready for them.

~

*A*fter nearly a full day in the saddle, sweat soaked through Biddie's undergarments. Mr. Leach led them along a narrow trail cutting through the desert mountains. Her horse ambled behind the pack horse carrying their trunks. Lucy's horse plodded behind her, bringing up the tail of their small train. They'd been riding for hours. Surely, they were close to the ranch by now. Biddie twisted and looked past Lucy to where the trail disappeared over a crest. The sun hovered just below the horizon, casting streaks of reds and golds across the sky. Had she made the right decision?

Lucy caught her eye and shared a knowing look. "He'll be fine."

Biddie forced a weak smile and faced forward again. Of course Father would be well. It was why she'd persuaded him to allow them to continue without him. Billy had left before dawn to fetch the doctor, and they'd arrived back at the Leach home just as the sun rose over the western hilltops. The doctor pronounced Mrs. Leach's setting of Father's leg to be as well done as anything he might have accomplished. He also instructed Father not to travel or use his leg for several weeks as it healed. An exception had been made for Mrs. Leach and Billy to transport Father to the Stevens's ranch. Richard and Clarinda Stevens, were good friends with her family. Although the Stevenses were back east at the moment, their medically skilled housekeeper, Teodora, would see to Father's needs. He was to remain abed there for at least six weeks until the doctor declared him healed enough to travel again.

Naturally, Father had expected Biddie and Lucy would remain with him, but when Biddie reminded him of the urgency of Ginny's need, he'd softened his stance. In the end, he agreed that Biddie could continue to the ranch if Lucy accompanied her and Mr. Leach guided and protected them. Father had offered to pay the man for his trouble, but instead the family asked Father to deliver a list of supplies to them once he was healed and on his way to the ranch.

Teodora had ample medical skills, a heart of gold, and— with the Stevens family currently in Massachusetts—plenty of time on her hands. There would be nothing for Biddie to do there but wait. It made no sense for her to have accompanied Father. At least, that was what she'd convinced herself of this morning.

She reined her horse to a stop. "This was a mistake. We need to go back."

Mr. Leach halted his mount at the crest of the slope they'd been climbing and twisted in the saddle to gape at her. "We're almost there."

Lucy guided her horse to a stop beside Biddie's. "Mr. Davidson is in good hands with Teodora."

"But what if she left to visit her own family? Who will look after Father?" Biddie ought to have at least escorted him to the Stevens's ranch and confirmed that the housekeeper was there. What had she been thinking to leave him so soon after his injury?

Mr. Leach frowned. "My Arvilla won't leave your pa untended. If the housekeeper ain't at home, she'll find someone else to care for him or else bring him back to our place and care for him herself."

Biddie exhaled. Of course the kind-hearted woman wouldn't leave an injured man to fend for himself. She was being silly. She closed her eyes and admitted the truth—if only in her heart. Father wasn't who she was really worried about. He was in good hands. But Biddie had no idea how Ginny would react to their unannounced appearance.

In San Francisco, the decision had seemed easy, even obvious. She'd been yearning to reunite with her long-lost siblings since the moment they'd vanished from her life, but never knew where to look. With Virginia's letter, the opportunity was finally within her grasp. Of course she should go. Yet with every mile traveled, her back had bunched, her neck stiffened, and her stomach churned. What if Ginny didn't want to see her? What if she'd only wanted the money she asked for? There'd been no invitation in her message. No expression of regret for their lost years together. Why hadn't Biddie considered that Ginny might be perfectly content in her life without a little sister to bother or burden her?

42

Biddie swallowed against the pressure climbing her throat and, for the first time, considered the ugly truth she'd been ignoring. Ginny had known where to send that letter. Which meant, she'd known all along where Biddie was and could have come to see her. But she hadn't.

Lucy's hand came to rest on her shoulder. "What's really bothering you?"

Trust her best friend to sense the truth. Biddie opened her eyes with a teary smile that quickly melted. "Ginny doesn't want me here."

Lucy's brow furrowed. "You don't know that. We haven't even found her yet."

"She knew where I was and didn't come to see me."

"Perhaps she couldn't afford the travel, or responsibilities on the ranch kept her from leaving."

"Then why didn't she write sooner?"

Lucy shrugged. "I don't know. But you can't jump to conclusions without at least giving her the chance to explain." She tipped her chin in the direction they'd been heading. "Besides, we've come this far. Do you really want to turn back now and always wonder what might have happened if we'd kept going?"

Lucy was right. If they turned back now, Biddie would always wonder. And the questions that had plagued her since that awful morning she'd awakened to Mama's sobs would go on hounding her for the rest of her life. She straightened her shoulders and wiped the tears from her face. "You're right." She nodded to Mr. Leach. "My apologies for the delay, sir. You may continue."

Mr. Leach nudged his mount forward, and Biddie followed him into the long, shallow valley nestled between the peaks. Unlike the mountains of Northern California which she'd twice visited with Father, these hills bore more rocks than trees. While there were plenty of shrubs and even some grass, every shade of green here seemed faded—like a cotton dress left too long in the hot sun. Perhaps that was the case. Was it possible these plants grew brighter with winter rains, only to fade in the summer? She squinted into the bright-blue cloudless sky. Did it even rain here? She chuckled at her own question. Of course it must. How else would the plants get their water? Still, with the heat quickly stealing the moisture from her skin, rain in this dry land was difficult to imagine.

"What's that?" Lucy's voice drew Biddie's attention.

She shifted to see what Lucy was looking at and followed her friend's gaze to a blackened area at the foot of an eastern slope near the center of the valley. Before she could wrap her mind around what she was seeing, Mr. Leach spoke in a hushed voice.

"That's where the ranch was. This looks worse than I expected. Where are all the men?" He lifted a staying hand. "You ladies wait here while I see if there's anyone about. If there's trouble, you two turn around and ride hard for the Rowland place."

Biddie's heart sped like the needle of Mother's new sewing machine. The precious pouch of money Father had entrusted her with weighed heavily in her hidden skirt pocket. She tried to recall how long it had been since Mr. Leach had pointed out Lupine Valley Ranch's nearest neighbor. Two hours? Three?

Not waiting for their agreement, Mr. Leach pulled his rifle from its scabbard and continued on. His head swiveled continuously, as though expecting an ambush.

She studied the blackened area again. Ginny had said there'd been a fire, but Biddie hadn't expected this much devastation. Could her sister have been living here among the ashes and charred plants? Surely not. She searched the stone-studded valley but saw no sign of Ginny.

Biddie glanced at Lucy. "There's nothing left. Ginny had to have found somewhere else to stay while she waited for my response." She squeezed the reins. "Why didn't I consider that? How will we ever find her?"

At that moment, a woman's voice called out. "Stop where you are and state your business."

Hope skittered in Biddie's chest. "Ginny?" Despite Mr. Leach's instructions, she nudged her horse deeper into the valley, trying to discern where the voice had come from. "Where are you? It's me, Biddie."

A tall blonde in a faded gray dress, coated with dust, emerged from behind a boulder taller than the house they'd slept in last night. Her short, braided pigtails might have given a youthful impression if it weren't for the hard gleam in her cold blue eyes. She aimed her rifle at Mr. Leach. "Who're you?"

Mr. Leach held still as a marble bust. "Name's John Leach. I was asked to see that Miss Davidson and her friend reached you safely. Ain't no need for that weapon you're holding."

Ginny didn't lower her rifle. She glanced at Biddie. "What're you doing here? I told you to send a reply so's I could make plans. I ain't got time for a visit, or whatever it is you've come for. So just leave the money and head on back the way you come."

A new fire started in the valley, only this one was inside of Biddie. She swung out of the saddle and landed with a thump among the desert shrubs. "You haven't time for a visit?" Thorns tugged at her skirts as she marched through the wild land separating her from her pigheaded sister. "Well, then, please enlighten me as to your busy schedule. Perhaps you've a meal to get on." She waved toward the scorched remains of the ranch buildings. "Wait, that can't be it since you've no kitchen. So perhaps it's curtains to hem or shelves to dust. Whoops. Those are gone too." She stopped two feet from the end of Ginny's rifle barrel, close enough to see the sparks of irritation in her sister's blue eyes. "So it must be you're too busy sweeping to find the time to speak with the little sister you haven't seen in eighteen years. That, I can understand." She waved her arm to encompass the valley surrounding them. "All this dirt will take years —decades, even—to sweep clear of the valley."

Ginny's mouth quirked up at the corner, and she snorted. "You always were full of sass."

She was? Biddie couldn't remember ever speaking to another person as she'd just spoken to Ginny. Her face flushed. What had come over her? She should apologize. What a first impression to—

Ginny stepped sideways, reestablishing her 'aim at Mr. Leach. "Don't you move." She tipped her head toward Biddie. "I might not shoot her, but I ain't got no call to spare you. Men"— she spat the word like a bug had flown into her mouth—"ain't welcome here."

"But he's our escort, and he helped Fath—"

Ginny didn't take her gaze or her aim off poor Mr. Leach. "I don't care who he is or what he's done. I said men ain't welcome here, and I meant it." She gestured with the barrel toward the trail they'd ridden in on. "Now get."

Biddie gasped. "Ginny!" Her big sister had apparently lost all sense since they'd last seen one another. "You can't go around threatening people. Especially not men like Mr. Leach who has been nothing but kind and generous toward us. He had things that needed doing on his own ranch and his own family to care for, but they all dropped everything to help when Father was hurt yesterday. And now he's ridden all this way just to see that we came to no harm." Again she placed herself between Mr. Leach and Ginny's rifle. "Without his assistance, you'd still be waiting on me to bring the funds you so desperately need."

Ginny's eyes narrowed. "Ain't no need to be spouting my business around strangers."

Biddie winced. "You're right. I'm sorry. But that weapon you're aiming has me all flustered and"—she grabbed the barrel and shoved it toward the ground—"would you put that thing away already? Mr. Leach means you no more harm than Lucy or I do."

Ginny spared a glance for Lucy before turning attention back to Mr. Leach. She didn't set the weapon down, but at least she didn't raise her barrel again.

Biddie sighed. "It took us all day to reach you. If Mr. Leach leaves now, he'll be riding through the night. Surely, you can allow him a few hours' rest before he goes home."

Ginny finally looked at her. "You mean, before you *all* ride back."

Biddie pinned Ginny's gaze with her own. "Where have you been living since the fire?" There weren't any structures in sight, but Biddie had a sneaking suspicion what her stubborn sister's answer would be. Even as kids, Ginny had always felt she had something to prove. And no wonder with Pa knocking them down time and again with both his words and his fists. Well, he'd never landed a physical blow on Biddie. Thanks to Ginny's interference.

Her big sister scowled. "Right here, of course. This is my land now that Oliver's gone"—she shifted her glare to Mr. Leach again—"and ain't nobody going to take it from me."

"I got no interest in your land, Miss. I got a homestead of my own." He jerked his thumb toward the west. "'Bout twenty-five miles or so thataways." He surveyed the valley with disdain. "And it's a sure sight prettier than what you got."

Mr. Leach's land *had* been greener with more oak trees and wild grasses, but Biddie didn't think it wise of him to point it out.

To her surprise, Ginny relaxed. "Fine. You can sleep there." She pointed to a cleared patch of dirt in front of the scattered ash piles. She tucked the butt of her rifle beneath her shoulder. "But I'll be watching. And at first light, you go." She met Biddie's gaze once more. *"All* of you."

Mr. Leach shook his head. "No thanks." He looked at Biddie. "Miss Davidson, I think we ought to head back to the Rowlands' place before it gets too dark. Clyve's got the manners and a heart Miss Baker's clearly lacking." He sneered at Ginny. "Of course, I wouldn't expect much better of anyone related to that snake, Oliver Baker."

Had Mr. Leach not heard Biddie call Ginny her sister?

He continued, seemingly oblivious to her frown. "No doubt the Rowlands' cook'll have a warm meal to share too. Then we can hit the trail at first light."

Biddie studied her sister. Something wasn't right. "Where's Preston?" Had their brother been anywhere in the vicinity, he'd have showed himself by now.

"Took off years ago." Ginny's stone-like expression wavered for a heartbeat before firming again. "I wrote him same time I wrote you."

Biddie swallowed the disappointment that her brother wasn't here. "Did he respond?"

"No. And he ain't got money like you, but he'll come help now that Oliver's gone."

"Where are your vaqueros?"

Ginny glanced to where a large mound of dirt was topped by a rickety cross made from branches. "Dead."

All of them? Didn't a ranch usually need at least half a dozen men to run it? Cold washed through Biddie.

Mr. Leach cleared his throat. "I don't mean to rush you, Miss Davidson, but if we don't leave now, it'll be dark before we make the Rowlands' place. It ain't wise showing up unexpected after dark in these parts."

Biddie sucked in a breath, widened her stance, and crossed her arms. "I'll not be going back." She hadn't fully made the decision until the words left her mouth, but they felt right. She couldn't leave her sister here with no home and no help. Not that Biddie knew the first thing about construction, but she could learn.

Ginny scowled. "'Course you are. This ain't no place for a city gal."

Mr. Leach fisted his free hand. "I promised your father I'd see you here and then take you back. That was the deal."

"I'm sorry, Mr. Leach, but my plans have changed." She gestured to the empty valley. "My *sister* clearly needs help to get this ranch back on its feet." She raised a questioning brow toward Lucy, who nodded as Biddie had expected. "We're staying."

Mr. Leach moved to dismount. "Now hold on. You—"

The rise of Ginny's rifle cut off his words. "Stay on your horse."

Biddie grimaced. She was putting the kind man in a terrible position. "I'm so very sorry. Please don't worry about my father. He knows I have a mind of my own and can be unreasonable at times." Not that she felt she was being unreasonable, but no doubt Mr. Leach and Father would see it that way. "If you'll wait, I'll retrieve my writing utensils from my pack and send you with a letter for my father. Will that help?"

"Fine." Mr. Leach turned his mount to face their back trail and reached for the reins of Biddie's horse.

Ginny's rifle swung toward Biddie once more. "No need for a letter. You go with him. Like I said, I don't got time to babysit you. I just need your money." She nodded toward a large stone beside Biddie. "You can leave it there and go."

Biddie ignored her and crossed to where Mr. Leach waited with the horse she'd purchased from the Gaskill brothers. She extracted a sheet of paper, her bottle of ink, and her pen. Using the nearest rock as a writing surface, she began forming her explanation. As she wrote, Lucy removed their bags and trunks from the horses.

Ginny squawked. "What are you doing? I told you, you're not staying."

Both Biddie and Lucy ignored her and continued with their tasks. By the time Biddie had finished her message to Father, Lucy had removed the last bag and looped the reins for both horses through the branches of a large shrub.

Mr. Leach accepted the folded letter she gave him and glanced at Ginny, then back to Biddy. "You sure you want to stay?"

"Positive."

He shrugged. "Well, all right." He tipped his hat to her and Lucy. "It's been a pleasure, Miss." With a nudge to his horse, he started back the way they'd come.

Behind her, Ginny spluttered. "Call him back. You need to get on that horse and go, or..."

Biddie faced her, chin raised. "Or what?"

Ginny cocked her rifle. "Or I'll shoot you for trespassing."

Lucy gasped, but Biddie laughed. "You already admitted you wouldn't shoot me."

Ginny scowled. "I said I *might* not shoot you. Didn't say I for sure wouldn't. But if you don't leave—"

"If I leave now, you don't get the money I brought you."

Ginny laughed. "This is exactly what I mean. Twice now you've said you brought me money." She waggled her rifle. "And I'm the one holding the gun. You ain't got the sense it takes to survive out here." She waved to Biddie's filthy gown, the skirts riddled with tears from traipsing through the shrubs. "Your fancy dress couldn't even make it one day."

Biddie stepped forward. "Don't underestimate me."

Lucy's hands landed on her hips. "Your sister's tougher than you think."

Ginny's face hardened into an expression Biddie didn't recognize. "Neither of you has any sense." She jerked her chin to where Mr. Leach had disappeared over the valley's rim. "Now that he's gone, what's to stop me from shooting you both and taking everything you brought?"

Memories of nine-year-old Ginny's bloodied face flashed in Biddie's mind. She grabbed the end of Ginny's barrel and held it against her chest. "Then do it. Pull the trigger."

Eighteen years may have passed, but there was no way the sister who'd sacrificed herself to protect her younger siblings could have changed so immensely that she would actually pull the trigger. Was there?

CHAPTER 5

From his lookout position, Gideon ground his teeth as the lone male in the group of newcomers disappeared from sight. Had everyone in this state lost their mind? What were three women going to do on their own in such a desolate, isolated place? Had that man no honor? Didn't he know bandits and hostile Indians roamed this land?

The women resumed arguing.

Wonderful. He resisted the urge to throw something. The newcomers ought to have solved his dilemma by removing the first woman—whose name was apparently Ginny. Instead, the cowardly Mr. Leach had tripled Gideon's trouble by leaving two more women behind. And what was worse, these two were clearly citified ladies with no clue of the danger that might find them out in the middle of nowhere. The one named Biddie— Ginny's sister, if he'd heard right—wore a dress better suited to an afternoon tea than a hard ride through the desert. Her skirts bore enough ruffles to clear the valley of dust.

Suddenly, Biddie grabbed the end of the rifle and held it to her chest.

Gideon leapt to his feet. It was official. They were all insane.

He drew his rifle and stepped forward, intent on intervening before someone got hurt. But just as he opened his mouth to shout, Ginny lowered her rifle.

Biddie reached out and drew Ginny into her arms.

Gideon stood frozen as the two women hugged. Well, the crazy woman was hugging. Ginny just stood there, allowing it to happen. He shook his head. The world had flipped upside down. That was the only explanation for this madness.

His small movement must have caught Biddie's eye, because she turned toward him.

He dove behind the nearest bush and waited for shouts of alarm to echo in the valley.

Several long seconds passed in silence.

His calves screamed for relief from his crouched position, but he didn't dare move. The branches of the bush might disguise him, but they probably weren't thick enough to hide movement.

Calm feminine voices began to chatter, followed by the crunch of boots on dirt. The sounds faded toward the opposite side of the valley.

He tipped onto his knees and peered out.

Their backs to him, the three women carried bags toward the same large boulders Ginny had disappeared into the night before. What were they planning to do? Sip tea in their stone garden? As if Wild Ginny had a tea service hidden back there.

With a frustrated huff, he fell onto his haunches.

Now what?

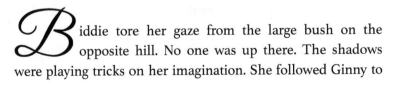

*B*iddie tore her gaze from the large bush on the opposite hill. No one was up there. The shadows were playing tricks on her imagination. She followed Ginny to a narrow gap between two giant boulders that held up a third boulder.

"Watch your head," Ginny called as she stepped down into the narrow passage.

Biddie ducked and moved her arms so they held her bags with one before and one behind her. After a few feet, the space widened and the ceiling rose. She found herself standing in a cave-like space tall enough to stand upright and wide enough that the three of them didn't feel terribly crowded together. She studied how the large rocks balanced over, under, and around one another. Most of the gaps had been filled with dozens of smaller rocks. The only exceptions were the slot they'd just come through, a crack to Lucy's right, and an opening above what looked like a small firepit. A lot of work had gone into making these stones a livable structure. Had Ginny done all the work herself?

At the far end of the space, two small crates held an assortment of supplies. Beside them, a pickaxe, a handle-less shovel, and another tool Biddie didn't recognize leaned against the curved stone wall.

"This way." Ginny turned and squeezed through the other crack in the rocks.

Biddie followed her with Lucy just behind.

They came to another open space similar in shape to the first, but considerably smaller. She could still stand upright, but the walls pressed in so that the three of them stood almost shoulder to shoulder.

At one end, a rough blanket was stretched across the packed dirt with a second blanket piled to one side. Two metal buckets sat nearby. One was filled with water. The other appeared empty, but judging by the stench, it was being used as a chamber pot.

Ginny snatched it up and nudged past Lucy. "Be right back."

Lucy's wide eyes caught Biddie's. "She's living in these rocks?"

Biddie winced. "I'm sorry. I should have asked more questions before I committed us to staying. If you want to leave, we can try to catch Mr. Leach. It may not be too late if we hurry."

Lucy's head tilted. "You'd never leave your sister in such a situation."

"No, but if you want to go—"

"If you stay, I stay." Lucy's gaze traveled around the space, and she shuddered. "I just didn't expect this. Where are her food stores? I didn't see any—"

Ginny's reappearance cut off Lucy's words. "Food stuffs all burned with the house and..." Her face contorted. "Everything that wasn't metal."

Lucy gasped. "How do you survive?"

"If you know what to look for and how to prepare it, this land's got plenty to get by on." Ginny retrieved the two dirty blankets from the floor. "Here. You two can have these." She thrust the wadded fabric at Biddie.

"Isn't that your bedding?" Biddie asked.

Ginny shrugged. "I'm used to sleeping in the dirt."

Biddie exhaled. Despite her gruff exterior, Ginny's heart hadn't changed. "Thank you, but we've brought our own bedrolls." Biddie looked for a place to lay out their blankets and spotted another narrow opening not blocked with rocks— about two feet long, one foot wide, and maybe four feet tall. The top of the slot was only as high as her waist because the bottom sat below the ground on which she stood. "What's through there?"

"Nothing." Ginny stepped down into the hole and stooped to pass through the opening. "It's just another little cave."

Biddie laid her bags aside and dropped into the gap. "Can you stand up in there?"

"Almost."

Biddie passed through and found Ginny standing upright with her head tipped sideways to avoid scraping it on the rock ceiling that hung just an inch or two lower than was comfortable. However, the space was twice as wide as the last room. "This will do nicely."

Ginny snorted. "Right. I'm sure it beats the pants off that fancy house you live in in San Francisco."

Biddie pressed her lips tight. How did Ginny know what her home looked like? How long had she known where to find Biddie? Why hadn't Ginny contacted her sooner?

Ginny waved to the slot they'd just passed through. "It's not too late to change your mind. If I fire my rifle in the air, that Mr. Leach might come back." She tipped one shoulder up. "Then again, he might not. He is a man, after all."

"I'm staying." What had happened to make her sister so bitter toward men? Sure, their pa was the worst example of the opposite sex, but Ginny must have known others who were better.

Setting her questions aside for another time, Biddie retrieved her bags from the other room and focused on settling in. At some point, while they were laying out their bedrolls and arranging their personal possessions beside them, Ginny disappeared.

Biddie found a spot between two small rocks to hide the heavy money pouch. Would the funds Father had sent her with be enough to replace all Ginny had lost? Obviously, money couldn't bring back the dead, but would it be enough to rebuild the ranch? She nibbled her lower lip a moment, then shook off the worry. God would help them find a way. He always did.

She found a third plate-sized rock and set it in front to completely disguise the bag. She scrutinized her choice. "Can you tell that's a hiding spot?"

Lucy turned and examined the pile of rocks blocking the

only sizable opening in their section of the rock cave. "Not at all."

A minute later, Biddie exited the boulder home and gasped. Far above, brighter and more resplendent than anything she'd ever seen, a blanket of stars covered the sky as dusk fell into night. Biddie stared in awe. The same God who created those stars, set them in their place, and knew each of their names, was watching over her right now. Peace stilled her.

Lucy stopped beside her. "There she is."

Biddie followed Lucy's gaze to where Ginny was striking steel against a small rock. Biddie closed the distance to stand beside her sister. "Mr. Leach said open fires at night drew bandits."

"This valley's sheltered from view." A spark caught the small bit of charred cloth atop the rock Ginny held. Smoke wafted from the glowing edges of the fabric. "Unless they're sitting on the ridge, no one's going to see the glow. I took your horses to the spring. They should be fine for the night."

"Thank you." Recalling the movement she thought she'd seen earlier, Biddie examined that portion of the valley's rim once more. Though it was nearly full dark, a thin line of the sun's radiance remained along the western edge, battling the deepening blue. Dark silhouettes of the desert flora stood stark-black in contrast.

There. Another subtle shift in the shadows. She squinted. It could be a trick as she'd thought earlier. Or a branch swayed by a breeze they couldn't feel in the valley. But her gut said otherwise. She opened her mouth to ask Ginny's thoughts, but Lucy spoke first.

"Are you sure it's safe?" She rubbed her arms as the fire grew. "Mr. Leach said there were rumors of a bandit gang in the area."

Ginny added a thicker branch to the growing blaze. "Probably true. But there's no reason for them to come this way." Her lips curled. "They've already taken everything they want from this ranch."

Biddie watched her sister's expression in the flickering light. "Is that what happened? A bandit gang attacked the ranch?"

Ginny gave a curt nod, her gaze fixed on the fire.

Biddie stepped closer. "Did they hurt you?"

Ginny pushed to her feet. "I'll fetch fresh water from the spring."

Before Biddie could protest, Ginny had snatched a pail and stomped off into the dark.

Lucy patted Biddie's back. "Give her time. If something did happen, it won't be easy to talk about."

Biddie let her shoulders sag. "I know. I just wish..." Too many ways to finish the sentence tangled her tongue. She wished Ginny would trust her. She wished Father were here. She wished Pa had never taken Ginny and Preston away.

"It'll be all right. You'll see." Lucy wrapped her arms around Biddie's shoulders, squeezed, and then released her. "I'm going to find my Bible while we have firelight to read by. I didn't see any candles inside." She returned to their temporary home.

Biddie glanced again to where she'd noticed the strange movement. She might not be able to make her sister talk, but she could at least make sure they weren't being spied upon. She lifted the rifle Ginny had left behind. Her sister probably wouldn't like Biddie borrowing the weapon, but if there *was* someone on the ridge, Biddie wasn't going to meet them empty-handed.

~

*G*ideon didn't know whether to laugh or punch something. The woman was a fool. After the wild one left with a bucket, Biddie had claimed her rifle and started up the hill in the opposite direction from where he knelt behind a bush. At first, he'd thought the naive city girl planned to try hunting in the dark.

The truth was worse.

Once beyond the fire's light, her shadow had turned and circled back in his direction. He'd already suspected she'd spotted him, but why hadn't she alerted the others? And now to come after him on her own? She must be out of her mind. He could be a bandit, for all she knew. He could have a gang of men hidden up here. Yet here she came, tromping through the brush like a mama cow in search of her calf.

At least she wasn't bellowing.

Judging by her slow movements and crouched posture, she probably thought she was being sneaky. He bit back a laugh. Then he scowled. If he were anyone else—anyone with foul intentions—she'd be delivering herself right into trouble.

With true stealth, he slipped from his position to stand behind another rock and wait.

Her borrowed rifle aimed at the bush he'd originally hidden behind as she crept past him.

In one swift move, he gripped the butt of the weapon, jerked it from her grasp, and slid his other arm around her so that her back was pinned to his chest. He dropped the weapon and clamped his hand over her mouth just as she screamed.

His fingers muffled the sound. Good. Let her be scared. Maybe she'd think twice before trying such a fool thing again.

She writhed in his grasp, trying to break free.

He took a few elbow jabs to his ribs before he adjusted his grip to pin her arms. The tremble in her limbs convicted him, but if he turned her loose now, she was liable to wallop him good. He risked a murmur. "You can calm down. I'm not going to hurt you." Careful not to hold too tight, he waited for her to relax. The scent of rosewater met his nose. He hadn't smelled that since—

A sharp pain in his shins cut short the thought. He sucked air through his teeth.

She'd kicked him and was rearing to try it again.

He wrapped one leg around both of hers. "Didn't you hear me? I said, I'm not going to hurt you. Just calm down and I'll let go."

She twisted and squirmed to break free, threatening to topple them both.

He leaned against the boulder behind him to keep them from tumbling down the hill. She was a feisty thing, he'd give her that. Still, her small frame was no match for his larger one. "Listen, I don't know what other weapons Ginny's got down there, but if I let you scream, I'm sure to find out the hard way. So just calm down and we can talk. I promise, I mean no harm to any of you."

He may as well have been talking to the rocks.

She continued to fight him, and he struggled to maintain his hold. Not because she'd suddenly grown stronger, but because the smell and feel of her was almighty distracting. Never in his life had he held a woman so close. Nor had he ever before had cause to restrain one against her will. Keeping his hands in chaste positions and trying to avoid bruises weren't things one needed to consider when wrestling with a man.

Something deep inside sprang to life—a feeling he'd thought long dead.

He thrust her away and scooped the rifle from the ground.

Let her scream. It was safer.

He rushed to put several feet between them and braced for her shout.

It didn't come. Rifle aimed at the ground, he risked a glance over his shoulder.

She stood where he'd left her, her wide eyes catching the faintest hint of moonlight. Her heavy breathing seemed loud in the quiet valley, but not another sound escaped her lips.

He pivoted back to face her. "Are you hurt?" He didn't see how she could be, but why else wouldn't she move or call for help?

"No."

Guilt weighed his conscience. "Look, I'm sorry. I shouldn't have scared you like that, but coming up here the way you did was straight foolish. I thought—"

"Who are you?"

He ran his free hand down his face. He was making a mess of things. "My name's Gideon Swift. I was hired to cook for the ranch, but when I got here, the place was in ashes and Ginny ordered me to leave."

"So you decided to spy on her and...what?" She thrust one arm toward the sad remains of the ranch. "She has nothing of value left. What could you—" Her words cut off with a gasp, and she backed away from him.

It took him a moment to catch up to the horrific conclusion she'd jumped to. "No!" His adamant protest only seemed to encourage her retreat. A short cactus stood in her path.

"Look out!" Dropping the rifle, he lunged forward, grabbing her elbows just as the back of her fancy dress pressed into the fuzzy-looking spindles.

She jerked to free herself, but he held firm. "Unhand me."

He drew her away from the danger before releasing her. "You need to be more careful." He pointed to the sharp plant. "Even the plants will try to hurt you out here. Why didn't you go back with that Mr. Leach?"

"No!" She shouted, raising both arms and charging toward him.

No, not toward him. Toward something behind him. He spun in time to duck the swing of a pickaxe.

"I told you to get off my land." Ginny raged and swung again.

Gideon sidestepped her strike. "I did but—"

"Wait!" Biddie threw herself between them.

It was a noble gesture, but another foolish one. Ginny was already drawing the weapon back for another attack, and rage muddled a person's thinking. There was no guarantee she wouldn't hurt Biddie in her attempt to reach Gideon. He grabbed Biddie's arm and thrust her behind him.

Her head popped into his periphery. "He didn't hurt me."

"You screamed." Ginny swung again.

Gideon stepped back, keeping Biddie behind him and his hands up.

"He startled me." Biddie's fingers gripped the back of his shirt and tugged left.

He stepped back and to the left.

Ginny lifted the pickaxe. "He put his hands on you." Swing.

Tempted to go for the pistol at his waist, he resisted. Drawing a weapon would only make matters worse. He continued pressing them backward as Biddie guided him around brush and rocks. "I was trying to protect her."

Biddie spoke up again. "I almost fell into a cactus. He saved me."

Ginny finally hesitated, and Gideon took the opportunity to snatch the tool from her grasp. She lunged for it, but he hurled it far down the hill. With a feral cry, she reached for him, but Biddie once again placed herself between them.

"Enough! Ginny, stop. You're acting like Pa after he'd emptied a bottle."

Ginny's palm flew toward Biddie's face.

Gideon caught her wrist. "I don't think so." Fire burned in his gut. "What kind of woman goes from defending her sister to attacking her?" Then again, she had threatened to shoot Biddie earlier.

Ginny flinched, though her body remained rigid. Chest heaving, she lowered her chin and glared at Biddie. "Don't *ever* compare me to that monster."

"I'm sorry, but..." Biddie seemed to think better of finishing her sentence. Her mouth opened and closed before she spoke again. "Mr. Swift didn't hurt me. I couldn't let you hurt him."

A sudden twist of Ginny's arm broke Gideon's grip. In a blink, she yanked his pistol from its holster and aimed the barrel at his chest.

He braced for the shot.

CHAPTER 6

"*N*o!" Biddie lunged to block her sister's aim, but Mr. Swift blocked her.

Instead of shooting, Ginny stepped back and considered Mr. Swift. "You haven't explained what you're doing, still on my land."

Obviously braced for a shot, the man gave a small shrug. "Ma taught me never to leave a woman alone in a vulnerable situation."

"I'm no damsel in distress. I can take care of myself."

Mr. Swift nodded. "I can see that. But I can also tell you have no food and no time to hunt. What are you doing with all those rocks?"

Ginny jerked. "You've been watching me?"

He nodded toward the ridge of the valley to the west. "At first. But when I realized you were out of food, I set some traps and caught you a few rabbits. I was headed back to leave them for you when your visitors arrived."

Biddie crossed her arms. "I knew I'd seen someone."

Ginny gave her a sharp look. "And you didn't say anything? Where's my rifle?"

Biddie stiffened. Wasn't the one weapon aimed at the poor man's chest enough? "What do you want it for?"

"It's mine."

"Then you aren't planning to shoot anyone with it?"

Ginny heaved a sigh. "Not at the moment."

Biddie waved her hand in the direction she'd seen Mr. Swift drop the weapon. "It's somewhere over there."

"Biddie?" Lucy called from beside the fire, her gaze searching the darkness. "Is everything all right?"

"Yes," Biddie replied at the same moment Ginny yelled, "no."

"We'll be down in just a minute," Biddie assured her. "We have a guest."

"You mean a trespasser." With one eye still watching Mr. Swift, Ginny found the rifle hidden in the deep shadows beneath a nearby bush. She checked the load, then tucked the butt under her arm. "You heard her. Get down there." She motioned with the pistol for Mr. Swift to precede them toward the fire.

He hesitated. "Can I have my pistol back?"

Ginny laughed, though there was no humor in the sound.

Biddie injected a warning into her tone. "Ginny. Mr. Swift is not a threat."

"So he says." Despite her reservations, Ginny lowered the barrel to point at the ground. Though she kept her finger near the trigger. "When I believe him, I'll return his weapon."

Mr. Swift offered a stiff smile and waved for Biddie to go ahead. "Ladies first."

She stepped forward, but Ginny caught her elbow. "No, thank you."

His smile vanished and he stomped ahead of them into the valley.

Lucy saw him coming and backed away, her brown eyes rounding. "Oh."

Biddie pulled free of Ginny's grip and followed him. The fire's light danced across the waves of Mr. Swift's golden blonde hair, drawing her eye to a raised white scar behind his left ear. His dust-covered, travel-worn shirt and trousers spoke of long days on the trail and his leather holster hung empty around his hips. As she joined Lucy, his chocolate gaze met hers and her stomach flipped. She swallowed. "Lucy, this is Mr. Gideon Swift. He's the ranch's cook."

"He's a trespasser with no business sneaking about my property." Ginny stood at the edge of the fire's light like a guard on duty.

Biddie sighed. "He brought you food."

Ginny scoffed. "I see no rabbits."

Mr. Swift pointed to the western ridge. "They're up there, hanging from a tree, if the coyotes haven't found them yet. I'm happy to fetch them." He started in that direction.

Ginny lifted the pistol, bringing him to a halt. "How do I know you ain't got a rifle or friends hiding up there?"

The man threw his hands up in exasperation. "Then you get them."

"And leave you here unguarded?" Ginny shook her head. "Nope."

Biddie stomped the way he'd pointed. "Then I'll get them."

"What if there's more men up there, waiting for you?" Ginny called after her.

Biddie ignored her. Mr. Swift was at least a half foot taller than she was and three times as strong. She'd felt the flex of his muscles beneath his shirt as he held her. He could have hurt her in any number of ways when he caught her. Instead, he'd held her gently but firmly until reason had returned to her panicked brain. He hadn't even drawn his pistol the whole time Ginny was swinging that confounded ax at him. If her sister weren't so blinded by her unfathomable hatred of the male gender, she'd recognize that Mr. Swift had already proven himself trustworthy. If there were other men waiting in the dark at the top of this valley, he'd have said so.

No doubt he'd have made himself known instead of lurking in the shadows had Ginny not already warned him off her land. That he'd stuck around to see Ginny was safe and even hunted food for the ungrateful woman made him a saint in Biddie's book.

With it being so dark, it took her a bit of looking, but she found the rabbits hanging exactly where he'd said they'd be. She worked the knotted rope free and carried them back to the fire. Without a word, she held them aloft until Ginny acknowledged them.

"So he hunted rabbits. How do we know he wasn't going to eat them himself?"

Rolling one's eyes is uncouth, Biddie. The memory of Mother's voice kept Biddie's expression in check. "Two whole rabbits? By himself?"

"Desert rabbits ain't got much meat on them."

It was true the rabbits were small and unlikely to provide a filling meal for the four of them, but it was more than what they'd had before Mr. Swift's gift. Biddie turned to him. "Do you know how to prepare and cook these?" Despite her own culinary skills, rabbit was not something they'd ever eaten at home.

"Of course. And I'd be happy to prepare a meal for all of us with whatever else you have available."

"There ain't any other food," Ginny groused.

Biddie set a hand on her hip. "You said your land provided ample sustenance. Surely, you have something we can add to the meal."

"I got dried mesquite, a few dried juniper berries, and one wild onion."

Was that all? Biddie handed the animals to Mr. Swift. "Your assistance is greatly appreciated." It galled not to be able to assist with their meal. Although baking was her forte, cooking of any kind was one of Biddie's greatest pleasures. Unfortunately, she knew nothing about preparing the wild ingredients her sister had on hand.

About an hour later, Biddie savored the last bite of her less-than-filling meal and surveyed the starlit valley. There was much to do before this land could become a home. "Wouldn't it be easier to start over some place new?"

Ginny sat on a nearby rock, her rifle within reach and Mr. Swift's pistol in her lap. "Spoken like a spoiled rich kid."

Biddie's face warmed. "There's nothing here but ash and rock."

"That just shows how little you know. This land is filled with gifts you'll never understand." She tossed her tin plate into the coals of their fire. "Why don't you just give me the money you promised and go back to your fancy home in the city?"

Lucy straightened. "It was a fair question. You don't have to be mean about it."

Mr. Swift set his own plate aside. "I'd be happy to escort you all to the city in the morning."

Ginny stood. "The rest of you can go. I'm staying." She turned to leave.

Biddie intercepted her. "But why? You could come with us to San Francisco. Mother and Father would be happy to have you. They promised Mama—"

"This land is all I have." Ginny crossed her arms, the pistol pointed to one side. "I'm not giving it up."

Mr. Swift rose to meet her glare. "Then it'll be taken from you."

Ginny cocked the pistol and aimed it at the man. "Is that a threat?"

"Don't be daft." A muscle flexed in his jaw. "A woman alone out here doesn't stand a chance of making it."

"She's not alone," Biddie protested.

"Sorry, but your presence only makes matters worse. Once men discover there are three unattached females living alone out here, you won't be able to keep them away." Ginny uncocked and lowered the weapon as she opened her mouth, but Mr. Swift continued before she could speak. "Most of those men will be honorable, or at least decent enough to offer marriage in exchange for taking this land from you. But some won't be. And those are the ones who'll sneak into your home in the dead of night and catch you sleeping."

Lucy made a quiet sound of distress.

"But no one knows we're here except you, Mr. Leach, and Father." Biddie moved to put a comforting arm around Lucy's shoulders. "Father certainly won't spread the word, and I doubt Mr. Leach is the gossiping sort."

Mr. Swift crossed his arms. "Are you saying you didn't stop at the store I was told is about twenty miles west of here?"

"Well, of course we stopped." They'd needed to replenish their food. "But what does that matter?"

"You don't think the owners will notice Mr. Leach rode east with two unfamiliar city women, then came back without them?" He raised an eyebrow.

"But they can't know where he left us." Lucy looked to Biddie. "Can they?"

Biddie recalled Luman Gaskill's keen interest in their travel plans. At the time, she'd seen no reason for discretion and had told him they were headed to the Lupine Valley Ranch to visit her sister. The man had suddenly recalled a task needing his attention and left her alone. "I...told Mr. Gaskill we were coming here." She gave Ginny a quizzical look. "He had a strange reaction to the ranch's name."

Ginny scowled. "Oliver wasn't well liked in these parts. It's one of the reasons I've been left alone since the fire. No one bothers calling."

Mr. Swift nodded. "That's why the stage manager didn't know about the fire."

"Only ones who knew were the Rowlands." Ginny shifted her feet. "They saw the smoke when they were out riding their range and came to check on the place."

"And they didn't offer to help rebuild?" Lucy placed a hand over her heart.

Ginny looked away. "I didn't give them the chance. Saw them coming and hid out till they left."

Mr. Swift frowned. "You don't trust them?"

Her expression darkened. "They're men."

"Ginny..." Biddie inched toward her sister. "What happened here? You've never said—"

"And I ain't going to say. There's no point chewing old cud. What's done is done and can't be undone."

"Yet you're determined to stay?" Biddie couldn't understand why her sister would want to remain in a place with memories so terrible she wouldn't speak of them.

Ginny only nodded.

"Fine." She turned to Mr. Swift. "My sister may not have the funds or the desire to hire you, but I do."

Ginny squawked.

Biddie ignored her. "As you've correctly pointed out, we are three women in a rather vulnerable position. While I agree that our wisest course of action is to return to the city, you can see that my sister would not come with us, and I cannot leave her here alone. Therefore, I humbly request that you remain with us as our protector."

Mr. Swift stumbled back a step. "You don't know me from Adam."

"I know that you've had ample opportunity to do us harm, should that have been your aim. Instead, you provided us with food and resisted the urge to shoot my rather obstinate sister, even when she's repeatedly threatened to do the same to you."

Ginny's gaze shot from Biddie to Mr. Swift and back again. "Absolutely not. I—"

"Need my money." Biddie glared her big sister down. "Isn't that right? And the only way you're going to get it is over my dead body or by agreeing to the reasonable assistance of myself, Lucy, and Mr. Swift."

Ginny glowered. "Just because he ain't hurt you yet don't mean he won't."

Biddie crossed her arms. "Be that as it may, those are my terms. Take them or leave them."

Mr. Swift raised a hand. "Now hold on. I haven't agreed to stay."

$\sim$

*G*ideon readjusted the final stake for his tent and pounded it into the ground. He squinted in the dimming light of the fire's embers and eyed the triangular canvas. It had kept him out of the weather since leaving Montague—mostly—but a tent was never as secure as a true building. He'd looked forward to trading the drafty thing for a lumpy bed in the ranch bunkhouse.

He considered the charred remains of that structure. What was he doing here? How had Biddie talked him into agreeing to help with the harebrained notion of rebuilding this ranch? She'd said there was an accident with the freight wagon they were traveling on. Her father had been injured but would soon heal and join them. She'd made it sound as though the man would be right as rain in a matter of days, a couple of weeks at the most. By the time she'd stopped talking, it had seemed downright unreasonable for Gideon to refuse his assistance.

So, of course, he'd promised to remain until her father joined them. And it had absolutely nothing to do with the fire in her sky-blue eyes.

With that settled, the women had bid him good night and disappeared into their boulder cave.

Well, Biddie and Lucy had. Virginia—as she'd told him to call her—remained outside, her rifle in hand. It seemed she still didn't trust him and had insisted on standing guard. All night.

He tipped his hat toward her shadow, hovering just outside the dwelling's entrance. Then he ducked inside his tent and began setting up camp. As he laid out his bedroll, it occurred to him Biddie hadn't given any details regarding her father's injury. He frowned. What was she hiding?

Not that Gideon had been entirely forthcoming either.

But he was only going to be here a few days. The women didn't need to know about his vision troubles or the headaches that sometimes knocked him off his feet for days at a time. The last one had been brought on by the heat, strenuous work, and not drinking enough water. But Virginia had confirmed she had a spring that supplied plenty of fresh water, and he wasn't here to work as a ranch hand. All he had to do was keep a lookout for trouble and help fix their meals. Cooking wasn't exactly strenuous work—not as ranch jobs went. Which was why he'd responded to Oliver Baker's ad in the first place. So long as he was careful, Gideon could avoid any episodes during his stay here.

That's what you thought before. Gideon ignored the small voice in his head, snatched up his canteen, and shoved through the canvas flap to check on Legend, whom he'd moved into the valley. The horse happily munched on the green grass surrounding Virginia's hidden spring, alongside the women's horses. Thankfully, the fire didn't appear to have spread as far as the spring and there was still plenty of feed for their animals. Gideon ran a hand down the gelding's side, battling the invasion of memories.

"What were you thinking, climbing into that corral?" Mother's anguished cry dragged him into the past.

Sitting on the worn settee in their once-elegant parlor, Gideon's throat constricted against any defense. He'd been thinking Father needed help. The aging man couldn't run their entire ranch by himself, and hired men were thin on the ground. Besides, Gideon had felt fine when he hopped over the fence. He hadn't had an episode in weeks. Still the doctor insisted that increased activity would trigger the pain. But with both his elder brothers buried at Gettysburg, Gideon was the only son left to help.

He released a harsh laugh, his fingers pressing hard into the sides of the canteen. The truth was, he hadn't been able to stomach lying abed another day while Father worked himself to death. In his arrogance, Gideon had decided to defy doctor's orders and take back the ranch duties that had once been his.

Instead of helping, he'd pushed Father into an early grave and broken what was left of Mother's heart. She was never the same. He sometimes thought her passing four months ago was a blessing. At least now she was reunited with the ones she loved.

Gideon closed his eyes and pressed his forehead against Legend's neck. Father's death was six years ago, and this situation wasn't the same.

Gideon had learned to control his headaches—mostly—by recognizing the signs when one was coming on. He could take precautions. Besides, there weren't even any cattle on this so-called ranch. He was perfectly capable of babysitting a few foolish women.

Unless trouble came while he was having an episode.

Which was why he needed to stay hydrated and well-rested. Gideon shook the lingering guilt from his shoulders and strode to the spring to refill his canteen.

~

*B*iddie dipped her washcloth into the bucket of spring water and rubbed it against her bar of soap. Once she had a good lather, she handed the soap to Lucy.

Lucy lathered her own cloth. "It'll be nice to be clean again." She sighed as she washed. "It was so hot today."

"The cold water does feel good." Biddie scrubbed her face, then used water from a second bucket to rinse it. She watched the water stream across the stone floor and trickle through a small crack in the corner. "It's odd letting the water spill on the ground like that."

"Less work, though. No dirty basins to haul outside."

"True. But I still miss our tubs." At home, there were two rooms with large porcelain tubs that all the women, including Biddie and Mother, took turns using. Wood stoves had been installed in the rooms to save trips to the kitchen for heated water. She considered the sparse rock room in which she and Lucy stood. "Do you suppose it gets very cold here in the winter?"

Lucy shrugged.

Ginny's voice came through the entrance where she stood guard. "Snows most years."

Lucy gaped. "Snow? In the desert?"

"Up here, it does. Flatlands don't get any, though. Just rain and lots of it."

Biddie imagined bathing in this way during a snowstorm and mentally shivered.

Lucy wrung her cloth and began wiping the soap from her skin. "I thought the desert was supposed to be dry."

Ginny's shadow shifted in the entry. "Some parts are drier than others, but all of it gets some rain. Else nothing could live there. Not even cactus."

Biddie pictured the beautiful valley her sister called home.

Despite the desert's incredible summer heat, huge patches of golden grass confirmed Ginny's claim of wetter seasons. The year-round spring hidden among the rocks alleviated any concerns about keeping a herd watered. She didn't know much about ranching, but if the ranch had been successful before, it stood to reason that it could be again. Ginny must think so, too, or she wouldn't be so adamant about staying.

An image of the Stevens's large sheep ranch near San Diego flashed in Biddie's mind. The Stevens family had two large houses, a smaller house for their foreman, a bunkhouse, an enormous barn, too many corrals to count, and even their own school. Biddie's fingers tingled with hope for what Ginny's future could look like. She dropped her washcloth into the bucket and reached for her drying towel. "How much lumber do you need to rebuild? Luman Gaskill offered to place an order for us, but I didn't know how much to send for."

"None."

Biddie turned to face Ginny. "Did you say *none*?"

"Wood burns."

"Then what will you use to build?" Surely, Ginny didn't plan to live in these caves forever.

"Rocks."

Biddie put on her nightdress and considered the rocks blocking the gaps in the cave room surrounding them. Building with rocks would significantly lower their building costs. "But they let in so much wind. Won't you be cold in the winter?"

"I didn't bother mudding these rooms since I don't plan to be in them long. I'm still working on getting enough stones to start building my new house and barn. Those will be mortared with the stuff Indians and Mexicans use in their adobe houses. If you build them right, rock houses stay cooler in the summer and warmer in the winter."

Biddie had seen adobe houses in San Diego. Even one of the Stevens's large houses was built of adobe. Father said they were made of large bricks formed from mud and straw or other grasses. "Why not build an adobe house?"

"Rocks are better at stopping bullets."

What had her sister endured when the ranch burned? It was on the tip of her tongue to ask, but now wasn't the time. She should be able to see her sister's face when they discussed what was clearly a sensitive subject.

Forcing her mind back to the task of rebuilding the ranch, she withdrew her brush and began undoing the damage wrought on her hair by the day's adventures. "What about corrals? Won't you need wood for those?"

"Rocks will do for those as well, and rocks are free." Ginny glanced over her shoulder. "I told you, I don't need much. Ranching suits me, but I'm smart enough to know I can't run a large herd by myself. I won't owe more than I can repay."

"You can't mean to continue on your own forever." A ranch as large as the Stevens's required many people to keep it running. "Won't you hire men to help you run the ranch?" The funds she'd brought covered the salary Mr. Swift had been promised, but would the money stretch to as many men as her sister needed to make this place a success?

"No man's ever going to be welcome on my ranch." Ginny's head turned toward where Biddie knew Mr. Swift was setting up his tent, though she couldn't see him. "I still ain't sure how you talked me into letting that one stay."

Biddie hid a smile. When they were younger, she'd been able to talk Ginny into almost anything. It seemed that hadn't changed.

Ginny continued, "But as soon as Mr. Davidson comes, you're all leaving. Then it'll just be me again. The way I like it."

Biddie tried to ignore the sting of her sister's words. Wasn't she at all glad Biddie had come? Hadn't she missed her even a little? "What about Preston?"

Ginny snorted. "Preston's not a man."

"He turned twenty-eight last May."

"Still don't count."

Perhaps she should change tactics. "You might marry. I've heard there are many single men out here. Any husband would expect to help you run the ranch."

"Take it over, you mean. No thanks. I've had enough of taking orders from *men* to last me three lifetimes."

"Ginny, be reasonable." Biddie marched toward the entrance. "You can't run a successful ranch by yourself. And even if you could, what kind of life is that?" She grasped her sister's shoulder. "What happened to make you so—"

"Nothing happened to me, and nothing's wrong with me." Ginny pulled away. "Not everyone needs servants, silly clothes, and fancy washtubs to be happy." She stomped into the darkness.

Lucy sighed. "You shouldn't have pushed her. She's been through a lot."

Biddie spun to face her friend. "Yes, but *what* has she been through, and why won't she talk about it?"

"It can be difficult to speak of things that hurt us." She gave Biddie a piercing look. "I know you know that."

"But you know that I know because I've told you about all the things that hurt me. Just like you've told me all the things that have hurt you."

Lucy turned to collect her soiled clothes. "It's different for us. We're close and—"

"She's my *sister*." Biddie yanked her brush through her hair.

"Yet before today you hadn't seen her for eighteen years." Lucy dropped her dirty clothes into the corner they'd designated for keeping the garments until they could be washed. "You can't expect to pick up where you left off as children."

The hard truth of Lucy's words created a hole in Biddie's chest. Why had Pa done this to them? It wasn't fair. Whatever she'd done to make him leave her and Mama behind, she'd been only a child. She hadn't meant for any of this to happen. A tear slipped free, and she wiped it away.

Lucy's arms came around her, drawing her close. "Just give it time. Everything will be all right."

Biddie returned Lucy's embrace. "But I don't have time. When I told Mr. Green about this trip, I assured him I'd return in time to place orders for the bakery's supplies."

"Then he's freed up the funds? I thought he told you it'd be months."

"He did. But what if something changes? If he's able to purchase the property sooner and I'm not there to—"

"Don't go borrowing trouble before it comes." Lucy held her at arm's length. "What would your mother say?"

Biddie sighed. "To trust in God's provision and timing." She knew in her mind the right thing to do. Why couldn't she feel it in her heart?

Lucy patted her shoulders and released her. "Right. Now, can we talk about the handsome man you've hoodwinked into helping us?" She grinned and waggled her eyebrows before ducking into the next room.

Biddie laughed at her friend's obvious attempt to cheer her and followed Lucy through Ginny's room and into the space they'd claimed as their own. "I didn't hoodwink him."

"Psh. You made it sound like Mr. Davidson scraped his knee and would be along as soon as the doctor finished applying his bandage."

Biddie's face warmed as she crawled onto her bedroll. "As opposed as he was to three women rebuilding this ranch, do you think he'd have stayed if I admitted Father's injury would keep him away for"—she glanced toward the opening and lowered her voice just in case their words echoed beyond the stone walls—"at least six weeks?"

"Hmm. Probably not, but you still should have been honest with the man."

Conviction pinched at Biddie. "It's not like he has somewhere else to be. He *was* planning to work here."

"As a cook."

"He'll be cooking."

Lucy's voice took on a knowing tone. "And hauling and building and whatever else you find for him to do."

"You're making a big deal out of nothing." Biddie shifted, trying to get comfortable on the hard stone floor. "He appeared perfectly capable of doing anything that needs doing around here. And he has a good heart. I'm sure he won't mind the extra work at all."

Lucy giggled. "He *did* look capable."

The way she said it reminded Biddie of the strong muscles that'd held her close when she first sneaked up on him. The remembered warmth of his chest against her back did funny things to her stomach. Surely, such a strong, kind man wouldn't mind such a small change of plans. Would he?

CHAPTER 7

*B*efore the sun had fully risen the next morning, Biddie followed Ginny to the ridge of the valley, her stomach still rumbling for food. Mr. Swift had combined the last of Biddie's oats with the dried and ground mesquite Ginny had on hand to create a palatable mush. Still, there hadn't been enough to satiate everyone's appetite. They'd all agreed a trip to the Gaskills' store in Campo was necessary, and purchasing food would be their first priority.

In order to better assess what else they might need to purchase, Biddie had requested that Ginny give them a tour of the ranch and explain her plans for its future. Ginny protested that the running list in her mind was sufficient and a tour was a waste of time, but Biddie insisted. If they were going to invest their energy, sweat, and money into this land, they deserved to understand what they were working toward.

Ginny hadn't been able to argue with that.

She stopped at the peak and waited for everyone to join her before pointing down to the largest burn spot. "That's where the barn stood." She shifted her hand to the right. "That was the house." She continued to point out the places where structures had once been but were no more.

Then she faced away from the valley and swung an arm to encompass the magnificent view of the desert floor stretching away from them. "Lupine Valley Ranch holds claim to nine hundred and seventy-nine acres, almost twice what most places around here can claim."

Mr. Swift crossed his arms. "Why's yours so much bigger?"

"The man who owned it before Oliver came here with his brother. They each claimed a homestead, some timber land, and squatted on more till they could buy it from the government. Then the brother died, and his land became part of this ranch."

What would it have been like to come here with her siblings and then be left alone in this desolate place? Biddie swallowed. "That's so sad."

Ginny shrugged as if to say that was just how life was and pointed left. "To the south, my land is bordered by a long narrow gorge. At the bottom is a small creek. If you follow that creek west to the foot of the mountains where the water sinks into the sand, you'll find a bunch of desert willows. They mark the southern point of my western boundary. To the north, there's a line of rock sticking out of the mountain. And if you head east from the valley's eastern ridge, you'll fall down a sharp slope. The bottom of that near-cliff is our eastern border."

Biddie tried to wrap her mind around so much land and failed. The three-quarters of an acre owned by the Davidson Home for Women and Children was considered huge by San Francisco's standards. It would look like a speck on Ginny's ranch. "And you plan to run it all by yourself?"

Mr. Swift broke a twig from a nearby shrub and plucked the leaves from it. "It's not the land that creates most of the work.

It's taking care of fencing, structures, tools, and most of all, the animals."

Ginny studied him. "You sound like a man with experience."

Mr. Swift dipped his chin. "I grew up on a ranch in Texas."

"Why'd you leave?"

"My father died and the bank foreclosed."

"I'm so sorry." Biddie laid a hand on his shoulder.

Ginny snorted. "You couldn't keep your own ranch going, but you want to tell me how to run mine?"

Biddie gasped. "Ginny, be kind."

"Staying isn't my idea. It's yours and your sister's." Mr. Swift shifted away from Biddie's touch to scowl at Ginny. "I'd rather escort you to the nearest city."

Lucy stepped forward. "I'm sure Mr. Swift's experience will be useful."

Biddie nodded. "Yes, you won't need to explain to him how to do everything the way you will Lucy and me. So—"

"Now hold on." Mr. Swift raised a staying hand. "I agreed to cook and make sure you ladies were safe. That was all."

"Surely, you don't mean to watch three women do all the heavy labor?" Biddie leveled a challenging glare at him.

"I came here to cook. For men."

"I see." Biddie's shoulders drooped. Had she overestimated his goodness?

Ginny huffed. "Can we get going to the store now?"

Biddie shook off her disappointment and faced her sister. "You haven't told us your plans for rebuilding."

"What's to tell?" She pointed into the valley again. "We need a new house, a new barn, new corrals. We need new pipes for watering the garden that needs replanting. Then, of course, there's the troughs and a new herd."

Biddie's head swam with the details, and she again worried whether Father's loan would be enough to pay for it all.

Mr. Swift had nodded with each item Ginny listed. "And a defensive perimeter."

Ginny studied him. "What do you mean?"

Pointing, he drew a large circle encompassing a significant portion near the center of the valley where Ginny had indicated she wanted to put her new house and barn. "If you build a fence along here, it'll slow down anyone trying to get at the home." His eyes traced the rim of the valley. "It'd be better to build a second one here to protect the cattle, but that'll have to wait until later since it'll take so long."

Ginny nodded. "That ain't a bad idea. Except a stone wall would be better than a fence."

Because, again, a wood fence could be burned.

Mr. Swift shook his head. "Nope. A wall provides cover for the attackers. A fence slows them down but doesn't stop your bullets from hitting their mark."

An expression of grudging respect appeared on Ginny's face. "You learn that in the war?"

"Yep."

Ginny's nose wrinkled. "I suppose being from Texas, you fought for the Confederacy."

He squared his shoulders. "No, ma'am. I mustered up with the 2nd Regiment, Texas Calvary."

Ginny's brows rose. "Fine. We'll build a fence, *after* the rest of the structures are done. Cutting enough willow poles for a project that size will take a long time, but I'm not buying lumber for a fence." She turned to Biddie. "Now let's go."

≈

*G*ideon reined Legend to a halt in front of the Gaskills' store and switched the bridle for a lead rope. Biddie and Lucy stopped beside him and did the same. The two women had ridden double on Lucy's mount so Virginia could ride Biddie's horse. The offer by Biddie was another example of the crazy woman's generous heart.

During their ride to Campo, she'd explained why she'd come to Lupine Valley Ranch. The story left him speechless. He couldn't think of another person alive who would drop everything to come help a relative they hadn't seen or heard from in eighteen years. Well, maybe a mother would for her child. But Virginia was Biddie's sister. And an ungrateful, grumpy one at that. Staying on a ranch with no men about to protect them was still a foolhardy notion. But he could see now that it came from a generous, if foolish, heart.

He checked that Legend had enough rope to reach the water-filled trough, then strode past the women to hold open the store's entrance. The clang of a hammer against metal resounded in a nearby building as Gideon followed them inside. He paused to allow his eyes to adjust to the dim interior. Relief to be out of the sun's harsh rays was overwhelmed by the almost choking scent of dust and garlic. He glanced left and spotted several braids of the pungent herb strung from the ceiling.

After greeting the proprietor, Gideon joined Biddie near a soap display in the back corner. "Didn't you say you wanted some herbs?"

She added the soap to the bag she'd brought and glanced up at him. "Yes, why?"

"Did you see the garlic by the door?"

"I could hardly miss it." She chuckled and tucked a stray lock of sunshine-colored hair into her bonnet.

"You have a nice laugh." As soon as the words were out, he wished them back. She'd get the wrong idea.

Those sky-blue eyes widened. "I—I do?"

"Uh—" He cleared his throat and stepped back. His backside bumped into something soft.

"Hey." Virginia's startled exclamation accompanied a return shove, sending him forward into Biddie.

His arms instinctively went around her as they toppled toward the display. The back of one hand was crushed between her head and the wooden shelf, while the other protected her back from the impact. "Are you all right?" He tipped his head down to assess whether she was hurt and felt her breath tickle his lips.

As though he'd been burned by a campfire, Gideon jerked back, releasing her.

Biddie blinked at him. "I—I'm fine, I think. Thanks to you."

"Good." Gideon pivoted and strode toward the front door. "Let me know when you're ready to load. I'll be outside."

Large oaks scattered around the settlement provided shade for the waiting horses. Gideon stroked Legend's mane, then decided to stretch his legs with a walk around the property. The women would be a while collecting the supplies. The trickle of a nearby creek drew him. He stepped down the bank to the water's edge and followed its oak-lined path.

Several minutes later, the crunch of weeds alerted him to the presence of another human. He turned.

Biddie waded through the tall underbrush, skirts held above the snagging thorns of tumbleweeds and fox tails. Her gaze was fixed near her feet as she made her way down the gravelly slope.

He started toward her. "Finished already?"

"No, but I wondered if—"

A distinctive rattle sounded from the weeds near her.

She turned toward the sound.

"Don't move."

She froze.

Gideon drew his pistol and crept forward, trying to get a look at the rattlesnake. "Can you see it?"

Her lips barely moved as she whispered. "See what?"

"That's a rattlesnake's warning, sure as I'm a Texan."

Her eyes scanned the brush. She gasped, her eyes fixing on a spot about four feet ahead of her and to the left. "There." The dip of her head was almost imperceptible.

"Okay. Stay calm and slowly back away." Keeping his distance, Gideon skirted the area until he could clearly see the snake.

Biddie did as he'd instructed.

Gideon cocked his weapon and took careful aim at the coiled, rattling creature. As soon as Biddie was a safe distance back, he pulled the trigger.

The rattling stopped.

Gideon looked at Biddie. "Are you all right?"

Her lower lip trembled along with her fingers as she wrapped her arms around her middle. "Yes, thank you." Her gaze remained glued on the corpse. "It's still moving. Are you sure it's dead?"

He stepped to block her view of the animal's death throws. "I'm sure." Her gaze grew unfocused. He needed to get her mind off what had just happened. "That's three times in two days, now, you know."

Her gaze cleared and met his. "Three times?"

"That I've saved you." He tipped his head. "I'm beginning to think you place yourself in harm's way on purpose."

Her mouth fell open. "Of all the ludicrous...of course I'm not—"

"Then you've changed your mind and decided to let me take you to San Diego or wherever your father's recovering?" He'd meant to tease and distract her, but the reality of the danger surrounding the naive woman stole his humor. She hadn't even recognized a rattler's warning. This city girl had no business being out here.

She closed her mouth and lifted her chin. "One has nothing to do with the other."

"That only proves my point." He crossed his arms. "You have no idea how dangerous it is out here—especially for an unprotected woman." He jerked a thumb over his shoulder. "Look at what just happened."

"Nothing happened. I'm perfectly well."

"Because I—*a man*—was here to protect you." He'd heard of women tough enough to live alone on the frontier, but he'd never met one. And those women—if they truly existed—weren't beautiful city gals used to lace, teas, and fine-mannered gentlemen.

She offered a smug smile. "Which is exactly why we've hired you to stay on at the ranch."

"I can't be around all the time." Especially if he suffered another episode. "Do you even know how to shoot?"

Her cheeks flushed. "Mr. Gaskill has agreed to sell us two rifles."

He opened his mouth to respond but held his words as the sound of running boot-steps drew closer. He looked past Biddie. Virginia—rifle in hand—was crashing through the tall oaks, mesquite, and thick desert shrubs lining the creek. Luman and Silas Gaskill were on her heels.

Virginia drew to a stop beside Biddie. "Are you hurt? What happened? We heard shooting."

Biddie raised calming hands. "I'm unharmed. Mr. Swift saved me from a snake, that's all."

Luman's gaze met Gideon's. "Rattler?"

Gideon shifted to allow view of the deceased animal.

Luman grinned. "They make good eats, so long as you cut off the head."

Gideon had already considered that. This trip to the store would replenish the ranch's larder, but it was always wise to use what was available. Besides, growing up on a ranch had taught him to value the life of all creatures—even the loathsome ones. Making use of the snake's body was the respectful thing to do.

~

*a*n hour later, Biddie tightened the cinch on the saddlebag and eyed their six laden animals. Thank the Lord, Mr. Gaskill had been willing to sell them three horses at very reasonable cost—one for Ginny and two more to carry additional supplies. Without the pack horses, they'd probably not have been able to transport their purchases back to the ranch. As it was, they'd need to return in a few weeks for the rest of the wood they'd ordered. Mr. Gaskill's inventory was meager, and they could only strap so much to a horse's side.

She finished cinching the final strap on the second pack horse and turned to join the others beside the fire Mr. Swift had built in a cleared section of land behind the store. Lucy kept watch over a pan of chicken Biddie had seasoned while Mr. Swift used a stick to turn the snake meat in his own pan. Biddie took over watching the chicken, and Lucy began pouring coffee in everyone's mugs.

Watching Mr. Swift's fingers, she remembered the feel of them cradling her head, the tickle of his breath as he'd looked down at her. An unfamiliar warmth had enveloped her in that moment. Could it have been the attraction some of the women back home had described? She studied his profile. Had he felt it as well?

She forced her gaze away from his scruffy jawline. Whether he'd felt it or not was irrelevant. She had a bakery to start, and he...well, she wasn't sure what his plans were after leaving Lupine Valley Ranch, but the mental image of him in San Francisco felt wrong. Like a misplaced embroidery stitch.

The snake meat was turning white. A shudder passed through her. "Are you really going to eat that?"

"Of course. Rattlesnake tastes pretty good." He rotated the meat. "There's not much, but you're all welcome to share it with me."

Ginny grinned. "Count me in."

Lucy's nose scrunched. "Thanks, but I'll pass."

He quirked a brow at Biddie. "What about you?" His teasing tone told her he thought she was too squeamish to accept. "If I remove the bones and cut it into small pieces for you, I think it should be safe."

As if she were an infant who couldn't be trusted to chew her food properly. "Don't be ridiculous. I'll have it exactly as you take it." She ignored the queasiness in her stomach and faced Ginny. "Now that we have our own rifles, I was hoping you could teach Lucy and me to shoot."

Ginny shook her head. "Rebuilding the house will take days. Weeks, maybe. I can't afford to waste time teaching you something you don't need to know. I told you not to spend your money on them weapons."

Biddie pressed a fork against the top of the chicken. It needed more cooking. "And I told you that if Mr. Swift decides to leave sooner than promised—as you keep telling me he will —we're going to need a way to defend ourselves should trouble arise."

"I'm not going to—" Mr. Swift protested at the same time Ginny said, "There won't be any—"

Biddie cut them both off. "Men aren't the only source of trouble. Look at what happened today. If I'd had a rifle and knew how to use it, I wouldn't have needed Mr. Swift's assistance."

He snorted. "It takes years to hone the kind of skill I have. You're not going to learn to shoot with that sort of precision under pressure from a few target lessons."

Biddie checked the chicken again. Done. She began scooping it onto their plates as she spoke. "I've got to start somewhere, and being able to shoot poorly has to be better than not being able to shoot at all."

Mr. Swift removed his own pan from the fire. "Not if you

shoot me in the backside because you don't know how to properly handle a weapon."

"Then *you* teach me." She thrust a plateful of chicken at Lucy but kept her eyes on Mr. Swift. "Clearly, you have the skills and experience to show Lucy and me how to properly handle and shoot our new rifles."

"I didn't sign on to—"

"Or would you rather we teach ourselves?" She stabbed her fork into her own serving of chicken and ripped a chunk free. "Because one way or another, we *will* learn." She shoved the meat into her mouth and chewed. Why must the man be so contrary? There were moments when she could see his kind heart. Like his efforts to bring Ginny rabbits and how he'd sacrificed his own hands rather than allow Biddie to crash into the shelf. But then he'd call her a fool or point out the number of times she'd needed saving. Which was he—an arrogant dictator or benevolent protector?

~

*G*ideon smacked his hat against his thigh and glared at Virginia. "You can't stand guard three nights in a row." The obstinate woman had stayed awake again while the rest of them slept on the trail last night. He'd wanted to take her place as guard then, but a headache forced him to swallow his protest. But tonight the headache was gone, and he'd be hanged if he let her lose any more sleep. "You hired me to protect you. So go to sleep and let me do my job."

Virginia's bloodshot eyes glared at him as she stabbed a finger toward Biddie. "*She* hired you. I don't trust you." Her lip curled. "I don't trust any man."

Again, the word *man* sounded vile on her lips. "Yet you'll dress like one."

Biddie and Lucy had gasped in apparent horror when

Virginia emerged from their boulder cave five minutes ago wearing a pair of men's trousers she'd purchased from the Gaskills.

Virginia jutted her chin. "Trousers are more practical than skirts."

Why had she decided to change her clothing now? No matter. The topic was a distraction from his main concern. "Not all men are the same. I've caught and cooked your food, helped load and unload your supplies, and even saved your sister's life." As he spoke, her eyelids drifted shut. "What more do I have to do to prove you can trust me?"

She snapped her eyes open again. "Leave." She swayed on her feet, catching her balance by bracing the butt of her rifle against a nearby rock. "I can protect my ranch easier without you around."

He clenched the brim of his hat. "Like you protected your father and the other men from those bandits?"

Virginia visibly blanched. "I—"

He was a heel. "I'm sorry. I shouldn't have—"

"No." She sliced a hand through the air. "You're right. I failed then." Her posture straightened. "But I will not fail again." She turned on her heel and marched toward the valley rim, her rifle against her shoulder.

Gideon smacked his hat on his thigh again. Now why had he gone and lost his temper? Never in his life had he met a more stubborn bunch of females, but that didn't excuse his words. They'd been a low blow. Though she still hadn't shared any details about the attack, the mass grave and charred remains spoke for themselves. What had happened here wasn't something one woman could have stopped. In fact, her survival seemed nothing short of a miracle.

"She'll never make it through the night." Biddie's voice at his shoulder startled him.

He glanced at her. Without her bonnet, the golden curls of

her hair caught the sun's setting rays, adding a reddish hue. He turned back to where Virginia's silhouette moved through the shrub. "I know. I'll stand guard over there." He pointed to the opposite rim of the valley.

"Thank you." Biddie offered a steaming mug. "This should help."

He took a long drink of the hot coffee. The brew was good. Just as her herb-crusted chicken had been. Almost better than his. If it weren't for the sheer mountain of work it would take to rebuild this place and the ever-present threat of attack, his presence here would be unnecessary. The thought should comfort him. So why did it sting?

CHAPTER 8

June 17, 1873
Lupine Valley Ranch
Eastern San Diego County, California

Gideon swung the mallet and slammed its heavy head onto the chisel, ramming the pointed steel deeper into a crack in the large stone. He repeated the action, and the crack gradually widened. Eventually, the rock split, and Gideon carried the two large pieces to the wheelbarrow behind him. Lucy immediately lifted the handles and scurried off to dump the rocks onto the growing pile near the spot Virginia had chosen as the site of her new home. To his left, Virginia swung another mallet, working to break yet another stone. Biddie did the same on his right.

He paused to wipe sweat from his brow and shook his head. Never in his life had he imagined performing such grueling tasks alongside a bunch of females. It wasn't right. Men ought to be doing this work. Not that any of the women around him would agree. And he had to admit, he was impressed with their work ethic. They might lack the natural strength of men, but their perseverance and determination made up for it. Still, it would take them ages to gather and split enough rocks to build the size of home Virginia wanted.

Her plans weren't anything grand or oversized. If anything, she was being a bit short-sighted in not including a room for future children. Despite her bitterness toward men and her unusual behavior, he couldn't believe there wasn't a man somewhere who could soften her heart and maybe even win it.

Of their own accord, his eyes sought Biddie's profile. Her bonnet sagged, sweat dripped from her nose and darkened several areas of her ready-made brown dress, yet she continued swinging her mallet. Her strikes weren't as hard as his, but she was surprisingly strong for such a small woman. She'd caught him gaping when they first started that morning and explained that baking was a physically demanding task. He'd never thought of it that way, but it made sense. Still, he marveled at her diligence.

Biddie paused to take a drink from her canteen and glanced at him. "Something wrong?"

"No." He cleared his throat and reached for his canteen. "I was just wondering who's missing you in San Francisco. Aside from your parents, I mean." Surely, a woman as beautiful, skilled, and hard-working as Biddie had a man eager for her return. Perhaps, if he could get her thinking on whoever he was, she'd get to missing him and go home.

She winced. "I don't think anyone mi—"

"I'm sure Mr. Green"—Lucy huffed as she returned with the empty wheelbarrow—"would be happy to have you back."

Biddie avoided his questioning gaze. "He said he'd not be ready for several weeks yet." In a murmur, she added, "Maybe months."

"He asked you to wait?" Gideon took a swig of water and crammed the lid back onto his canteen. Was the man out of his senses? Sure, Biddie was stubborn and naive, but on only four days' acquaintance, even Gideon could see she'd make a wonderful wife despite those flaws. He moved to the next rock and chose a spot for his chisel.

Biddie's chin rose. "He's a very busy man. There are many things he needs to get in order before—"

"It don't matter what he's got to do." Gideon tapped the end of the chisel, seating it into the natural crack he'd found. "Any man who'd let his woman wander in the desert alone—"

"I'm not alone, and I'm not his woman."

Gideon's swing missed, and he hit his thumb. With a hiss, he popped it into his mouth. "You're not?"

"Oh! Are you all right? Let me see." Biddie rushed over and grabbed his wrist, prying his thumb free. "Oh dear, it's bruising already." She traced the tip of her finger across the swiftly swelling spot, the sensation entirely too pleasant.

He pulled away. "I'm fine." He wanted to repeat his question, but her relationship with Mr. Green wasn't really any of Gideon's business. All he needed was something or someone to persuade her to go home. "Have you written to Mr. Green about your change of plans? It's one thing to take a short trip under the protection of your father. Staying out here alone is—"

"I'm not alone. I have Lucy and Ginny and you. I am perfectly safe."

Virginia loaded more rocks into the wheelbarrow. "You going to split more rock or just keep yapping?"

Gideon opened his mouth to reply, but Biddie's reach for the wheelbarrow forestalled his next words.

She smiled at Lucy. "You take a break. I'll take this load. Then I want to grab a bite to eat."

Virginia rolled her eyes. "You do that. I'll just keep working while the rest of you finish your tea." Striding away, she called over her shoulder, "Remind me, why did you stay?"

It was obvious no answer was expected. Gideon looked

from Virginia's back to Biddie's retreating form, and then to Lucy who just shrugged and strolled in another direction.

Gideon worked in silence for several more hours before attempting another foray. He glanced over his shoulder at Lucy, who waited by the wheelbarrow. "I know why Virginia's here—it's her ranch—and Biddie's her sister, but why are you here?"

Lucy dusted dirt from her skirts. "Biddie's my best friend. I'm here to support her."

He swung the mallet. "Won't your parents be worried when you don't return as planned? Surely, your father wouldn't approve—"

"It's just Mum and me. And she's too...busy to worry."

"I've never met a mother too busy to worry about her child."

Lucy shrugged as Virginia and Biddie added their rocks to the barrow. Without another word, the quiet woman lifted the handles and headed back toward the house site.

Another defeat. Gideon slammed the mallet onto the chisel. He sneaked a glance at Virginia as he worked. Dare he attempt another conversation with her? Would it do any good?

The rock split, and he decided to go for it. "So...Virginia. I know your father passed on, and Biddie's your sister. You've got a brother named Preston who's coming, but you don't know when. Are there any other siblings? And what about your mother?"

Virginia exchanged a glance with Biddie but didn't speak or break the rhythm of her swing.

Biddie answered instead. "No other siblings. And our mama died when I was five."

"I'm sorry." His brow furrowed. Was there a delicate way to ask how one sister wound up educated, with the manners of a high-society woman, while the other sounded as though she'd had little or no formal education, and acted more like a man than a woman? Virginia's father died in the attack, but Biddie's was still alive, just injured somewhere near San Diego. "Then the two of you share a mother? What about your brother?" Perhaps it was impolite to ask such questions, but something told him the answers to more than their family ties lay within this mystery.

"Technically, Oliver Baker was my father as well." Biddie's mallet clanged against her chisel. "Though he never acted like one. Henry and Cecilia Davidson adopted me after Mama died."

"Oliver didn't object? And why you? What about Virginia and your brother?"

Virginia's rock split and she dropped her mallet. "I'm going to check the perimeter." She snatched her canteen and strode away before anyone could object.

Gideon cringed and offered an apologetic smile to Biddie. "It seems I've got a gift for discovering sore topics."

Biddie drank from her canteen. "It's only natural you'd be curious, given the circumstances."

He pulled his hat from his head and beat the dust off it. "Still, I shouldn't have stuck my nose in where it didn't belong." Hadn't his mother taught him curiosity killed the cat? There had to be a safe topic they could discuss. He recalled the smile Biddie had worn when she mentioned the Davidsons adopting her. "You seem fond of your adoptive parents."

"They raised me and love me as their own." The smile returned along with a new sparkle in her eyes. "And they gave me a little brother. Though, not one I share with Ginny and Preston. Charlie—or Charles as he's started insisting I call him—is Cecilia and Henry's only natural child. He was born shortly after they adopted me."

Gideon found a new rock and set to work. "That must have been tough. Did you worry they'd turn you out once they had their own child?"

"Never." She returned to swinging her mallet. "Mother and

Father have given me everything. That's why it's so important..."

Her words trailed off as her smile faded. Her entire body stilled as her gaze focused somewhere beyond the horizon.

He hammered his chisel again. "That's why *what's* so important?"

"The bakery." Her words were almost a whisper.

"What bakery?"

"My bakery. It has to be a success."

"Why—"

Lucy ran toward them. "Biddie, come look!" Chest heaving, she skidded to a halt and waved for them to follow her back the way she'd come. "You won't believe what I've found."

～

*W*ith Gideon at her side, Biddie followed Lucy through the valley and over a small rise. "Where are we going?"

Lucy's glance held more excitement than Biddie had seen in her friend for years. "You'll see." She stopped in front of a large juniper bush and scooped something from beneath its branches. She lifted her hand, revealing a palm-sized white rock embedded with many small brownish-red stones. "Look how they sparkle." Lucy tilted her find, causing sunlight to reflect off the angular surfaces.

Biddie ran a finger across one of the tiny reddish crystals. "Are they...what are they?"

Lucy laughed. "I'm not sure, but I think they're a gem of some kind. Look." With her empty hand, she pushed back the branches of a large juniper bush. Behind it, a narrow tunnel led into the side of the mountain. She pointed to a candle sitting on a bit of wrought iron stabbed into the wall of the cave at a point where the sunlight gave way to darkness. "I think it's a mine."

"It can't be." Biddie followed Lucy into the mouth of the cave with Gideon close behind. "Ginny would have told me." Wouldn't she? "Besides, even if it is a mine, it must be played out. Otherwise, Ginny wouldn't need Father's loan." She scanned the walls of the tunnel. "Did you find any more?"

Lucy shook her head. "But I haven't gone very far. I came to get you as soon as I realized it was a mine. There may be more deeper in." She lifted the white rock, a furrow in her brow. "Don't you think they're valuable?"

Biddie studied the shiny reddish stones again. "They do look an awful lot like Mother's ruby earrings, except...darker and a bit browner. Like cinnamon."

Gideon held out his palm. "May I see them?"

Lucy handed them over, and Gideon pivoted toward the sunlight. He lifted the rock to eye level, turning Lucy's find this way and that. "I think these are garnets."

"What are you doing here?" Ginny charged through the bush. "That's mine." She snatched the crystal-embedded rock from Gideon, strode past them all, and dropped it into a bucket Biddie hadn't noticed on the ground beneath the candle. Ginny turned to block them from further exploring the tunnel and shouldered her rifle. "Out!" She didn't aim at any of them, but the threat was clear. "Get out. You have no business here."

Gideon, Biddie, and Lucy dutifully exited the cave and skirted past the bush.

Ginny followed them out, her face nearly as red as the stones Lucy had discovered. "I turn my back for one minute, and the three of you quit working to start snooping."

Lucy gasped. "I wasn't—"

"A bunch of lazy thieves is what you are." Her glare pinned Biddie. "And you. My own sister. I thought I could trust you."

The accusation landed like a punch to her gut, but she straightened her spine. "That's a fine comment from the sister hiding a secret mine. You can't trust *me?* How can I trust *you?*

99

You've told me almost nothing about...about anything. Where have you been for the last eighteen years? How did you even end up on this ranch? How did you know where to find me? And why did you wait until you needed money to let me know where you were, or that you were even still alive?" She licked at the salty tears trickling across her lips.

"I—" Ginny's feet shifted along with her gaze. "It was complicated. You can't possibly understand. You, with your fancy clothes and fancy raising in the big city. You have no idea what it was like with Oliver and—"

"So *tell* me."

"I...he..." Ginny shook her head. "The point is, this is *my* ranch now, my land. If you want to stay, you follow my rules. And no one"—she aimed her glare at Gideon—"especially you —goes in there." She jerked her thumb over her shoulder toward the mine. "Ever."

Lucy looked deflated. "But—"

"And you are never to speak of it again." Ginny took a step toward Lucy. "Am I clear?"

Lucy's head dropped and she shuffled her feet.

Gideon scratched his chin. "But why?"

"Because I said so and this is my land. Break my rules and I will personally escort you off my ranch at gunpoint."

~

*B*y the time the sun set below the valley's rim, a dull throb had developed in Gideon's head. He squeezed his eyes against the pain but couldn't block out the words his family's old doctor had spoken just a week before Father's death.

"You served your country well, but it's come at a cost. It's time you accepted that."

Gideon had to finish emptying his stomach into the bedside bucket before he could respond. "Father needs my help."

"Be that as it may, your days of hard labor are behind you. Be grateful. Most men never came home, and too many of those who did are horribly disfigured or lost limbs. Many suffer from pains my medicines can't touch. Some have even lost their grip on reality. But for some reason, God spared you. A bit of missing peripheral vision and headaches that can be avoided simply by resting and foregoing strenuous work? Why, that's a gift, is what it is."

Gift? More like a curse. Gideon opened his eyes, grabbed the iron hook, and lifted the coal-covered lid from their new Dutch oven. The scent of beef, onion, and the other vegetables he'd added to their evening stew wafted up to him. His stomach rolled. Despite his not having eaten since breakfast, not a bite of this meal would stay down if he tried to eat any.

He took deep breaths to settle his insides and served up three bowls for the exhausted women.

Biddie's weary smile emerged from a dirt-covered face as he offered her one. "Thank you." She winced when her fingers pressed against the sides of the bowl.

He pulled the dish away. "Sorry, I should have warned you it was hot."

She shook her head. "It's not the heat." She lifted her palms and showed him the blisters covering several places, many broken and bleeding.

It was his turn to wince. "I warned you the gloves wouldn't be enough."

Her jaw firmed, and she retrieved the bowl from his grasp. "I'll be fine."

Virginia set aside her rifle to accept her serving. "A few more days and her hands will be tough as leather, same as mine."

Lucy grimaced as he handed her a bowl. Whether the

expression was from the blisters she undoubtedly bore or Virginia's words, he couldn't tell.

The enthusiasm the brunette had briefly shown over the mine's discovery had vanished with Virginia's steely declaration that no one was to enter or even speak of the mine again. The decision was so odd, Gideon had been tempted to question Virginia about it. In the end, he'd decided exploring the mine would only encourage the women to remain in this valley longer. And heaven knew he wasn't up to helping them mine it. So he left the topic alone.

Conversation among the women had been strained for the rest of the day, and as the women tucked into their meals, silence descended on their group. Gideon scooped his serving into the remaining bowl and covered it with a cloth. Perhaps he'd be able to eat it later.

With the Dutch oven now empty, he poured in hot water. As he scrubbed, he caught Virginia sneaking a glance at Biddie. It was clear the two needed to talk, but they hadn't said a word to each other since the confrontation at the mine. He'd half hoped Virginia's refusal to answer Biddie's questions would send the pretty city gal back where she belonged.

But he wasn't that lucky.

Not even bleeding blisters seemed enough to drive that filly home. And they looked painful.

Virginia cast several more glances at Biddie, then dropped her tin bowl in the dish bin and headed for the valley's rim with her rifle.

Yep. They were two stubborn women.

He should go after Virginia and tell her he'd take the night watch. As he'd expected, she'd fallen asleep the night they argued. When she woke the next morning to discover he'd stood guard without attempting anything nefarious, her attitude toward him seemed to shift a little. Not enough to let him keep watch alone last night. But enough to let him join her.

She'd fallen asleep just as the sun rose. He ought to insist she take tonight off. And he would. If he didn't know this infernal headache would have him heaving his guts out long before sunrise.

Some gift.

He finished cleaning the Dutch oven and returned it to the box they'd decided would act as kitchen storage until they'd finished the house. He added a sliver of soap and more hot water to the dish bin.

Lucy placed her bowl and spoon in the bin as he rinsed Virginia's. "You didn't eat."

He tipped one shoulder. "I'm not hungry."

Biddie brought her bowl and spoon to be washed. "After the work you did today?" She knelt beside him. "Let me do this. You need to eat."

He gritted his teeth against a harsh answer. His headache wasn't her fault. "Thank you, but no. You're exhausted. Go rest."

"No, really, I—" Her fingers tangled with his over Lucy's bowl.

He jerked away, and soapy water splashed them both. "I'm fine."

She jumped to her feet. "Fine." She pivoted to leave.

What was wrong with him? No woman's nearness had ever affected him this way. The sooner he could leave, the better. "You never said how your father was injured."

She faced him, obviously confused. "I told you, it was a wagon accident."

"Yes, but what type of injury did he sustain?" She'd made it sound like scrapes and bruises, maybe a sprained ankle. But instinct warned she'd downplayed the seriousness.

She clasped her hands behind her back. "He injured his leg."

"A sprain?"

"No, uh…" She glanced at Lucy, then dropped her gaze to the ground. "His leg was broken."

"Broken?" He bit back a foul word and dropped Lucy's dish into the suds. He rose and closed the distance between them, forcing her to meet his gaze. "That'll take weeks to heal."

Remorse covered her expression. Her voice was a whisper. "I know."

His fists clenched. "You tricked me. You made it sound like he'd be along in less than a week." He was a fool. Why hadn't he asked more questions?

The ocean-blue eyes staring back at him were the answer.

Shaking his head, he stepped back. Then back again. "I've changed my mind." He pivoted toward his tent. "You can finish the dishes." Pulse throbbing in his head, his vision swam as he sank onto his bed roll moments later. What had he gotten himself into?

CHAPTER 9

*G*uilt made for a restless night, and Biddie rose before the sun determined to rid herself of the pesky emotion. Ginny spotted her outside and headed for bed.

Biddie started a fire before gathering her ingredients from the cellar. As quietly as possible, she set to work creating a breakfast guaranteed to smooth any ruffled feathers.

By the time dawn arrived, the delicious scents of cinnamon and sugar wafted through the air.

As she'd hoped, Gideon was the first to join her beside the fire. He rubbed sleep from his eyes and took in the scene. "You made breakfast."

"I thought you could use some extra sleep."

He sniffed. "Is that...cinnamon?"

She removed the cloth covering the pan she'd moved from the fire moments before. "I hope you like cinnamon rolls."

A grin split his face. "I love them."

She separated a roll from the bunch and drizzled her glaze over the top.

He accepted the bowl from her and immediately took a bite.

His moan of delight released the tension in her shoulders. "This is incredible." The roll was gone in seconds.

She held her hand out for his plate. "Would you like another?"

"If there's enough."

She took his plate and served him a second roll. "I made two batches. This one"—she felt her cheeks warm—"is just for you."

He gave her a knowing look. "An apology."

She dipped her chin. "Yes."

He heaved a loud sigh and just stood there, holding his second roll as he studied her.

She shifted her feet. "Aren't you going to eat it?"

"Depends." He tipped his head to one side. "Are you going to lie to me again?"

"I didn't lie. I just—"

"Withheld the truth."

Her shoulders slumped. "Yes, but only because I knew you wouldn't stay if I told you how long Father would be recovering."

His brows rose. "That's manipulation."

"It is and I'm sorry. I promise it won't happen again." She swallowed hard. "But I'll understand if you decide to leave."

Please don't let him abandon us, Lord.

His eyes narrowed. "I don't suppose I can convince *you* to go home?"

She squared her shoulders. "I'm staying until my brother comes. I can't leave Ginny here alone, and there's no chance I can convince her to move to San Francisco."

He made a sound of agreement. "She's even more stubborn than you."

She crossed her arms. "I'm not stubborn, I'm—"

"Stubborn as an old mule." The sting of his accusation was erased by his teasing grin.

She released a laugh. "Well, maybe a little. But sometimes being stubborn is the only way to get things done."

He opened his mouth to reply just as Lucy emerged from the boulder cave. "Do I smell cinnamon rolls?"

~

*B*iddie set aside her mallet and reached for her canteen only to find it empty. Tipping her face to the sky, she noted that it was nearly noon. "I'll go make us a meal and bring it out to you."

Lucy slammed her mallet onto the chisel. "Thank you."

Gideon set his tools aside with a frown. "Making meals is my job."

"I don't mind." She gestured toward his growing pile of split rocks. With Ginny still napping, they'd decided to pile their rocks here and transport them to the build site later. "You're faster at this than I am, and cooking will give my hands a break."

"I could make the meal, and you could still take a break." He wiped sweat from his forehead with the back of his sleeve.

"Ginny wouldn't like that. And I truly don't mind cooking." Without waiting for him to protest further, Biddie turned and started the walk back to their boulder cave.

She entered the first room and paused to allow her eyes to adjust. Ginny's snores echoed from the next room. Stifling a giggle, Biddie stuck her head through the opening to check on her sister. Fully dressed down to her boots, Ginny slept spread across a thin blanket. One of her hands was tucked under the pillow, the barrel of her pistol peeking out from beneath it.

Could that be safe?

With a shrug, Biddie retreated to the first room and gathered her ingredients. She quickly assembled three sandwiches of cold beef left over from last night's meal and wrapped them in a cloth. After filling their pitcher at the spring, she carried the water and sandwiches back to where Lucy and Gideon still worked at splitting rocks.

They each found a spot in the scant bits of shade beside large shrubs and settled in to enjoy their meal.

Lucy finished her sandwich first. "Ginny's still asleep?"

Biddie nodded. "She didn't so much as flutter an eyelash when I checked on her."

Gideon returned the cap to his canteen. "She can't keep staying up all night."

Biddie swallowed her bite. "I've tried talking to her, but she won't listen. Did you know she sleeps with her pistol under her pillow?"

Lucy nodded. "And her boots on."

"I knew men who did that during the war." Gideon frowned. "From what I've heard, the ones who survived the worst battles still do it."

A chill traveled down Biddie's spine. What had her big sister endured?

~

A week later, Gideon and the women set out for Campo to collect the supplies they'd ordered during their previous visit. As they neared the settlement, he squinted. He tried to count the number of wagons and horses kicking up dust. Thirty, maybe forty people were gathered in front of the Gaskills' store and blacksmith shop. They didn't look happy. He slowed his mount. "Maybe you ladies ought to wait here. I can—"

"Must be trouble." Virginia nudged her horse faster, and the other women followed suit.

Gritting his teeth, Gideon urged his horse to catch up.

Within minutes, they'd drawn close enough to overhear talk of bandits and stolen horses.

Virginia brought her horse to a stop beside a man about her age with sun-tanned skin and a pale hat topping dark-brown hair. "What's happened?"

The man's mustache and full beard moved as his scowl turned to a smile at the sight of Virginia. "Well, look who's here. Good to see you're still alive, Gin. Some of the boys were starting to wonder, but I told them you were too tough and stubborn to die." The man's gaze flicked over Gideon before moving to Biddie and Lucy. "And who are these lovely ladies?"

Virginia scowled. "Never mind them. Tell me what's going on."

The man's perusal lingered on Lucy, and he winked.

Gideon's spine stiffened. This one bore watching.

Raised voices drew the man's attention back to the crowd. "Bandits stole half a dozen horses from McCain's place last night."

Virginia eyed Rowland. "Anyone get a look at them?"

His expression turned knowing. "Nah. But reports say the bandits who hit your place are still up north. Valadez raided the store at Firebaugh's Ferry. This bunch came from Mexico, and we mean to catch them before they make it back." He aimed an assessing stare at Gideon. "Could use as many *good* men as we can get." There was a question in the way he emphasized the word *good*. "I'm Clyve Rowland, Gin's neighbor."

Too far away for a handshake, Gideon simply nodded. "Gideon Swift. I'm helping out at Lupine Valley Ranch."

Both Clyve's brows rose as his gaze shifted to Virginia. "I thought you said—"

"It's a long story." Virginia turned her mount to maneuver around the crowd. "I've got supplies to fetch."

Lucy and Biddie followed her, and Gideon turned his mount to trail them.

As he passed Rowland, the man lifted a staying hand. "You won't join us?"

Before the war, Gideon would've been the first to volunteer. In his current condition, he'd be more hindrance than help—especially if one of his migraines came on. He stared at a tangle in Legend's mane. "I've got the women to protect."

Clyve's laugh was short and harsh. "Gin hasn't ever needed or wanted a man to protect her. Most of the women around here know how to look out for themselves. They've got to. But Gin's especially tough. She can look out for those other two."

"Maybe so, but I aim to do the job all the same." Not waiting for the man's reply, Gideon urged his horse onward. Pausing outside the store, Gideon took a long drink from his canteen. He needed to stay well hydrated. Because, regardless of Virginia's protests, Gideon was determined to stand watch tonight.

CHAPTER 10

$\mathcal{T}$he next night, Biddie dropped her dirty dishes into the warm, soapy water of the dish bin. Rather than camp in the open the previous evening, it had been decided to set up their tents behind the Gaskills' hotel and spend the night in the relative safety of the building's shadow. Virginia and Gideon argued over who would stand watch. In the end, both had stayed awake all night.

Remaining in Campo instead of starting back the night before made for a long ride home. By the time everything was unloaded and the evening meal eaten, everyone was exhausted. Biddie turned from the bin and caught Ginny dozing against a boulder.

Biddie gently pulled the empty bowl from her sister's hands. "You look done in. Why don't you go to bed?"

Ginny's eyes flew open. "What?" Confusion clouded her blue eyes.

"It's late. You should get some rest."

"Can't." Ginny struggled to her feet. "Got to stand watch. Those bandits—"

"Gideon can watch for them."

She shook her head. "You're too trusting. He—"

"Gideon is a good man." Biddie resisted the urge to shake her obstinate sister. Why couldn't she see his true character? She sucked in a long breath. Now wasn't the time for a lecture. "But how about this?" She retrieved her rifle from where it was propped against a rock and faced Ginny. "I'll stand guard at the cave entrance while he guards the valley. Will that suit you?"

Ginny scoffed even as fatigue forced her to place a steadying hand against a nearby boulder. "You still don't know how to use that."

Biddie shrugged. "I may not be able to shoot well yet, but this thing is heavy." She swung the weapon for emphasis. "I promise I can keep any intruder out long enough for you to wake up." Not that she'd have any need for such an action with Gideon also standing guard.

Ginny glanced toward the spring where Gideon had gone to fetch more water, then heaved a heavy sigh. "Fine. But if anything happens..."

"I'll wake you at once. I promise."

Two hours later, Biddie watched Gideon's silent silhouette slip along the valley's ridge from one stack of boulders to another. He was skilled in moving stealthily, but she knew where to look, and the brightness of a full moon made his task difficult. The situation would be different if they had enough men to station them at intervals along the valley's rim. Then, the men could choose the best spots and remain in place. There'd be no need for movement that might reveal a guard's location to a watching bandit.

Not that she felt they were in any real danger. Were she a bandit, she certainly wouldn't be out on a night so bright. She'd wait for the cover of a new moon when shadows would hide her dastardly deeds. Gazing up at the star-studded sky, she struggled to imagine any evil could persist beneath the glow of such glory. It made her want to sing praises to the God who'd created it all, but singing would awaken Lucy and Ginny, who desperately needed their sleep.

Tired of keeping her own company, Biddie crept toward the shadow that disguised Gideon's watchful form.

When she reached the cluster of boulders, however, Gideon was not there. Turning, she began scanning the ridge in either direction. How had she missed his movement?

"What are you doing up here?"

Gideon's close whisper made her jump, and she barely managed to swallow a scream. She whirled to face him. "You scared me half to death."

He raised his hands. "Sorry." Despite his apology, a smile split his face and mirth danced in his eyes.

She huffed. "I was bored and thought I'd see how you were doing."

"I'm fine. You could go to sleep."

"Ginny would be furious."

"True." He scanned the slopes leading toward their valley, then turned back to her. "I could come wake you before dawn. Then she wouldn't—"

Biddie shook her head. "My bed is farthest from the entrance. You'd never reach me without waking her." Not to mention the impropriety of his presence in her...sleeping area. She couldn't call it a bedroom without real walls, a proper floor, or even a door. But still, it would be improper. Father would never approve, and she shuddered to think what might happen if Ginny caught him sneaking toward Biddie's bed. A shiver ran over her.

"Are you cold?" Gideon looked around as though a coat might appear.

With the temperature still warm enough to bring a sweat to her skin even at this late hour, neither of them wore outer garments. "Definitely not. I was only thinking of what Ginny might do if she caught you in our cave."

He winced. "Good point." He pulled his hat from his head and ran a hand through his hair. "I don't suppose you want to sleep outside."

"No, thank you. I'll be fine." She turned her gaze toward the stars. "Aren't they beautiful? We can't see nearly as many back home. Of course, I noticed them once we were out to sea and a few times since, but somehow here..." She searched for a way to explain the difference.

He tipped his face toward the sky and whispered the words she could not find. "They seem crisper, brighter. Somehow closer and yet farther away at the same time."

"Yes, exactly. Doesn't it remind you of how great our God is? To think that He created all of this"—she waved her hand to encompass the sparkling dome above them—"and set every star in its place. And He also created each of us, setting us in our place, and guiding us through our lives like a loving Father." She turned toward Gideon, eager to share this moment. "It's so humbling, I—" Her joy fled at the look of pain and anger flashing in his eyes. "What?"

He blinked, and the anger was gone, leaving only sadness. "Nothing." He turned away. "I should move to the next point."

She followed him to the next lookout spot, doing her best to be as quiet as he was and failing miserably. When they finally stopped beside another set of boulders, she whispered, "How are you so quiet? I can hardly hear the dirt beneath your boots."

He shrugged. "It's something I learned for hunting. We all have our skills. Like you with baking. Those cinnamon rolls were incredible. Will you sell them in your bakery?"

She blinked, surprised he'd remembered her plans. They'd not spoken of the bakery since before Lucy discovered Ginny's mysterious mine. She'd been trying to avoid worrying about Mr. Green's reaction to her delayed return. Surely, he wouldn't mind, given how long he'd said it would take to procure the funds. "I will sell them occasionally, though my focus will be more on the desserts coveted by San Francisco's social matrons. Those are the women with the most money to spare for delicacies and with the right connections."

Gideon frowned. "If money and status are so important to you, what are you doing out here?"

She crossed her arms. "You make it sound sinful, but money and status open doors that would otherwise stay closed. Charity homes cannot run only on love and good intentions. They must have supplies and the means to attain them."

Gideon's brows rose. "You're going to open a charity home *and* run a bakery?"

"Of course not. I'm speaking of the charity home my parents run, the Davidson Home for Women and Children."

"But if it's their charity, what's that got to do with you?"

The weight of her past pressed against her chest. "My parents sacrificed a lot to adopt me. Few people understand how much. Helping them with the charity is the least I owe them."

"You're lucky you *can* do something for them." His tone grew intense. "You shouldn't take that for granted."

She stiffened. "I'm not, but right now Ginny needs me and—"

"Then take her with you." He scanned the slope below them. "You'd all be safer in San Francisco with your parents."

Why was he so eager to be rid of her? "Is that all you ever think about—how to convince us to leave so you can move on with a clear conscience?" She stepped back, her shoes slipping on the loose gravel.

His hands caught her arms. "Four."

His gentle tone and the warmth of his touch stilled her for a moment. "Four?"

"Times I've saved you."

"I only slipped."

He smirked. "Still counts. Who knows? You might have twisted an ankle or tumbled down the hill without me."

"Well..." Why couldn't she formulate an intelligent response? She broke free of his grip. "I'm staying. But Father should be along any day now, so feel free to leave."

~

Several days later, Gideon shoveled dirt from the trench that would hold the footing for the front wall of the new house. Each of the three women had chosen a wall and were working on their own trenches. He'd offered to do all the digging, but they'd insisted on doing their part. No matter that he could dig twice as fast as either Biddie or Lucy.

However, their decision turned out to be a good thing. The late morning heat was making his head ache.

He set his shovel aside. "I'll get started on our noon meal." He retreated to the shaded patch of dirt he'd dubbed 'the kitchen.'

After Biddie's suggestion that he leave, Gideon had taken a break from rock collecting. Instead, he'd collected logs and branches. Getting the curvy sticks to stay where he wanted them took many patient adjustments, but eventually, he'd created a shady covering for the area where they prepared their meals. It wasn't at all like a real kitchen, but it provided some relief from the relentless desert sun. Which was exactly what he needed at the moment.

He took a long drink from his canteen, then carried the pitcher back to the women and made sure each of their canteens were full. He returned to his makeshift kitchen and spotted two riders cresting the valley's rim. They each trailed a horse behind them.

"Company," he shouted to the women as he snatched his rifle and pistol holster from the stone he'd laid them across earlier. He searched the surrounding hills for more intruders. The men seemed to be alone. Gideon secured his pistol at his waist and strode forward, rifle lowered but ready.

Virginia shouted from somewhere to Gideon's right, "That's far enough. State your business."

With no peripheral vision, Gideon couldn't see her, but he had no doubt her rifle was trained on the strangers.

The men immediately halted, only one-third of the way into the valley. The older of the two removed his hat, revealing straight black hair, dark brown eyes, and tawny cheeks. An Indian. "I'm looking for Miss Bridget Davidson and Miss Lucille Arlidge." His speech carried a slight Mexican accent.

"What do you want with them?" Virginia's tone wasn't a bit softer. If anything, it'd taken on a sharper edge.

"Mr. Davidson sent me to fetch them."

Biddie hurried past Gideon. "Why hasn't he come himself? Has he taken ill?"

"Biddie, get back," Virginia ordered. "You're in the line of fire." She sidestepped, trying to regain a clear shot.

Biddie ignored her and continued toward the men.

The older man's gaze settled on Biddie. "My name is Eduardo and this"—he swung his hat toward his companion—"is Manuel. We work at the Grand Valley Ranch. Your father is well, aside from his leg, but Doc says he can't travel." Eduardo withdrew a paper from his saddlebag. "He sent you a letter. May I bring it?"

"Yes, please," Biddie answered before Virginia could object.

Still, the man didn't move.

Gideon turned and, sure enough, Virginia still aimed her rifle at the newcomers.

Biddie huffed. "For heaven's sake, Ginny. Put your rifle down."

Virginia scanned the valley, then slowly lowered her weapon.

Eduardo and Manuel took it as permission and led their mounts the rest of the way into the valley.

Biddie accepted the letter and quickly read it. "Oh no. Father disobeyed the doctor's orders and attempted riding too soon. He re-injured his leg. Now the doctor says he can't travel for at least four months." She lowered the paper to look at Lucy. "He wants us to stay at the ranch with him while he heals."

Gideon expelled a breath of relief. At last, a voice of reason. These women couldn't possibly last on their own out here for four months. He turned back to their food supplies. "I'll prepare food for your journey while you pack."

"That won't be necessary," Biddie assured him.

"It's no trouble." He reached for the rolls she'd baked the previous day. "I can help strap your bags to the horses when you're ready too."

"Thank you for your offer, Mr. Swift." Her tone sounded anything but grateful. "However, your assistance is not needed since Lucy and I will not be leaving with these gentlemen."

Gideon left the rolls in their basket and faced her once more. "Is the letter not from your father?" His finger twitched toward the rifle's trigger. If these men were tricksters—

"It is from Father, but his news does not change our plans." She looked to the two newcomers. "Father is well cared for at your ranch, is he not?"

"Yes, Miss. Teodora takes excellent care of him." He crimped the edge of his hat. "But he was clear in his desire that you should return with us." He gestured to the horses they'd brought with them. "We brought these for you, and there is a separate tent for your comfort while we travel." He pointed to a bundled canvas strapped to the side of one mare.

"That was very considerate of you, and I'm terribly sorry for your trouble, but I'm afraid I must insist on staying. As you can see"—she gestured to the partially dug trenches—"there is far too much work here for a single person to accomplish. It makes far more sense for us to remain here where we can be of use than for us to return and do nothing but sit idly at Father's bedside." She looked to Lucy. "Don't you agree?"

Lucy nodded.

Gideon resisted the urge to kick the dish bin.

His gaze collided with Biddie's questioning blue eyes.

He answered her unspoken question with a short nod. He would stay. Tempted as he was to mount Legend and ride off, the women had made it clear they would remain with or without his protection. And he'd never be able to live with himself if something happened to them in his absence.

Biddie's responding smile fanned the attraction he'd been trying to smother since he'd stopped her from falling in the Gaskills' store. He'd done his best to keep his distance, but there was only so much he could do under the circumstances.

Her father's request that she return had seemed a gift from God. He should have known better.

Now, instead of being stuck for a few days or even a few weeks, he faced four long months of headache-causing labor and dodging this strange pull toward the mule-headed angel. What was he going to do?

CHAPTER 11

Sweat soaked Biddie's bodice and dripped down her face as she worked with Lucy and Virginia to fill their wheelbarrow with clay from the banks of the narrow creek bed. They'd had to dig a few feet to reach the clay, but the thick reddish-gold material was needed to create the mortar that would bind the stone walls of their new house.

Biddie paused to wipe her face with the back of her sleeve. She must look a fright. Mother would be appalled, but there wasn't much Biddie could do about it. Rebuilding the ranch was dirty work.

At least since their trip to the store, they had a hip bath for bathing. It was a great deal better than the tiny bucket and cloth Ginny had been using when Biddie and Lucy first arrived. But how she missed the convenience and comfort of the big porcelain tubs they had back home.

As the women dug, Gideon rested in the shade of a nearby

shrub and sipped water. He'd already made more than two dozen trips to empty the wheelbarrow. As soon as the women finished refilling the cart, he would again push the heavy load up the slope and down into their valley.

Biddie stabbed her shovel into the clay and whispered another prayer of thanks that God had sent them such a generous man. He was the only one of them strong enough to push a full load. Had he not been here, they would have been forced to make trips with the barrow half full.

As if he'd read her mind, Gideon said, "If we had a second wheelbarrow and another man to push it, this job would go faster."

Ginny's rhythmic shoveling didn't so much as stutter. "No men on my ranch."

"Virginia, you're tough and the hardest worker I've ever known. But men are stronger. That's just a fact. And having more around would make—"

"I said, no men." Ginny dumped a scoop of clay into the barrow. "They don't all work as hard as you. And I haven't met one yet that I could trust."

A compliment followed by an insult. Biddie winced as Gideon grabbed another shovel and drove it into the hard-packed clay.

Biddie studied her sister. "Was it so bad before the attack?"

There was a long silence.

Biddie stuffed down the pain of another ignored question and stuck her shovel into the clay.

Then Ginny spoke, her voice hard and bitter. "You think those ash piles are what's left of a nice home, a sturdy barn, and everything a ranch is supposed to be." She hurled another scoop of clay toward the barrow and missed. "But that ain't never been here." She used the side of her boot to scrape the stray clumps back onto her shovel. "It was just a bunch of rickety shacks that leaked rain and snow and sand. When we got here in '65, the place was already in bad shape. Oliver cursed the man he'd won it from till he was blue in the face and emptied his gun into the side of what passed for the house. Next morning, he rode off, swearing he was going to kill the liar." She dumped another shovelful into the barrow. "I knew better."

Biddie nodded, her sole memory of Pa pushing toward the surface of her mind. "Pa was a mean drunk, but he wasn't a killer."

Ginny's bleak eyes met hers. "Not when you knew him."

The words sent cold shock through Biddie. Had Pa's temper gotten so out of control he'd actually killed someone? Who? Why? Had he gone to jail? Why hadn't he been hung as most murderers were? Biddie swallowed. Could she truly be the daughter of a murderer?

Without further explanation, Ginny turned back to digging. "No, I knew he wouldn't do it because there were too many saloons between here and Fort Colville's gambling houses. Sure enough, Oliver came back three days later, with empty pockets." She released a harsh laugh. "What I didn't expect was the wagonload of drunks he brought with him. Every one claimed they had experience working cattle." She shrugged. "I think some did. But not one put in an honest day's work once they got here." Her lips tightened as she scraped her shovel through the clay. "All they wanted was cards, drinks, and..."

Ginny didn't finish her sentence, but thanks to the stories Biddie had overheard some of the rescued women tell back home, she could imagine what else men like those might be interested in. Ginny's entire body was tense as she worked—her jerky movements at odds with the smooth rhythm she'd been using until now. Horrible suspicions formed in Biddie's mind, but she didn't dare breathe them. No wonder Ginny loathed men. Fathers were meant to protect their daughters, yet Pa had done anything but. "How did you survive if none of the men worked?"

"There was a big herd of cattle here when we arrived. It took me a while to figure out how to manage the beasts. I lost too many to dumb ignorance. And of course, a herd that size needed more than one person caring for them. But I survived."

Lucy's nose scrunched. "I thought the place was abandoned when you got here?"

"No, the previous owner left four men to keep the herd alive while he was gone."

"Do you mean your father left you alone with four strange men?" Gideon stood. "What about your brother? How much younger is Preston?"

Biddie searched her memory. "He's a year younger than Ginny, four years older than me." She raised her brows at Virginia. "That's right, isn't it?"

"Yes, but in any case, Preston was fighting in the war when we came here, and the men that were here lit out quick once Oliver started shooting."

Lucy gasped. "He shot them?"

Virginia returned to digging. "Nah. I distracted him long enough for them to get out of sight."

Heaviness settled on Biddie's shoulders. This was the man whose blood ran through her veins? "Those poor men."

"Of course, the ranch was rundown." Gideon's lip curled. "Any man who'd gamble his land isn't to be trusted. My father would have died—did die—before he let someone else take his ranch."

Virginia shot him a pointed look. "Then you should understand why I'll never leave Lupine Valley Ranch."

"This isn't a ranch. It's a patch of scorched desert." He shoveled more clay into the nearly full wheelbarrow. "Ours was a true ranch built by the blood, sweat, and tears of generations."

Emotion flashed in his eyes, but he turned before Biddie could discern what it was.

With the tip of her shovel, Ginny smoothed the piled dirt to make room for a few more scoops. "Every legacy starts somewhere. Your great-great-grandfather, or whoever, had to buy that land at some point. Back then, it wasn't anything but a patch of raw land, same as this." Virginia nodded as if to punctuate her point. "This place is the start of my legacy."

Biddie smiled. "A new beginning for the Bakers?" What a wonderful thought.

Virginia dumped the final shovelful of clay onto the barrow. "One not soaked in gin and sin."

Despite her dark comment, the idea of starting a legacy was the first bit of optimism Biddie had heard her sister express. To Biddie's mind, a legacy required children and grandchildren to carry it into the future. Was it possible Ginny wasn't as set against men and marriage as she'd declared? Biddie tried to remember the faces of the men who'd gathered in Campo to form a posse. Surely, one of them would see the treasure her sister would be as a wife.

~

*G*ideon dumped the wheelbarrow's contents onto the pile near the trenches ready to hold the house's new walls, then turned back the way he'd come. As he walked, Virginia's talk of legacy rubbed at his memories like sand inside his socks.

She'd misunderstood what he'd meant about his family's ranch. Father hadn't purchased their land in Texas until Gideon was thirteen years old. Still, Father never missed a chance to remind Gideon of the ancestors who had risked everything to come to America, and those who'd sacrificed and saved to drag their family out of poverty—giving the next generation a chance at a better life.

From childhood, it had been drilled into him that it was his responsibility to continue that legacy and see that the next generation of Swifts would do even better. Their Texas ranch should have been the means of seeing that through. Father had worked hard to improve the land and ensure the future happiness of his children and grandchildren.

But in Gideon's arrogance, he'd ruined it all.

From the rim of the valley, Gideon looked toward his tent and grimaced. Dirty canvas, a bed roll, and enough supplies to last a week on his own were all that remained of generations of hopes, dreams, and sacrifice. Worst of all, his would be the last generation since there was no way he could take a wife in good conscience. No matter how a certain pair of blue eyes and golden curls tempted him. For once in his life, he would deny his own desires and put the safety of others first.

If only he'd learned his lesson sooner.

He shook himself. Standing around moping wouldn't undo the past, nor could it change his future. He started down the slope toward the creek.

The women stood at his arrival and began refilling the wheelbarrow. He took his canteen to a shady spot and sat. Still, the memories plagued him. He needed a distraction. "So... Virginia. You never did say how you survived the attack that killed every man on this ranch." It was a mystery he hadn't been able to figure. It might have made sense were her father the type to send her to hide or Virginia the type to cower in the shadows. But he couldn't picture either being the case.

Virginia froze at his words, and the glimpse of pain she failed to conceal before smoothing her expression made him instantly regret his thoughtless inquiry. He opened his mouth to take back his question, but Biddie spoke first.

"I've been wondering the same thing."

"I wasn't at the house when they came. I was busy and didn't hear the shooting until it was too late."

Gideon rubbed at his brow. With the way sound echoed off the boulder-strewn slopes surrounding the ranch? It didn't seem possible a single shot could go unheard, let alone the number it must have taken to kill so many men. What was Virginia hiding?

CHAPTER 12

Gideon shoveled sand onto the wet clay in the wheelbarrow, then used the blade of his shovel to mix the mortar. Meanwhile, Virginia set the first layer of stone into the bed of mud mortar spread across the bottom of the nearest trench. It felt good to finally be starting on the foundation for the house. Too bad the echo of hammers slamming against chisels filled the valley, reminding him this house was far from their only project. Biddie and Lucy were already hard at work, splitting more rock for the troughs they'd build next. After that, they'd need to start gathering branches to form corrals.

An unusual scattering of gravel brought Gideon's head up, his eyes searching the valley's entrance. Sure enough, a rider was headed down the trail toward them. He braced himself for Virginia's shout of warning.

Instead, she muttered, "What is he doing here?"

Gideon looked closer and recognized Clyve Rowland, their closest neighbor. What *was* the man doing here?

As the rider drew nearer, Virginia continued setting stone as though she hadn't noticed their visitor. It was the calmest reaction to a new face in the valley Gideon had ever seen her display. Was it a show of trust? If so, why hadn't she asked her neighbor for help after the attack? Why not ask him for help now?

Clyve's gaze took in the signs of work scattered throughout the valley's basin as he brought his horse to a stop in the yard and dismounted. "Howdy." He nodded to Gideon.

Gideon set his shovel aside and crossed the distance to shake the man's hand. "Did you catch the horse thieves?"

"Afraid not. They crossed into Mexico, and we lost their trail." He turned to Virginia. "Hello, Gin. Need a hand?"

Virginia glanced up long enough to glare at Clyve. "I'm not paying, if that's what you're after."

Clyve laughed off her rude response. "I didn't expect you were. I'm just trying to be neighborly."

Virginia didn't respond as she stood and went to choose another rock from the nearby pile.

Clyve waited a second more, then offered, "How about I bring the rocks to you and you can place them where you want them?"

Virginia shrugged as she returned to the trench and knelt to set her stone into the mortar.

Clyve must have taken her gesture as agreement because he went and chose two rocks from the same pile. By the time he reached the trench, Virginia was done setting her stone in place. He offered her both stones. She chose one and turned to put it in position while Clyve left to get another rock from the pile.

Gideon couldn't believe how easily Virginia accepted the man's assistance. Did the two have history? Was it possible she had a romantic interest in the man? Gideon studied their interaction for another minute or two before turning back to his job of mixing the mortar and keeping it wet until Virginia was ready for more. If there was interest on her side, Gideon couldn't see it, but there was definite speculation on Clyve's part. Each time Virginia turned her back, the man watched her with a clear look of appreciation.

Frowning, Gideon added more water to the mortar. Hadn't the man winked at Lucy in town? What was he doing watching Virginia like that? Gideon gave the mortar another stir, then cleared his throat. "Was there a particular reason for your visit today?" Maybe it wasn't his place to question Virginia's guest, but he couldn't put his finger on what was happening here, and he didn't like feeling in the dark.

Clyve gave him an assessing look. Did he think Gideon was interested in Virginia? He returned the man's look.

After a moment, Clyve nodded. "I came to speak with Gin."

Virginia's head popped up. "What about?"

"Well..." Clyve glanced at Gideon, clearly hoping he'd leave.

Gideon widened his stance and crossed his arms.

Clyve turned back to Virginia. "I've been thinking. This here's a lot of work for one person." He waved to indicate the valley. "And you and me, we get along." He set aside the rock he was holding, pulled his hat off, and squatted beside the trench so that he was on eye level with her. "Seems to me, we'd make a good team. So how about it?" He held his hand out as if to shake on a deal.

Virginia sat on her heels'. "How about what?"

Clyve's expression grew pinched. "You and me getting married, of course."

Virginia's head fell back, and for the first time since he'd met her, she genuinely laughed. Long and hard. "Oh!" She gasped between laughs. "Oh, that's a good one." She wiped at tears leaking from her eyes.

Clyve's face grew red, and he withdrew his hand. "I wasn't joking. I'm serious."

It took a few seconds for Virginia to bring her laughter

under control. She blinked at him with wide eyes. "You can't be."

"I am." His stern expression sobered hers.

She shook her head. "Clyve Rowland, you know full well I've no intention of getting hitched. Ever." Her hands landed on her hips. "What would put such a fool notion in your head? You been drinking?" She leaned toward him and sniffed.

He jerked away. "No, I haven't been drinking. Now, be serious, Gin." He slapped his hat back on his head. "You can't run this place on your own. It's too much for one person."

Her eyes narrowed. "You just want my land."

"Of course, I want this land. Every rancher around wants this land. You've got your own spring." He dragged his hand down his face. "But I'm not trying to take it from you. I meant what I said. We'd make a good team. It'd still be your land, we'd just—"

"Don't you treat me like a fool." Virginia stomped out of the trench and moved to stand mere inches from the man. "Ain't no married woman who's got any land. The second she says, 'I do,' the law takes everything she has and gives it to her husband. So I ain't gonna marry you"—she jabbed a finger into Clyve's chest —"or any man. Not now, not ever. So just go on and get." She turned on her heel and went back to the trench. "I got work to do."

Gideon slid his hand over the butt of his pistol as Clyve glared at Virginia's back. A vein throbbed near the man's temple, his jaw visibly clenched. He didn't move for several seconds. Then something seemed to switch in his mind, and he drew a hand across his face before heaving a loud sigh. "I told Pa you wouldn't listen."

Virginia snorted as she passed him to retrieve more stone. "I should have guessed he put you up to it."

Clyve nodded and scuffed his boot across the dirt. The clang of Biddie and Lucy's hammering seemed to catch his attention, and his head turned in their direction, though a large bush hid them from view. "Are the other women over there?"

Gideon didn't like the renewed hope in the man's expression. He debated not answering, but it would do no good. "They're splitting stone."

Clyve stared at him. "Those little things?"

Virginia stepped into the trench and set another stone in the mortar bed. "Thought you knew better than to underestimate a woman."

"Not every woman is as tough as you, Gin." Clyve shook his head. "And those two seemed too delicate for such work."

Gideon gritted his teeth. Why did Clyve's words irritate him? He'd thought the same thing at first. But after weeks of watching Biddie and Lucy tackle almost any task they put their minds to, he was beginning to see they were tougher than they looked. He met Clyve's gaze. "You'd be surprised what they can do."

"Maybe so, but it don't set right with me, leaving women to do such hard labor." His look judged Gideon for not taking the task from them.

He opened his mouth to inform the know-it-all that stopping these women from doing anything they'd decided to do was about as easy as stopping a stampede, but the man spoke first.

"I'm going to help." Clyve picked up a mallet and strode toward the clanging.

As he passed, Gideon shot his arm out. "If you want to help, take this." He pressed his shovel against the man's chest. Clyve grabbed it reflexively, and Gideon used the man's surprise to yank the mallet from his grasp. "*I'll* help split the stone."

Gideon didn't wait for Clyve's agreement but hurried off to join Biddie and Lucy.

*B*iddie slammed her hammer against the chisel. *Clang.*

Her letter to Mr. Green weighed heavy in her pocket. How long until they could return to town so she could mail it? Would he understand her reasons for remaining on the ranch? What if it hadn't taken as long as he thought to procure the funds? If he'd already purchased the property, would he begin renovations without her input? What if he grew impatient and found another baker to run the bakery? She'd lose that perfect location, have more competition, and need to find a new investor. Was there even another one out there who'd believe in her enough to give her a chance?

Lucy's hammer clanged against her chisel, drawing Biddie's gaze. There was no obvious crack in the stone Lucy worked on. Instead, she chipped away at one spot, creating a small divot into which a wedge could be inserted. Then she'd create another divot and insert another wedge and continue on until there were a line of wedges stuck into the rock. Careful tapping against the top of each wedge would eventually form a crack that could split the rock. But it was tedious, exhausting work.

Biddie's gaze took in the golden valley dotted with white boulders and sage-green shrubs. Everything here took so long. If only Ginny would agree to hiring more help. But in the years they'd been apart, it seemed her sister had grown as hard as these stones. Few of Biddie's suggestions were heeded and even fewer questions answered.

She'd boarded their ship in San Francisco with such excitement. Her sister was alive, and at long last, Biddie would receive answers to the questions that had plagued her childhood. Where were Ginny and Preston? What had they been doing all these years? Why hadn't they come back for her? Why had they left her in the first place? Of course, she'd told herself time and again that, like her, they'd been children at the time. If Pa took them away, what choice did they have in the separation? Yet Ginny had long ago ceased being a child, and it seemed she'd known where Biddie was. So why hadn't she come? And why—now that Biddie was here and helping her in every way possible—wouldn't Ginny answer any of Biddie's questions? Why was her sister so determined to keep the secrets of the past to herself?

Heavy boot steps drew nearer. Biddie shook off her melancholy and put on a smile to greet Gideon.

He scowled at her in return. "You need to rest." He took the hammer from her hands and pointed to where she'd left her canteen in a spot of nearby shade. "Sit and drink some water." He took the hammer from Lucy as well. "You too."

Lucy looked at Biddie in silent question, and Biddie shook her head with a shrug. She sat in the shade as instructed and took a long drink while Gideon started to work on the rock Lucy had been chiseling.

Biddie waited for a pause between his strikes to ask, "Is something wrong?"

"No." *Whack.*

"You seem..." Biddie hesitated, searching for the right word. "Unhappy."

"I'm fine." *Whack.*

Biddie exchanged a look with Lucy. Sure, he was. She sighed. Was everyone in this strange land so obstinate?

Several more seconds passed with Gideon hammering while she and Lucy rested. With his sleeves rolled to his elbows, she could see the muscles working in his arms as he swung. Yet the movement seemed as natural and effortless as a cloud drifting across the sky. He was born for life on a ranch. As much as he grumbled about having to care for them, the work here suited him.

He spoke without breaking rhythm. "Your sister just refused to get married."

Biddie's chest constricted. He'd proposed? To Ginny? Well, it did make sense. Hadn't she just been thinking how well-suited he was for ranch life? And whether her sister wanted to admit it or not, Ginny did need help with such a large ranch. "I —" Why were the words so difficult to get out? It weren't as though she had an interest in Gideon. Attractive as he may be, a relationship between them would never work. Their goals in life were too different. Well, in truth, she didn't know what his goals were, but it was highly unlikely he'd be happy in a big city like San Francisco. "I didn't realize you felt..."

He turned then, eyes wide with apparent horror. "Not to me. To that Clyve fellow."

Air returned to Biddie's lungs. Why was she so relieved? This changed nothing. She'd still be returning to San Francisco as soon as Preston returned and Father was well enough to travel, and Gideon would move on to some other ranch. In all likelihood, their paths would never cross again.

Lucy's brows furrowed. "Mr. Rowland was here?"

"Still is." Gideon's gaze searched Biddie. For what?

Looking away, she stood. "You left my sister alone with a single man? One who just proposed to her?" Didn't he realize the impropriety of such a situation? Perhaps not. The rules of propriety seemed different out here. Anyone back in San Francisco would find the idea of a single male living alone with three unwed females positively scandalous, but the Gaskills hadn't blinked an eye when they'd learned of the situation. Out here, it seemed practicality won over propriety. Still, a true gentleman wouldn't have left her sister alone with Mr. Rowland. Yet another example of how poorly Gideon would fit in San Francisco.

She stepped forward, intent on chaperoning her sister, but Gideon caught her arm. "They're fine. I assure you."

She turned and realized how close they stood. His deep

brown eyes held hers. Warmth zinged through her. Her heart sped in her chest. Did he feel it too? This irrational connection?

~

*G*ideon released Biddie and stepped back. Touching her had been a mistake. He spun and retrieved her hammer. Then he turned back, careful to avoid her probing eyes as he extended the handle toward her. "Here. If you're done resting, we'd better get back to work."

She took the tool, and he turned away. No good came from considering what had passed between them. Best to focus on the task at hand. He set the chisel in place and swung his hammer.

In seconds, Lucy and Biddie were back to work as well. The afternoon passed with agonizing tedium.

As the sun neared the western horizon, Gideon set his tool aside. "I'm going to get started on our evening meal."

Biddie lowered her hammer. "I can hel—"

"No." He knew his tone was too short, but couldn't bring himself to apologize. "I can handle it." Avoiding her gaze, he walked back to the 'kitchen.'

Virginia had finished the first two layers of stone and was working on a third as he approached. Clyve stood beside her pouring a shovelful of mortar across the line of rocks.

Gideon met the man's gaze. "Surprised you're still here." After the humiliating way Virginia had rejected Clyve's proposal, he'd expected the man to make an excuse to leave long ago. Perhaps Gideon had misjudged him.

Clyve's voice hardened. "I said I'd help."

Gideon nodded and offered an apologetic expression.

Clyve responded with a nod of his own, clearly accepting the unspoken apology.

Gideon turned his attention to preparing their meal and made sure to add enough for Clyve as well.

By the time everyone had finished eating, the sun was well below the horizon but twilight kept the stars from shining.

Clyve stood. "Thank you for the meal, but I'd best head for home." Virginia busied herself with bringing her bowl to the wash-bin as he stared at her. He opened his mouth but closed it again without a word.

Lucy rose and reached for his empty bowl with a smile. "Thank you again for your help today".

His eyes lit with her words and his lips curved upwards. "It was a pleasure getting to know you." He glanced to Biddie. "Both of you."

Lucy's cheeks pinked, and she turned away.

Biddie returned Clyve's smile. "Your generous assistance was much appreciated. You're welcome anytime."

"He is not." Virginia's distracted protest seemed more automatic than sincere.

Clyve's smile widened into a grin, and he plopped his hat onto his head. "Until later, ladies."

Gideon jumped to his feet. "Let me help you with your horse." He didn't wait for the man to point out that a seasoned rancher hardly needed help fetching his own horse but instead hurried to where the animal waited beside the spring.

Clyve followed close behind.

Gideon was fairly certain they were out of earshot but kept his voice low just in case. "Why'd you help today?"

Clyve straightened, clearly insulted by the question. "I've been Gin's neighbor for close to six years. It's what neighbors do for each other." He put his fists on his hips. "The real question is what you're doing here. The Bakers couldn't afford to hire good men before the attack. And I know Gin's got a good head on her shoulders, so you wouldn't be here if she didn't think you could be trusted. But that still don't explain your motives. Where'd you come from?"

Gideon explained how he'd been hired by Oliver and arrived to discover Virginia living alone. He explained his plan to leave her the rabbits and Biddie's insistence he stay despite Virginia's protests, but he left out the part about wrestling with Biddie and Virginia's attempt to pickaxe him.

Clyve lowered his arms. "You're the noble type, huh?"

"Aren't you?" Gideon held his gaze.

Clyve faced the fire's glow. "I'm not saying I'm perfect, but I wouldn't hurt Gin for the world."

"And the other two women?" Gideon thought he knew the answer, but wanted to hear it just the same.

Clyve looked him in the eye. "I'd never hurt any woman."

Gideon relaxed. "Good. That's what I thought. Which is why I wanted to ask your help in watching out for them."

"I'm not sure what I can do." He shrugged. "Gin refused my proposal, and I've got my own ranch to run."

"Just let me know if you hear of those thieves heading back this way or notice any strangers in the area."

Clyve nodded. "I can do that."

They shook hands, and Clyve mounted his horse, then looked down at Gideon. "Tell Lucy, I just remembered Old Man Pearson's got a milk cow he's looking to sell. She mentioned Biddie wanted fresh milk for some of her recipes."

Gideon agreed and considered the man as he rode out of the valley. Now that Virginia had rejected his proposal, was Clyve turning his attention to Lucy...or Biddie?

CHAPTER 13

*A*nother blurry line formed in Gideon's eyesight, and he clenched his teeth. He didn't have time for this. Virginia and Lucy were busy stacking stones onto the layer of mortar he'd just poured for them. Biddie stood beside them with a trowel and a bucket of mortar, ready to fill the gaps between rocks. His job was to bring the stones they needed from the pile. But if this headache developed into the blinding pain that squiggly line promised, he'd be forced to lie down, leaving the women to do the work alone.

He started to hand Virginia the next rock but had to close his eyes as a strong gust blew dirt across the valley. Once it passed, he lifted the rock. "Will this one work?"

"Let's see." She took the stone and set it in place, adjusting it slightly to meet the edges of the rock beside it as closely as possible. "Looks good."

He turned to retrieve another stone but collided with something.

"Oh!" Biddie cried out.

He whirled in time to see her topple backward against the

wall, dislodging several recently placed stones. Her bonnet hung askew, and her limbs bent at awkward angles.

"Oh no!" Lucy's hands flew to her face.

Silently cursing his missing peripheral vision, Gideon slid one arm behind Biddie's shoulder and another beneath her knees. "I'm so sorry." He lifted her from the toppled wall and carried her to the blanket they'd sat on for their noon meal. "Show me where you're hurt."

"I'm fine. Just a few bumps and scrapes." Her dirt-covered cheeks were rosy.

"Are you sure? You didn't hit your head on the rocks?" He nudged her bonnet aside to check for bumps. Grit and sweat coated her hair. She'd been working so hard. If only they'd hire more men to help.

She drew away from his touch, her face even redder. "No. Nothing like that." She wiped the mortar from her palms and winced.

He caught her wrist and turned it. Harsh red lines embedded with bits of gravel and mortar marred her skin. "Wait here." He retrieved their wash bucket and a cloth.

Back at the blanket, he took the lid off the bucket and dipped the cloth into the water. Then he reached for her hand.

"I can do it." She tried to take the cloth, but he held it back.

"Please, allow me. It's the least I can do."

She bit her lip and glanced to where Lucy and Virginia were busily repairing the damage he'd caused. Then she nodded.

As gently as possible, he cleansed her wounds. She didn't make a sound, but her occasional flinch betrayed the pain he'd caused her. He wanted to punch himself. What was he doing here? This ranch may have no cattle, but his poor vision still posed a danger to those around him. Biddie's injuries were minor this time. Next time, they could be worse. Was the little help he could offer truly worth the risk?

~

*B*iddie spit dirt from her mouth and turned so that her bonnet blocked most of the blowing sand. The occasional gusts of the morning had transformed into an unceasing gale that threatened to push her over. An hour ago, the gusts had torn Gideon's tent from its stakes, and they'd barely managed to catch the canvas before it blew out of the valley. All four of them had rushed to move Gideon's belongings into the front room of the boulder cave.

By the time they'd finished, Gideon was clutching at his head. Moments later, he lost the contents of his stomach. She could tell it grated on him to be forced to lay down while they continued to work.

She lifted a stone from the pile and carried it to the half-finished front wall of the new house. At the opposite end of the valley, a small whirlwind spun dirt and tumbleweeds through the air. She turned from the sight and handed Ginny the rock.

Ginny added the stone to the wall, adjusting it until it fit snugly. Then Lucy scooped a handful of mortar and pressed it between that rock and the one before it.

Biddie turned back to retrieve another rock from the pile. Unlike Gideon, she could only carry a single rock at a time. So their progress was slower without his help, but at least they were moving forward. With the sun halfway to the horizon, they'd probably not be able to finish as much as they'd hoped to today.

Another gust drove stinging sand into her eyes. "Ah!" She dropped the rock to cover her eyes with her palms.

"Don't rub!" Ginny shouted. Her hand came to Biddie's shoulder. "This way."

Biddie blindly followed Ginny's guiding.

"Duck." Ginny pressed a hand to the top of Biddie's head.

The wind lessened and she blinked, trying to see where they were. Tears and stinging pain continued to blind her.

"What happened?" Gideon's alarmed voice echoed around her. They must be in the boulder cave.

"I'm all right." She held her hands in front of her, searching for anything she might bump into. "I've just got sand in my eyes."

His rough hands took hers, guiding her forward, then pressed her downward. "Sit here."

Lucy's hands cupped her head. "Tip your head sideways and open your eyes so we can pour water over them."

Biddie tipped her head but couldn't force her eyes to stay open.

"Let me help." Gideon's large fingers gently pried her lids open, and a second later, lukewarm water flowed across her eyes.

It took two rinses to clear all the sand. When they were finished, Biddie smiled up at them. "I'm sorry to make such a fuss over a bit of sand."

Ginny clucked her tongue. "I knew a man who couldn't see for two weeks after getting sand in his eyes. Can you see all right?"

Biddie glanced around the room to assess her vision and spotted a box turned on its side and topped with a plate of sliced bread. Beside it was an onion, two carrots, a bundle of herbs, and an open jar of broth. She looked at Gideon. "I thought you were resting?"

He shrugged. "I figured the least I could do was prepare the evening meal while the rest of you work." He pointed to a small bed of coals near the entrance. "I was about to make some soup."

"You didn't need to do that. I could have handled it."

He scowled at her. "Cooking is my job."

Biddie opened her mouth to argue, but Lucy cleared her

throat. "We'd better get back to work. We're running out of sunlight."

Gideon shook his head. "You'll just get more sand in your eyes if you go back out there."

Ginny turned from where she'd been rummaging in a sack and lifted three long strips of cloth. "Not with these."

Lucy's brow wrinkled. "What are those?"

Instead of answering, Ginny drew her knife and cut two slits in each of the cloth strips. She handed one to Biddie and the other to Lucy. "You put them over your eyes like this." Lifting her cloth, she tied it around her head like a blindfold. Except the two slits she'd cut aligned perfectly with her eyes.

Biddie squinted, trying to see Ginny's eyes. "Can you actually see through that?"

"Enough to get the job done. Tie yours on and let's get going."

With the cloth protecting their eyes, they were able to add two more levels to the stone walls before the gusts grew too strong to continue battling. They retreated to the boulder cave, where Gideon gave them each a bowl of warm soup and a slice of bread before collapsing onto the pallet he'd laid out at the far end of the small room.

Biddie leaned close to whisper in Lucy's ear. "I'm glad he finally laid down. The poor man looked ready to fall over."

Lucy murmured an agreement, then spooned soup into her mouth. Her cheeks immediately puffed and her eyes widened.

"What's wrong?" Biddie asked. "Too hot?"

A frantic look in her eyes, Lucy shook her head and seemed to search the room for something. Then she spun and charged for the entrance. She bent at the waist and stuck her head outside. As she returned, she wiped sand from her face.

What on earth? Biddie looked from Lucy to her own bowl of soup. It seemed fine. She looked at Ginny, who shook her head.

"I ain't tried it yet."

Lucy reclaimed her seat beside Biddie and cast a glance at Gideon, who hadn't stirred. Then she whispered, "It's full of sand."

Biddie frowned. "Are you sure?" They'd been covered in sand when they came in. Maybe the sand from Lucy's face had gotten into the soup when she ate it. Biddie cautiously spooned a small amount into her mouth. The flavor was delicious, but Lucy was right. The soup was filled with sand. She turned away from the others and carefully spit the soup back into her bowl. "You're right."

Ginny wrinkled her nose and set her bowl aside. She eyed the bread suspiciously. "Think this is safe to eat?" She made no effort to lower her voice.

"Hush!" Biddie warned her with a worried glance at Gideon. Thankfully, he appeared undisturbed. "The sand must have blown into the soup when it was cooking near the opening. I'm sure the bread is fine." At least her grumbling stomach hoped it was edible.

CHAPTER 14

July 23, 1873
Lupine Valley Ranch
Eastern San Diego County, California

*G*ideon exited the Rowlands' barn and turned Legend toward Lupine Valley Ranch. How had the women gotten on since he left yesterday? He'd hated leaving them unguarded, even for one night, but it had been the only way to secure the gift Biddie wanted to give Virginia for her birthday.

The story he'd given for needing to leave was that he needed some personal supplies from Campo. In truth, he'd been sent by Biddie to purchase Mr. Pearson's milk cow. She'd instructed Gideon to offer the man two-thirds his asking price plus a basket of baked goods she'd made. Thankfully, Pearson had accepted the offer and Gideon didn't have to return empty-handed.

Although Biddie wanted milk for her baking, the cow would belong to Virginia. Plus, it would be the first livestock animal brought to the ranch since the attack—not counting their horses. Biddie had said her sister would be happy with the gift. And that wasn't all Biddie had planned.

She'd also talked Gideon into inviting Clyve to join them for the special meal she was going to cook. As expected, the man had been all too eager to accept her invitation. He'd even promised to bring his fiddle along with the milk cow now safely hidden in Rowlands' barn.

So, assuming Biddie had managed to secretly bake the cake she'd wanted to make, everything was set for a surprise celebration of Virginia's birthday later that night.

A little over an hour later, Gideon rode into the mountain valley and surveyed the land. A strange sense of coming home tugged at him, but he shook it off. This wasn't home. It was just familiar. Not the same thing at all.

He spotted the women hard at work finishing the last wall of their rock house. As they'd built, wood frames had been added for a door and two windows. A fireplace complete with a chimney stood centered on the left wall. If they finished the back wall today, they'd only need to build the roof before moving in.

His gaze moved to the tent he'd pitched in a more sheltered spot following the windstorm. Perhaps he could exchange it for the boulder cave once the women had their house to live in. Guiding Legend down the trail into the valley, Gideon waited for the women to acknowledge his return. He was certain Virginia had spotted him, though she gave no outward sign. But he didn't think Biddie had noticed him yet.

He was nearly upon them when Biddie looked up with a wide grin. "You're back."

"You get what you needed?" Virginia tossed the question at him without looking up from the rock she was setting.

Biddie's eyes lit with a similar inquiry.

He answered them both. "I did."

Biddie set down the trowel she'd been using. "I'll help you unload."

Gideon bit back a laugh. Considering he carried no more in his saddlebags than what he'd left with, and Biddie knew it, she must want to speak with him about the cow where Virginia wouldn't overhear them. Still, it was a pretty thin lie. One glance by Virginia would reveal nothing that needed unloading. Fortunately, she seemed too preoccupied with her work to notice.

Lucy, on the other hand, held her lips pressed together in an obvious effort not to laugh. "That's fine. I can handle the mortar." With a wink at Biddie, she shooed the two of them away.

Just in case Virginia was paying any attention, Gideon led Legend to the cave entrance and untied his saddlebags. Biddie took them from him, and he took Legend to his spot beside the spring before returning to the cave.

The second he stepped inside, Biddie seized his arm. "So you got the cow?"

Gideon looked down into her sparkling blue eyes and gulped. "Yep." He cleared his throat. "You won't believe what the man named her."

"The cow?"

He nodded, effecting a sober expression. "Patty."

"Patty?" She sputtered. "As in a cow patty?"

"Exactly."

She burst out laughing. She had a wonderful laugh, so light and free. It reminded him of how Mother had laughed before the war.

He stepped away from Biddie's touch and glanced at the glowing coals in the fire pit. "Did you bake the cake?"

Biddie nodded, and her whole body jiggled with excitement. "I told Ginny I was baking bread." She hurried through the opening leading deeper into the cave. Virginia had warned him to never cross that threshold, but he understood it was where the women slept.

A moment later, Biddie returned with a cloth-covered plate. She lifted the blue fabric to reveal a pale round cake not much bigger than his hand. He glanced up and caught her nibbling her lower lip.

"It's too small, isn't it?"

"There's only four of us—"

"Five, including Clyve."

Right. "All right, five. I still think this is plenty for five people."

She set the plate on an upturned box and wrung her hands. "Are you sure it looks all right? I'm still getting used to cooking in a Dutch oven. And I've never baked a cake in one. Part of the bottom stuck. That hasn't happened to me in years. Back home, we have a great big oven and different-sized pans and—"

"Biddie." He grasped her shoulders so she'd look at him. "It's perfect. She'll love it."

"Thank you." Those sky-blue eyes held his with such trust it pulled the air from his lungs.

Had he ever met anyone so beautiful, inside and out? She leaned toward him, and his gaze dropped to her soft pink lips.

"Virginia, I'm sure they're fine." Lucy's loud voice reached him just as the sound of boot steps neared the cave entrance.

He blinked. What was he doing? He dropped his hands and stepped away just as Virginia entered.

She eyed him with suspicion. "What's taking so long?" Her gaze bounced between Gideon and Biddie before fixing on her sister. "You all right?"

Biddie's cheeks were bright red as she nodded. "Just fine. I was just telling Gideon what I planned for our evening meal."

Virginia's mouth pinched at one side. "Thought he was

supposed to do the cooking? Ain't that what you hired him for?"

"In part, yes. But today is your birthday, and I wanted to prepare something special for you."

Virginia blinked. "It is?"

Had the woman forgotten her own birthday?

Biddie nodded firmly and stepped forward with arms outstretched. "Yes, now get out of here so I can get started."

She tried to push Virginia out the entrance, but the wild one planted her boots. "If he stays, I stay."

Gideon lifted his palms in surrender and headed for the exit. "I'm going too. We've got a wall to finish, haven't we?"

"Not that you've been any help the last two days." Virginia grumbled as she followed him out.

Unable to resist a last look, he caught Biddie watching him go, a bemused smile on her lips and something in her eyes that dared him to consider whether he could have a future after all. But as soon as the thought came, truth crushed it like the hammers they'd used to split the rocks. He'd only had one truly terrible migraine during his time at the ranch. Biddie had no idea how broken he truly was. She couldn't know he was only half a man, unable to provide for a wife and family. Worse, any family he dared create would be in danger because of him. If she knew the full truth of what the war had done to him, she'd never look at him that way again.

~

*B*iddie laughed and clapped as Clyve brought his song to a close. "Did you write that?"

Firelight glowed on his cheeks. "No, one of our hands heard it from a fellow back in Texas."

Lucy leaned back, her palms pressed to the ground behind

her. "Seems like there's a lot of people from Texas around here."

Clyve set his fiddle aside and reached for his drink. "There are. People in San Diego have even taken to calling these parts 'Little Texas.'"

Biddie shifted against the rock supporting her. "Did they all come together?"

Clyve laughed. "A few families did, but most came at different times. Funny thing is, they all planned on going farther, but said something about this valley tugged at their Texan hearts and they decided to stay."

Gideon's gaze moved through the darkness beyond the fire's light. "Western Texas isn't all that different from this place. Maybe it reminded them of home."

Finished with his drink, Clyve picked up his fiddle and settled it in his lap. "Maybe."

Ginny scuffed her boot in the dirt. "Maybe they were just tired of wandering." She sounded as though she spoke from experience. How much had her father and siblings moved around before settling in this mountain valley?

Clyve tipped his head. "A bit of both, I'd wager."

Lucy watched Clyve with an expression Biddie couldn't read. "Where're you from?"

"Ohio. My family had a small farm there. Father wanted more."

"Are you happy here?"

"Well, our claim isn't near as big as Gin's, and I could do without the bandits and Indians thieving our stock and attacking our homes, but mostly, I can't complain."

Ginny's nose scrunched. "Your land's flatter, more usable."

"But our creek is fed by a spring on McCain's land. We don't have our own, like you."

"True." Ginny grinned and took a sip of her milk. "Thanks again for the cow."

"It was my pleasure to bring it, but it's your sister who paid for it and Gideon who rode all that way to fetch it."

Ginny turned her smile on the rest of them. "Thank you all. I—" Her voice cracked, and she cleared her throat. "I ain't never celebrated my birthday before. Near to forgot I had one."

Biddie's mouth dropped open. What was more shocking—that Ginny had never celebrated her birthday or that she'd shared such a personal detail and almost cried over it? No, surely, those weren't tears in her eyes. It had to be the firelight playing tricks. Her big sister never cried.

Ginny jumped to her feet. "I'm going to check that it's still tied up." Without another word, she strode toward the spring, where they'd left Patty tied near Legend.

Clyve plucked idly at his fiddle. "You're going to need something to protect that animal from the summer's heat if you want her to keep producing."

Gideon waved toward the nearly complete house. "Soon as we finish that, I'll build something for shade."

"What about a barn?"

"We're planning one, but Ginny wants to build corrals first."

Clyve made a sound in his throat. "'Course she does. Probably wants to rebuild her heard as soon as possible."

"You don't approve?" Biddie studied his tight expression.

Clyve sighed. "Your sister can do anything she sets her mind to, but cattle are mean. Taking care of them is hard, dangerous work. No one should do it alone."

"Agreed." Gideon shifted so that his arms rested on his knees.

Clyve shot him a hard look. "Are you after marrying her?"

The sudden question knotted Biddie's stomach. *Was* Gideon thinking of courting her sister? It would make sense. Ginny needed help running this ranch, and Gideon had the experience to help her. Nevertheless, the idea didn't sit right at all.

"No." There was adamant sincerity in Gideon's response.

Biddie relaxed. Of course, he wasn't hoping to marry her sister. How many times had he said cattle work wasn't for him? Still, the idea seemed odd to her. Wouldn't a man raised on a cattle ranch want to put his skills to use? Why was he trying to hide in a kitchen?

CHAPTER 15

*G*ideon joined Biddie beside the fire and rotated the spit. These birds had better finish before this headache grew any worse. Early that morning, he'd ridden to the Rowland Ranch and traded for two chickens. He'd been roasting them over coals for four hours. Their skin was perfectly crisp, and a quick press of his finger told him the insides were still moist. Perfect. He refused to hand over the last few minutes of their cooking to anyone else. This was going to be his best meal yet.

A bit less than an hour ago, Biddie had added her cake to the fire. She'd claimed that her cake for Virginia's birthday came out dry and she was determined to do better for today's celebration. The cake had tasted fine to him, and he'd told her as much. She'd thanked him but hadn't seemed the least reassured and stood staring at the coal-covered pot for several minutes before joining the other women in the rock house.

They'd finished the roof by noon, and Gideon had hung the door before starting the chicken. Since then, Virginia, Biddie, and Lucy had been busy cleaning and moving their things into their new home. Well, that'd kept Virginia and Lucy busy.

Biddie came back every five minutes to stand and glare down at her Dutch oven.

Which is what she was doing now.

He ignored his blurring vision and poked the potatoes he had buried in the fire. Still firm in the middle. He re-covered them and glanced at Biddie. "How's the cake coming?"

She turned her glare on him. "I don't know."

"Why not open the lid and take a look?" No doubt, the cake would be mighty tasty. But maybe looking at it and seeing it was fine would calm her down some. She seemed worked up as a mare about to foal.

"If I check too soon, the cake will fall."

"Huh?" Gideon scratched his forehead. Was his pain fogging his thoughts again? Biddie wasn't the overly clumsy sort. Why was she worried about dropping the cake? Maybe his suggestion wasn't clear. "Don't pick the whole thing out of the fire, just the lid."

"No, if I let cold air into the oven, the middle of the cake might sink."

"So?" He didn't much care whether a cake was flat on top and didn't think Virginia would care either. He wasn't sure about Lucy. But it seemed to him most folks cared more about how a cake tasted than how it looked.

"If it sinks..."

The throbbing behind his eyes doubled, forcing his lids shut. He missed the rest of what she said. "Sorry." He pressed at his closed eyes with the base of his palms. "What'd you say?"

"Gideon?" Her worried voice drew nearer.

He ordered his eyes to open but only managed a brief squint. The pain was too much, and the effort brought water to his eyes, but he'd seen she was just inches from his face.

Her palms settled on his cheeks. "What's wrong? Did ash get in your eyes?"

Despite his pain, her nearness drew him. He needed to get

away. He raised his hands to pull hers from his face, but she caught his wrists.

"No, don't rub. You'll make it worse."

"It's not ash." Did she know she was stroking her thumbs across his wrists? The sensation made him want to lean forward and—

He jerked free and stepped back. This had to stop. He was in no position to take a wife, and he refused to take advantage of a woman. Especially not one so kind and innocent. "It's my head. I'll be fine. It's just an ache. It'll pass." He finally managed to force one eye open enough to see the spit handle and stepped toward it.

"Look out!" Biddie's fingers wrapped around his arms, yanking him backward.

He lost his balance and reached for something to steady him. He found her shoulders and clung to her. It was too late. His stomach lurched and he spun away.

No. He would not lose control in front of her. He commanded his stomach to settle but had to force several slow breaths to keep himself from retching.

Why had she tugged at him like that? The question roared in his mind, and his fists clenched. Not that she'd had any way of knowing the consequences, he reminded himself. In any case, he didn't dare ask her. Talking might upset the delicate ceasefire he'd negotiated with his guts.

As if reading his thoughts, she placed a hand on his back and said, "You nearly stepped in the fire. I think you'd better lie down until the pain passes."

"The chick—" Arguing was a mistake. He barely made it around a large bush before his stomach ejected his noon meal. Defeat hung on his shoulders like an ox yoke. Once again, his body had ignored his commands. He was a prisoner of his own skin and bones.

∾

*T*he evening after they'd completed their new house, Biddie followed Ginny along the ridge of the valley. Gideon was still abed with his headache. So Biddie had persuaded her sister to teach her how to keep a lookout. They'd started with Ginny teaching Biddie just enough about her new rifle to fire a shot into the air. Ginny insisted that was all Biddie needed to know. She'd said the sound would wake Ginny and send any intruders running for cover long enough for help to arrive. Now, they were following the same path Ginny and Gideon had followed every night. Ginny wanted to show her where to stop and study the land, and where to take cover if trouble came.

Suddenly, she pivoted to face Biddie. "I don't understand you."

"What do you mean?"

"You don't make sense."

Biddie didn't make sense? Ginny was the one talking in riddles. "Did I do something to upset you?"

"That's just it. Why would you make such a fuss about my birthday? How did you even remember it *was* my birthday?"

"I thought you liked Patty and the cake and..."

"I've been nothing but rude to you since you got here." Ginny turned and kept walking. "I don't understand it. You were supposed to be gone by now."

It was like someone had their fist around Biddie's heart and was squeezing it. "I..." What was she supposed to say? She'd thought Ginny was getting used to her presence. No, if she was honest with herself, she'd foolishly started to believe Ginny was secretly happy she'd stayed. It seemed she'd been wrong. "I'm sorry, I—"

"Don't apologize. Just tell me what you want." Ginny stopped and faced Biddie again. "It can't be the ranch, or you'd

155

be waiting for me to give up and leave instead of helping me rebuild it. Not that I ever would give up."

"What I want?" Biddie was so confused. "Ginny, all I've ever wanted was my big sister back. I missed you every day you were gone. When I look in the mirror, I don't just see Mama, I see you."

"I don't believe it. Everyone wants something. You're getting interest on the money you're loaning me, but what about the work?" Ginny's hands landed on her hips, and she leaned toward Biddie. "Why are you helping me?"

Didn't she understand? "Because I love you."

Ginny reared back, her face wrinkled with confusion. "Why?"

"Why?" Biddie ran her palms down her skirt, searching for words to explain what should have been obvious. "Because you're my sister. Because you shoved me and Preston under the bed and took the blows that day Mama went to deliver the laundry and Pa came home early. He was so mad, but I don't remember why." Even now, the terror of that day sent a shiver down her back.

"He was drunk." Ginny shrugged. "He was always drunk. And he'd lost at cards again." She tipped her head. "You remember that? You were so little."

"I don't remember much from before you left, but I remember Mama hummed while she baked, Preston was always watching everyone, Pa smelled of smoke and whiskey, and"—Biddie took Ginny's hand in both of hers and squeezed—"my big sister protected me."

"So what? You think you owe me?" Ginny shook free. "You were just a kid."

"So were you."

Ginny sneered. "I was never a kid. It's why he took me with him."

Biddie's heart skipped a beat. Would Ginny finally answer her questions? "Where'd you go?"

Ginny stared out over the desert, her eyes not seeming fixed on anything. "Sacramento, at first. Then on to Fort Colville. Oliver'd heard of a new strike and talked about mining."

Biddie'd heard horrible stories about children in the mines. "Did he make you dig?"

Ginny gave a mirthless chuckle. "We never made it to the diggings. Oliver found a game that first night and started a winning streak that lasted a week. Then he lost all his money in a single hand."

That didn't make sense. "I thought you said he won the ranch at Fort Colville."

"He did. That was later." Ginny started walking again.

Biddie hurried to catch up. "But how'd he win if he didn't have anything to gamble?"

Ginny didn't look at Biddie, but her big sister's eyes grew hard and her jaw tight. "I said he'd lost his *money*. He still had me and Preston."

Biddie stuttered to a stop. "Surely, you don't mean—"

"You probably felt bad about being left behind." Ginny tossed the words over her shoulder. "Now you know better."

CHAPTER 16

*W*ith a groan, Gideon rolled onto his side. The pressure in his skull would not let go. Any amount of light sliced like a blade through his brain. Movement unsettled his stomach. But he'd been in bed for two days while the women built a shelter for their new cow, started the corral walls, and did all the cooking and cleaning. Not to mention taking turns standing guard at night.

He was as useless as the day he came home from the war. What was the point in him staying here if he couldn't at least help with the cooking?

Moving slowly, he forced himself upright. Then waited for the world to stop spinning. He stood, eyes still closed, with one hand against the cool stone wall and shuffled forward until his toes bumped the side of a wood box. Ever so carefully, he lowered himself to the ground and reached into the box. After some digging, he found one of the strips the women had used to protect themselves from the sand and tied it over his eyes.

He cracked one eye open. Only a faint strip of dim light showed through. He opened his eye all the way. It hurt. But he could bear it. He opened the other eye. This was progress.

Keeping his moves slow and careful, he made his way to their new fireplace. He added wood to the coals and set the coffeepot on to boil. Then he stood and shuffled toward the cellar. Thank goodness Virginia insisted the house be built around it. Even with the cloth blocking most of the light, he wasn't up for going out into the summer sun.

It took him three times longer than usual, but eventually, he had a pot of soup simmering over the fire and the coffee warming on a pile of coals. He set a knife beside a loaf of bread on the table. Then he shuffled back to bed. It was time for a nap.

~

*B*iddie adjusted her grip on the reins as she followed Ginny and Lucy toward Campo. Gideon had been madder than a hornet when Ginny announced their plans to ride to town without him. It'd been four days since the pain in his head sent him to bed. For the last two, he'd managed to cook simple meals for them, but that was all. The rest of the time, he slept.

Biddie nibbled her lip. "I can't imagine the amount of pain it would take to keep a man like Gideon in his bed. The only other person I've known to suffer with migraines for more than a day was a woman who lived in The Home for a year or two when I was young. But her pains came every month with her womanly troubles. That can't be his problem."

"Probably something from the war," Ginny suggested without looking back.

"Did he say something to you? I've considered asking him about his experiences but the time never seemed right."

"Don't. Men hate talking about their weaknesses and they hate talking about the war even more."

"Wasn't he the one that brought it up when we were making plans for the ranch?" Biddie frowned at her sister's back. "He suggested those outer fences."

"That's different. You go asking him about his injuries and you're bound to be poking into those nasty memories. Take my advice and leave him be."

Was Ginny right? Growing up in a home filled with women hadn't provided Biddie with much insight into the male mind. From the sounds of it though, in the years she and Ginny had been separated her sister had been surrounded by men. Biddy firmed her lips. Since the last thing she wanted was to cause Gideon more pain, keeping her questions to herself seemed the wisest course of action. For now.

'Lucy sent Biddie a concerned glance over her shoulder "It sure was courageous of him to mount Legend and try to come with us."

Ginny snorted, "Pure foolishness, you mean."

Either way, he'd made it no farther than the valley's rim before his stomach gave out and fatigue nearly toppled him from the saddle. Thankfully, Ginny had been close enough to keep him from falling to the ground. She'd been none too happy about the delay it'd caused helping him return to the house, though.

The entire way back, he'd muttered warnings of the many dire things that could happen to three lone women traveling through the desert. Biddie had to admit his words had gotten under her skin. Which was why Luman Gaskill's smiling face was such a beautiful sight.

She slid from her horse, tied him to the post, and removed

the bag of baked goods she'd attached to the saddle. "It's good to see you, Mr. Gaskill."

"Well, I'm sure glad to see you three ladies again." He searched the area behind them. "Where's Mr. Swift?"

"Back at the ranch."

Mr. Gaskill frowned. "He didn't escort you?"

Ginny frowned back at him. "Have the bandits been causing more trouble?"

The store owner's expression brightened. "I've heard reports they've moved up north." Then he sobered. "They robbed a stage station north of Los Angeles last week. Two men were killed." He glanced at Biddie and clamped his lips tight. "Sorry, I shouldn't speak of such in the presence of ladies."

Ginny shook her head. "Are you buffaloed? We need to know what's going on, same as the men." She stepped toward the store's entrance. "Did our order come in?"

Mr. Gaskill took the hint and moved into the store. "Sure enough." He pulled several boxes from one corner and set them on the counter. "Here you are. Did you need anything else?"

Ginny reached for the nearest box. "No."

Biddie set her bag on the counter beside the boxes. "Actually, I brought you a gift."

Mr. Gaskill's eyes lit. "Did you?"

Ginny and Lucy carried three of the boxes outside.

Biddie revealed the small cakes she'd made in the new brick oven she'd insisted they build into the wall beside the fireplace. It had taken a few tries to get the treats exactly right, but cooking in the new oven was immensely easier than using the Dutch oven. Being able to bake again was like a breath of fresh air. She hadn't realized how much she'd missed it until this batch of fine honey cakes came out so well it brought her to tears. "I thought you might enjoy these."

Mr. Gaskill thanked her and immediately took a bite. "Why, this is delicious."

Lucy came to her side. "Biddie's going to open her own bakery in San Francisco."

The store owner eyed her speculatively. "I don't suppose you'd be interested in baking more that I could sell in the store while you're here?"

"Yes. I mean..." Biddie clasped her fingers as Ginny lifted the last two boxes. "That is, I'd love to, but..." Biddie tried to catch her sister's eye for some clue as to what she thought of the idea. Their talk on the ridge hadn't changed much. Ginny still worked like a maid afraid she was about to get the sack, and her words were as straightforward as ever. But at least she'd stopped talking about when Biddie and Lucy would leave. She'd even smiled at Biddie a time or two.

As much as they could use the money, Biddie didn't want to lose that small amount of progress over the few coins her cakes might earn. Ginny wouldn't like Biddy stopping work on the corral walls to bake things they couldn't even eat. Unfortunately, Ginny left without looking Biddie's way. She looked back to Mr. Gaskill. "I'm not sure I'll have time to—"

Lucy set her hand over Biddie's fidgety fingers. "What she means is, we're not sure when we'll be in town next, but you can be sure she'll bring more cakes for you to sell."

Mr. Gaskill beamed. "Wonderful. Oh!" He reached under the counter and withdrew two envelopes. "I almost forgot, these letters came for you."

Biddie recognized Father's and Mother's handwriting. "Thank you." She withdrew the letters she'd written to Mr. Green, Father, and Mother, and handed them over. "I'd be grateful if you would see these are sent with the next post."

"Of course." He tucked the mail beneath the counter and surveyed the empty surface. "Looks like you're all set, then."

"Actually…" Biddie turned toward the back of the store. If she was going to do extra baking for the Gaskills' customers, she'd need more supplies. She nearly skipped toward the barrel of flour. Hopefully, Ginny wouldn't mind too much.

CHAPTER 17

One week later, Biddie set a rock on the corral wall they were building and something scraped her finger. She lifted her hand, spotted a tear in the glove, and held it out for Lucy to see. "I'm going to fetch my spare gloves."

Lucy nodded and Biddie returned to the house. She'd need to repair the torn finger this evening.

Heated words carried through the open door as she removed the ripped garment. Gideon was back on his feet and feeling well enough to argue with Ginny. This morning, they'd disagreed on how big the corrals needed to be. From the sound of their voices, they were at it again.

Most of the time, the cattle would wander free. But occasionally, Ginny would need to round them up for branding, castrating, and other ranch things Biddie didn't understand. When she'd asked Gideon what *castrating* meant, he'd turned red in the face and refused to answer.

She couldn't understand why her wanting to understand more about ranching would make him mad, but then she didn't understand much about men. Especially that man. Every time she thought she had him figured out, he'd do or say something to prove the opposite.

Not that she needed to figure him out. She was here to help Ginny, and then she'd go home. Of course, if she could better understand Gideon, maybe she could help him, too, before she left. It was plain to see something pained the man more than his head. She'd seen it in the quiet moments when he didn't know she was looking. He'd stare at nothing with an expression of such deep hurt, it made her want to go over and wrap her arms around him until whatever was hurting him went away. But of course, that wouldn't work. And would be highly improper. In fact, Mother would be shocked to know Biddie had ever considered such a thing.

But she needed to figure out what was hurting him. She'd been considering it all morning and finally might have landed on the answer. Gideon was a man raised to run a ranch who had no ranch. He'd said he didn't want to ranch anymore, but he'd also said his family lost their ranch. Maybe he was just afraid that if he got another ranch, he'd lose it again. And that would hurt. She could understand that. But being afraid of getting hurt was no reason to avoid what could make a person truly happy. And despite what he said, he must love ranch life. Why else would he look for work as a ranch cook?

She just needed to figure out how to help him find the courage to try again. Of course, courage wouldn't do him any good if he didn't have the ranch to try running. Perhaps there was a rancher in the area who was looking to get out. Did Gideon have any money for buying a ranch? Probably not. But that was no problem. But perhaps she could convince Richard Stevens to loan him the money, same as Father was loaning money to Ginny.

Father. How was he doing? He'd written that the doctor said he was healing well but still couldn't travel. Father's frustration was clear, though he'd not written a word of complaint. Hope-

KATHLEEN DENLY

fully, he wouldn't try to come here sooner than the doctor thought was wise. As much as she missed Father, he wasn't getting any younger, and he shouldn't risk his health for her. He and Mother had already given her so much.

Had Mr. Green received her letter? She nibbled her lower lip. How often was mail taken from Campo to San Diego? If he had received it, was he displeased? Surely, if he were, he'd write and give her a chance to argue her case before offering the building to someone else. Or would he? He was a man of business, after all. It likely didn't matter to him who ran the bakery, so long as he made a profit.

Lord, have I made a mistake staying here?

Ginny had seemed pleased but confused by the birthday celebration and Gideon clearly needed a nudge in the right direction. No, there was too much need on this ranch for her presence here to be wrong. Which likely meant God had a purpose in her being here. She ought to trust Him to work out her dreams for the bakery and returning the social status her parents had lost when they'd adopted her. After all, God was almighty. If He wanted her to have that bakery, He'd make it happen. And she'd prayed and prayed over her plans for years. He wouldn't let her down.

Still, restless energy coursed through her.

Her eyes landed on the cellar door. The small, underground room was fill with the supplies she'd brought back from the store last week. There'd been no time to bake since then, and no pressing need since they wouldn't be returning to town anytime soon. But her fingers fairly tingled with the urge to plunge into a bowl of flour. Surely, Gideon's recovery was enough reason to celebrate. She wouldn't make a dessert this time. Their sugar was too precious. But she could make a few harlem cakes. They had enough of the ingredients for those to spare what she'd need.

She crossed the room and lifted the square wood door.

Something furry and brown skittered across her foot, and she screamed.

∼

*G*ideon turned from the spring with a bucket of water in each hand. He started back to where Lucy and Virginia worked on the newest section of corral fencing. It was coming along well, but the sun threatened to dry their mortar in the wheelbarrow before they could apply it to the wall. He quickened his pace.

A short scream ripped the air from the direction of the house. *Biddie.*

Gideon dropped the buckets and sprinted to the front door. He threw it open and charged inside, gun drawn but pointed at the ground. His eyes took a second to adjust to the dim light. A quick look around told him Biddie wasn't there.

He turned back to the open door. She wasn't in the yard either. Hadn't her scream come from the house?

He scanned the room again. This time, his gaze landed on the open cellar door. He was across the room and bending over the opening in a blink. "Biddie?"

A loud sniff preceded her answer. "It's all ruined." Her voice wobbled, and there was more sniffing.

Was she crying?

Candlelight flickered over the steep dirt stairs. "Is there someone down there with you?"

"I thought Lucy and Ginny were outside with you."

That wasn't who he'd meant, but it told him what he needed to know. He holstered his pistol and descended into the small space that held their foodstuffs. "What's wrong? Did you scream?"

"Yes, I'm sorry. It just startled me." She knelt in a corner with the broom in her hand. Candlelight shimmered across her damp cheeks.

His gut clenched. She *had* been crying. He crouched in front of her. "What startled you?"

"The rat," she said with such venom, he almost backed up. Then she pointed, and he spotted a small furry body lying on the ground. It wasn't moving.

He glanced at the broom. Did she feel bad about killing it? "It's all right, Biddie. You did what you needed to. Rats don't belong in a cellar. They might get into the food and then—"

"They did." To his horror, new tears welled and spilled down her cheeks. She pointed again, this time to the large sack of flour the women had brought back from Campo. "Those horrid vermin chewed through the bag and dug through all my flour."

So that's what she'd meant about something being ruined.

Her watery gaze met his. "What am I supposed to bake with now?"

Unable to resist, he pulled her against his chest. With one arm around her, he stroked her soft hair. "Shh. It'll be all right."

He resisted the urge to say it was just flour. Obviously, it meant more to her than he understood. Since she was a baker, maybe it was like a rancher losing his herd. Although he couldn't recall a man that'd ever shed a tear over a lost cow.

The sack of flour sat in a crate on the floor, the lid leaning against its side. "How'd they get through the box?"

"The lid was already off when I came down." She glanced up at him, her brow furrowed. Then she looked at the crate. "I've never heard of rats that can open lids. But I haven't had time to do any baking. So I couldn't have left it open."

With sudden clarity, Gideon recalled searching for the box of onions yesterday when he'd still been battling his head pain. He'd opened several boxes before finding the right one. He must've left the flour crate open then.

He released her. This was his fault.

He stood and spun toward the stairs. "I'll get you more flour. I'll leave now and be back by breakfast." It'd be a hard, long night's ride, but he could do it. Legend had done nothing but rest for days. He could handle the journey.

"Gideon, no. Wait, I—"

He ignored her protests and stormed out. His condition had hurt too many people. There wasn't anything he could do about Pa's death or losing their ranch. But buying Biddie more flour was something he *could* do.

CHAPTER 18

Gideon's eyelids drooped like stones were tied to his lashes as he rode into the valley at dawn the next morning. It was later than Biddie usually woke to start her baking, but he'd made it.

He led Legend straight to the front door of the house and raised his hand to knock.

Before his knuckles hit wood, the door flew wide and Biddie stared up at him. "You're back." The bundle under his shirt squirmed, and her eyes widened. "What's that?"

He reached into his shirt and carefully pulled the mama cat from where she'd ridden for the past six hours. He'd originally stowed her in a saddle bag, but her nonstop caterwauling almost made him drop her in the middle of the desert and leave her. Instead, he tucked her inside his shirt with the hope that being close to him would calm her. It'd been a risk. She just as easily might have dug her claws into his skin and climbed right out. Instead, she'd curled into a tiny fur ball and settled in for a nap.

Now, he lifted her for Biddie to see. "I got her to help with the rats. She's set to have a litter soon. I figured you could keep her in the house and let her roam the cellar now and then. And when her kittens are big enough, they can move to the barn and keep the rats out of there too."

Before he knew what was happening, Biddie shifted onto her toes and planted a kiss on his cheek. "You're wonderful." She leaned back and beamed at him like he'd just hung the moon.

His gaze dropped to her curving lips, and his mind filled with notions he had no business thinking. He shoved the cat into her arms. "Hold her while I get the rest." Without waiting, he went to Legend and removed the large bags of flour, salt, and sugar he'd purchased for her. He set them on the ground and untied the saddlebag he'd filled with pouches of baking soda, cinnamon, and any other spice Luman Gaskill had said women liked to bake with. It'd cost him every penny in his pocket, but the joy in Biddie's eyes was worth it.

Lucy came to the door. "What's going on?"

Biddie beamed at her. "Gideon brought us a cat."

Gideon handed Lucy the saddlebag. "Here. I'll be back to carry the rest inside once I've got Legend settled."

❧

A few hours later, Biddie pulled a fresh tray of harlem cakes from the oven. The round rolls were perfectly golden with a thin crust on the outside. She split one open and confirmed it remained soft and moist on the inside. "Perfect."

She slathered on a thick layer of strawberry preserves before replacing the top slice and wrapping it in a napkin.

Outside, Gideon was stirring the soup he was cooking for their noon meal. His back was to her, and she took the opportunity to study him. When he'd hurried away after she kissed him that morning, she worried that she'd upset him with her thoughtless show of gratitude. But he acted normal when he returned to carry in the heavy sacks of flour, sugar, and salt he'd brought her. So it must have been her imagination. Likely, he'd just wanted to get things settled quickly so he could nap. He'd clearly been exhausted after riding all night.

Guilt pricked at her conscience. If she hadn't made such a fuss over the ruined flour, he wouldn't have felt the need to drive himself so hard. She needed to find a way to make it up to him.

She caught her lower lip in her teeth. If she was going to figure out how to help Gideon see that he didn't need to give up on his dreams of running his own ranch, she needed to get to know him better. Was now a good time to talk to him? She glanced back to where Ginny and Lucy were still working on the corral wall farther down the valley. No. They'd likely be coming to eat soon. He'd never open up with Ginny around.

As if sensing her presence, Gideon turned.

She offered him her precious bundle. "I hope you like it."

"Thank you. I'm sure I will." He unwrapped the roll, took a bite, and released a soft moan. "This is delicious." In seconds, he'd finished the treat and dabbed at his lips with the empty napkin. "Wish I could bake like that. My biscuits aren't bad, but they're nothing compared to yours."

An idea popped into her mind. She clasped her hands together. "These aren't hard. I could teach you, if you want."

He glanced toward Ginny and Lucy. "I don't think your sister would like that."

"Whyever not?"

"Uh—" He tugged at his collar. "There's still a lot of work to do on the corrals. When I'm not cooking, I should—"

"Don't be silly." She waved her hands in dismissal. "If two of us know how to bake these, we can make them more often."

"I think your sister would rather I worked on the corrals than bake more rolls."

Hadn't he been arguing from the start that he'd only come

here to cook? Maybe he'd been lying about how good the rolls were and didn't think she had anything to teach him. But they'd *looked* perfect. "Did I add too much salt? Or was it dry?" They'd appeared moist, but looks can be deceiving. She should have tasted one before she brought him his. She was still getting used to their new oven, and it was poss—

"No. The roll was perfect."

Her shoulders lifted. "Then why don't you want me to teach you?"

"I do. I just—"

"Wonderful. We can get started after the meal." Ideas rose in her mind as she turned toward the house. "After the harlem cakes, I can teach you my favorite potato bread recipe. Lucy's especially fond of that one, and we can use the bread for sandwiches tomorrow. Oh! And I can teach you how I make my special pancakes. The women back home are always asking me to make more. And with your help I can make twice as much to sell Luman for our next trip to town."

～

hey'd built the house entirely too small. Gideon pressed himself against the wall, but it wasn't far enough to escape Biddie's enticing scent of cinnamon and something sweet. Or maybe that was the smell of the cake batter she was mixing.

In any case, three days of being cooped in this tiny space with her was getting to him. The room seemed to shrink as she went on and on about the proper way to measure and mix ingredients, and how to tell if the oven was at the right temperature, or if something was finished baking. Her incredible passion for the subject sparkled in her eyes, drawing him closer. Twice since they'd started this nonsense, he'd caught himself reaching for her.

Now, the urge to brush flour from her cheeks wouldn't leave him alone. Not that doing so would be all that bad. But he knew better than to think he'd be able to stop there. If he gave in to the temptation, he'd wind up cupping her cheeks. Then he'd draw her close and find out for sure if those pretty pink lips of hers tasted the way she smelled.

He clasped his hands behind his back.

What had he been thinking, agreeing to let her teach him? He hadn't been. That was the trouble. Whenever Biddie got to looking at him with a plea or a sparkle in those big blue eyes, his common sense took a nap. It was why he'd stayed at Lupine Valley Ranch in the first place.

Oh, he'd told himself it was for the women's safety. And it was. Partly. But mostly, he'd stayed because she was the first person since the war to look at him with such absolute trust and confidence in his abilities. Too bad her belief in him was born from ignorance of the severity of his condition.

After his latest head pain kept him abed for four days, he'd expected a change in her behavior toward him. But if she valued him any less for his weakness, she didn't show it. Still, it was only a matter of time before he did something that destroyed the admiration in her eyes. Not that he'd ever intentionally betray her. But his intentions hadn't mattered in the past. Why would they matter now?

If only he could pray and ask God to heal her father faster or send her brother sooner. He needed to get off this ranch before his condition led to true disaster.

～

*B*iddie gave the batter a final stir. "There. Now that the ingredients are fully mixed..." She glanced to her right, but Gideon was no longer beside her at the table. She turned. He stood against the wall, hands behind his back, with a strange expression on his face. "Gideon? Is something wrong?" She set the spoon down and moved closer to him. "Is your head hurting again?"

"No, I'm fine. It's just..."

Her stomach fluttered as he reached for her.

His thumb brushed her cheek just as Ginny stormed inside. His hand fell, and he seemed to be trying to melt into the wall.

Ginny glared at them. "What are you doing?"

Biddie blinked several times, striving to move her thoughts from the exhilaration of Gideon's touch to the ire in her sister's eyes. Honestly, her sister had the worst timing. And she always seemed to be mad about something. "I told you I wanted to teach Gideon to make Mama's chocolate cake."

Ginny's face pinched the way it did any time Biddie mentioned Mama. "Who are you trying to fool?"

"What?"

"The two of you were cozier than two doves in their nest when I walked in."

Gideon straightened. "Nothing happened. Biddie just had some flour on her cheek, and I was wiping it off for her."

She had? He was? Biddie's heart sank as she stared at him. Although why she should be disappointed that the moment hadn't been the romantic one her foolish heart had assumed, she couldn't imagine. It was good that he hadn't been thinking about kissing her. There was no way the two of them could ever have a life together. A rancher lived on hundreds of acres, and there certainly wasn't any land like that available near San Francisco. Even if there were, she needed to live in the city, preferably in a small apartment above her bakery. It was what she'd dreamed of, worked for.

She shook herself from her thoughts and met her sister's gaze. "He's right. Nothing untoward occurred. Nor would it. Your concerns are misplaced."

"Uh-huh." Ginny's tone made it clear she didn't believe either of them.

"Look." Biddie pointed to the batter-filled bowl. "I was just showing him the proper way to mix the ingredients."

Ginny snorted. "What for? He's a ranch cook, not a fancy baker for rich folk."

"Mama wasn't rich or fancy, but she still loved that cake and—"

"And she didn't have a ranch to rebuild. I do. And I need you both outside helping me build it."

Part of Biddie wanted to cheer that her sister had finally admitted to needing help. The other part didn't appreciate being bossed around. "We can come out as soon as the cake is in the oven. We'll have about an hour before—"

"Oh, no." Ginny marched forward and grabbed Biddie's wrist. "I'm not leaving you alone with him for one more minute."

Her big sister dragged her toward the door, but she dug her heels in. "Ginny, I told you noth—"

"And I told *you*, he doesn't need your fancy cooking." She let Biddie's arm go with a huff and planted her hands on her hips. "I thought you were here to help me, but it seems all you care about is your fancy baking and how soon you can go back to the big city where they pay heed to more than just filling their bellies and getting on with things that matter. You've got no real care for this ranch or me." Her lips twisted in an ugly sneer. "You're just here to prove what a good person you are." She pivoted and stepped outside, flinging words over her shoulder as she went. "You've done your bit of charity work now, so you can go. I'll get on just fine without you."

Biddie felt as though the air had been sucked from her lungs. She bent and gripped the edge of the table to keep from crumpling. What was wrong with her sister? How could she say such hateful things? Hadn't they been getting along better since their talk on the ridge? Hadn't Ginny believed Biddie when she'd said she was here because she loved Ginny? Staying here put everything Biddie had dreamed of and worked for at risk. What more did she have to do to prove herself?

"She has no business speaking to you like that." Gideon's voice startled her. She'd nearly forgotten he was there. "I'm going to talk to her." He started toward the door, but she caught his arm.

"No, don't." She released him and ran a shaky hand over her hair. "This is between me and my sister."

Gideon nodded, though judging by the clenching and unclenching of his fingers, he still wanted to say something.

She looked away, and her gaze landed on the half-stirred bowl of batter. Fire burned through her, and she snatched the bowl from the table. Stomping to the doorway, she stopped and hurled the batter into the dirt.

Gideon's appalled voice followed her as she whirled back into the house. "What are you doing?"

Ignoring him, she seized the basket of rolls and small cakes she'd baked to take to the store and stomped back to the door. With the flick of her wrist, everything she'd baked for the past three days landed in the dirt.

Ginny jogged into the yard. "Have you gone loco?"

Biddie wiped at the moisture blurring the sight of her sister's shocked face. "I don't care about these things," she shouted and pointed at the spoiled goods. "I care about you."

Ginny's expression hardened. "Only a rich person would waste food to make a point."

Biddie gave up. With a sob, she ran away. It was childish and she knew it, but she couldn't take one more second of her sister's coldness. What had happened to the big sister who'd loved her enough to suffer in her place?

CHAPTER 19

*V*irginia bit the sides of her tongue as Biddie ran away in tears. She shouldn't have said such awful things to her little sister. But didn't Biddie know the danger she put herself in, staring at a man all moon-eyed like that? No, of course she didn't. Sheltered as she must have been in that big fancy house, Biddie most likely had no notion of the thoughts such a look put in a man's head.

Virginia should have put a stop to Biddie's plans to teach him baking the moment she announced them. Instead, she'd let herself be swayed by the excitement in her little sister's eyes. More fool, her. But then, Biddie had always had the power to make Virginia agree to foolish things. So she'd told herself checking on them regular would keep Biddie safe. She'd failed to consider her sister would fall in love with the man. But Virginia recognized the emotion she'd seen in Biddie's eyes when she'd walked in and found Gideon holding her close. It was the same look Mama had given Oliver.

In Virginia's experience, love was the most dangerous thing a woman could feel. It stole her common sense and left her vulnerable, weak. The notion of her sister suffering such a fate had made Virginia see red, and she'd lost her temper. Could Biddie have been right? Was Virginia just like Oliver?

Gideon stormed toward her, his fists clenched.

Virginia drew her pistol.

He stopped and threw his arms up. "I'm not going to hurt you. Though heaven knows you need a good shaking. The only one hurting anyone around here, is you."

The sting of his words hit their mark, but she held her expression. Preston had once said Virginia's face could be mistaken for stone. At the time, they'd been arguing over whether to run away. In the end, there'd been no choice. He'd had to leave and she'd had to stay.

Gideon paced the dirt in front of her. "Your sister has done everything to show you how much she cares about you, but you just keep shoving her away. Her, and everyone else." He stopped and eyed her.

She widened her stance and made herself hold his gaze. No good ever came of showing weakness.

"I don't know what happened to you to make you so afraid to trust people, but Biddie deserves your trust. If you never believe anything else I say, believe that." He started to turn away, then paused and peered back at her. "I'm going after her now, but you owe her an apology. So start thinking on what you're going to say when she gets back."

He kicked up dust as he took off in the direction Biddie had disappeared.

She ought to go after him. She might not know much about big-city propriety, but she knew those two shouldn't be alone together. That was just common sense. She didn't *think* Gideon would hurt Biddie. But she'd misjudged men before.

She looked over her shoulder to Lucy. The quiet young woman stood by the wall they'd been building. She was too far to have heard what was said, but no doubt she could tell something was amiss. "Are you all right here?" She yelled the question to be sure Lucy heard her.

Lucy nodded and went back to work.

Virginia retrieved her rifle, hurried past the house, and headed for the ridge. Most likely, Biddie had gone to the spring. Not much else lay in the direction she'd run. There was a rock outcropping near the top of the valley that would give Virginia the perfect spot for spying on them. She definitely needed to have a talk with her little sister about men and what happened to the women foolish enough to trust them. But for now, if Gideon turned out to be anything other than the gentleman he seemed, she'd have her rifle ready to stop him.

~

*A*s he neared the spring, Gideon felt eyes on him and resisted the urge to search the slopes around him. No doubt, Virginia lurked somewhere in the shadows. The woman didn't know the meaning of the word *trust*. She'd probably dismissed what he'd said to her as easily as she swatted a fly.

He turned his focus back to Biddie. She sat beside the puddle surrounding the spring, her arms wrapped around her knees and face buried in her skirts. Her shaking shoulders made him want to go back and punch Virginia.

Well, not really.

He could never actually hurt a woman, but it drove him crazy seeing Biddie in so much pain. He sat beside her. What could he say to make her feel better?

No words came to mind, so he decided to just sit and wait for when she was ready to talk. The temptation to take her in his arms again was strong, but the feel of someone watching them held him back. Perhaps it was unwise to assume the watcher was Virginia. Without turning his head, he searched the valley slopes to his left. No figure revealed itself. He cursed his lack of peripheral vision that kept him from discretely checking the valley slopes on his right. He pretended to stretch his neck, first one way and then the other, using the different angles to get a better look.

There. Near some rocks close to the top of the valley. Virginia sat in the sun with her rifle across her lap. She tipped her hat, clearly not fooled by his neck stretching. She wasn't making any attempt to hide her spying, but at least she wasn't demanding he leave Biddie alone. And she was far enough that they could speak without being overheard. He turned away.

Biddie's tears were slowing.

He tugged the cloth from his neck and offered it to her. It was filthy, but probably better than having to use her sleeve.

She sniffed. "Thank you, but I have a handkerchief." She pulled the small cloth from a hidden pocket in her skirts and dabbed at her face.

He crammed his bandanna into his own pocket. "Are you all right?" What a dumb thing to ask. "I mean, is there anything I can do to help?"

She shook her head. "I'm sorry for what my sister said."

"Don't be. You've done nothing wrong. Your sister's the one who needs to apologize."

Biddie returned the handkerchief to her pocket. A wince marred her face as she withdrew her hand. She turned her palm up and examined it.

"What is it? Are you hurt?"

"I think there's a cactus needle in my hand, but I can't see it."

"Let me look." Gently, he took her hand and tipped it one way and then the other until sunlight caught on a tiny yellowish thorn. "I see it." With his free hand, he withdrew the tweezers he'd taken to carrying in his pocket. With all the cactus around, catching a needle or two had become a regular occurrence.

He bent over her hand, angling the tweezers to pinch the thorn. Twice it evaded him.

"Do you need help?" Biddie bent closer.

Her loose curls tickled his cheek. He jerked back. "Uh, maybe you'd better get it." He handed her the tweezers, resisting the urge to check the spot where Virginia was watching.

~

*V*irginia didn't like it. What were Biddie and Gideon doing with their heads so close together? She jumped off the five-foot rock to the hard dirt below and let the momentum hurry her steps down the slope to the spring.

Gideon jumped to his feet. "Biddie had a needle in her hand."

Virginia ignored him and focused on Biddie, who was fiddling with some tweezers. She didn't look up or acknowledge Virginia in any way. She cleared her throat. "Can I talk to you?"

Biddie shrugged.

Virginia gave Gideon a pointed look, silently ordering him to leave.

He gave her a look of warning, then headed back toward the house.

She squared her shoulders. "I'm sorry I lost my temper." Saying that she believed Biddie's claim to love Virginia would probably make Biddie happy, but Virginia refused to lie to her sister. No one had ever truly loved her. Even Preston, who Virginia knew cared about her at least a little, had eventually left her behind. It wasn't fair to hold that against him. It wasn't like he'd had a choice. But she felt abandoned, just the same. And he rarely wrote to her.

The only way she even knew how to reach him was the letter he'd sent last year explaining he'd joined a new traveling show after the last one had gone belly-up. He always addressed his letters to Clyve so Oliver wouldn't discover Preston's where-abouts and come after him. Had he received her news that Oliver was dead and she needed Preston's help? Would he come if he had? She shook the questions away and looked at Biddie. "I just don't want you getting hurt."

Biddie's face scrunched. "Baking isn't near as dangerous as running a ranch."

"That's not what I mean."

"What, then?"

"Gideon. You can't trust him."

Biddie groaned. "I thought we were past this. Hasn't he done enough to—"

"No. I know you don't understand. But you need to hear me when I tell you that no man can ever be completely trusted. No matter what they say or do."

"You seem to trust Clyve."

"Clyve was here when we came to this valley. Despite Oliv-er's nonsense, Clyve didn't turn his nose up at me the way most others did, and he's helped me out of a bind more than once. I trust that Clyve won't kill me to take my land. He's not the thieving or murdering sort. And most times, I trust him to tell it straight. But that's about as far as I trust him. I still wouldn't let you alone with him, and I don't want you falling in love with him either."

Biddie's brows shot toward her hairline. "Falling in love?"

"I seen the way you look at Gideon. You need to quit that. It's dangerous."

Biddie's cheeks reddened. "I don't know what you mean." She couldn't quite meet Virginia's eyes as she said it.

"'Course you do. You're smart. So stop acting stupid."

"I'm not."

"Love makes women stupid."

"I don't love him. I can't. I'm going back to San Francisco soon and—"

"Good. Remember that. Men don't want their wives working outside the home. If you marry him—assuming he offers—all your bakery dreams will be no more than a pile of ashes. Just like this ranch after the bandits came." It was far from the worst she could tell Biddie about marriage, but hopefully, it would be enough. Her little sister didn't need to know the worst of it.

Biddie's face paled, and for a heartbeat, Virginia regretted her words. She hated seeing the light fade in Biddie's eyes, but her little sister needed the truth. It was the only way Virginia could keep her safe.

CHAPTER 20

SEPTEMBER 10, 1873
LUPINE VALLEY RANCH
EASTERN SAN DIEGO COUNTY, CALIFORNIA

*B*iddie slid the tray of harlem cakes into the brick oven, then went into the cellar for more flour. At the bottom, the cat she'd named Pepper was stretched out in the fabric-lined crate they'd made for her. The animal was panting, with her tongue hanging from her mouth.

Biddie rushed back up the stairs and out the door. "Ginny! Gideon! Come quick." Gideon and Lucy were working on the corral wall, but Ginny was nowhere in sight. Biddie skidded to a stop beside them, panting almost as hard as Pepper had been. "Where's Ginny?"

"She went for more water." Gideon grasped her shoulders. "What's wrong?"

She drew strength from his confident blue eyes. "There's something wrong with Pepper."

He released her and started toward the house. His stride was quick, but he didn't run.

185

She hurried to catch up with him. "I've never seen anything like it. She was just lying there as she was all morning, but now she's panting as though she ran the length of the valley."

Gideon didn't slow, but his shoulders relaxed. "Sounds like it may be time for those kittens to make their appearance. But I'll take a look to be sure."

Excitement fluttered through her as they entered the house. She followed Gideon down the steps. "Do you mean it's normal for her to act like that when the kittens come?"

"Completely." He knelt beside the crate and studied Pepper. "Yep, I'd say that's what's happening." He grinned up at her. "Hope you're ready to lose your peace and quiet, and maybe a touch of your sanity to the tiny noisy things."

His words made her chuckle even as she clasped her fingers together and twisted them. She'd never seen any animal give birth before. What if Pepper needed help?

"I'd say she's in for a long day." Gideon rose and turned to leave.

Biddie pressed her hands to his chest. "Don't leave. I won't know what to do if something goes wrong."

He covered her hands with his. He held her gaze and spoke gently. "The process usually takes hours, and I've got work to do. Besides, you know your sister wouldn't like me being in here alone with you."

An entirely different flutter tickled the inside of her ribs. "But—"

He removed her hands and stepped around her, then paused beside her. He lifted one rough palm and cupped her cheek. "Try not to worry. These things usually go on without a hitch."

Unable to speak, she nodded, and his hand lowered. She caught it as he stepped onto the first stair. "Pray with me before you go?"

Wrinkles formed at the corners of his eyes. "God and I aren't on speaking terms. Sorry."

"I don't understand. Are you mad at Him?"

Gideon hesitated, then sighed. "More like He's mad at me."

"Do you believe Jesus is Lord?"

"Of course."

She let out a breath and smiled. "Then ask Him to forgive you, and He will."

He closed his eyes. "It's not that simple."

"Of course, it is." She gently squeezed his rough fingers. "The Bible says that if we confess our sins to God, He is faithful to forgive us."

"The Bible also says that we are to repent of our sins and not repeat them. I cannot be sorry for what I did. And I wouldn't act any differently if I were put in that position again." He pulled his hand free of hers. "I'm sorry."

Gideon turned and walked out of the cellar before she could think of a response. A moment later, she heard the front door close. She turned back to Pepper and began to pray, not just for the mama suffering to bring her babies into the world, but for the suffering man who'd stolen her heart.

∾

*E*ager to deliver her latest batch of baked goods to the Gaskills' store, Biddie woke before dawn the next morning and hurried down to the cellar to check on the five kittens and Pepper. She needed to ready breakfast, but she couldn't resist peeking at the new little family first. All were well and sleeping, so after a quick stroke across each tiny back and an extra few strokes for Pepper, she grabbed a hunk of cheese and left the cellar.

When they were preparing to travel, Gideon would cook breakfast over a fire in the yard since the women were usually still sleeping and no one wanted to heat the house more than it already was. In fact, Biddie almost wished she'd listened to Virginia and had her brick oven built outside. Baking in the house the last two days had been rather unpleasant. The stone walls kept most of the outside heat from warming the room, but they also trapped the heat from her oven. However, cooking indoors kept the sand out of her food. For that, she'd soak a thousand chemises.

As Ginny and Lucy dressed, Biddie slid a thick slice of cheese between three rolls and wrapped them in paper.

Patty would still need milking, and Biddie was nervous leaving the kittens alone so soon after being born. So someone needed to remain at the ranch and look after the animals. None of them liked the idea of any of them being alone at the ranch, but Biddie's baked goods needed to be brought to town while they were still fresh. Gideon refused to let Biddie go alone, and Ginny refused to let Biddie and Gideon travel so far without her. The argument over who should go had taken most of the evening until Lucy volunteered to stay behind and Ginny was convinced to accept the solution.

A rap at the door startled all three women. "We've got a problem." Gideon's voice seemed grave through the thick wood.

Biddie hurried to let him in. "What's wrong?"

Rather than enter, he waved for them to come out. "The cow's gone."

"What?" Ginny hopped outside, still yanking on her left boot.

A moment later, they were gathered beneath the cow's shade cover. He held the frayed end of a rope in his hands. "It seems this was rubbing against there." He pointed to a somewhat angular rock several feet away.

Ginny turned to scan the valley around them. "She can't have gone far." Her chin tipped down, and she moved toward the outer edge of where Patty had been able to wander with her tie down. "Here's her tracks." She pointed to hoof prints the size of Biddie's palm and followed a trail leading northeast. "She went that way." Ginny headed for her horse.

Biddie rushed after her. "Where are you going?"

"To get the cow, of course."

"But we're supposed to leave for town this morning."

Ginny saddled her gelding. "I know. This won't take long. Just wait here."

Biddie held her tongue. Of course, they needed to find Patty, but if they didn't take her goods to the store today, they'd be unacceptably stale before a customer could purchase one. As it was, they would lack the usual freshness she preferred to offer. Ginny and Gideon had both assured her, customers out here wouldn't mind day-old baked goods. They'd be grateful to find *any* available at the store. But they couldn't possibly want two- or three-day-old cakes and rolls.

～

*B*iddie's hopes sank as the sun rose higher over the horizon. Standing on the valley ridge, she searched the desert below but could not spot her sister. "Where is she?" Ginny had been gone for hours. If they didn't leave for Campo soon, the store would be closed before they arrived.

Gideon came to stand beside her. "I'm sure Virginia will be back as soon as she can. It may be Patty has gotten herself tangled or stuck somehow. Or maybe she's just being ornery about coming home."

Biddie thought of the hours she'd worked to create her goods for the store and the supplies already wasted during her argument with Ginny. Her sister hated seeing supplies wasted and they needed whatever money she could earn from the goods she'd baked. Biddie pivoted. "I'm not waiting any longer." She marched back toward the house.

Gideon caught up to her. "You can't go by yourself."

"So come with me."

"Virginia wouldn't like that, and you know it."

"She won't be happy if everything I baked goes to waste either."

"True, but—"

"I've made up my mind. You can come with me or not, but either way, I'm going." She didn't like putting Gideon in a tight spot, but really, Ginny's concerns about him were baseless. Perhaps if she saw they'd traveled to town together and Biddie returned unharmed, her sister would begin to trust Gideon more. Because there was no way he'd let Biddie make the journey alone. She pressed her lips against a smile. He really was a good man.

"Fine. But we'll take my tent and spend the night in town. You can sleep inside the tent, and I'll sleep outside by the fire. That way, there won't be any question of propriety."

Biddie made no argument.

In less than half an hour, they were loaded up and heading out of the valley. Lucy remained at the house as planned and would inform Ginny of their whereabouts.

Anxious to reach the store as soon as possible, Biddie set a faster pace than usual. Gideon and Legend matched her. They rode in silence for several miles before the horses needed a break. They stopped to water the animals from the canteens they'd brought along, then continued at a walk. Finally, she worked up the nerve to ask the question she'd not asked during their baking lessons. "What happened to your family's ranch?"

Gideon's face whipped toward her. "Why do you ask?"

Why *did* she ask? It really wasn't any of her business. Yet something told her the story was part of what held Gideon back. From their conversations over baking, he didn't seem to have any plans for the future. His only plans beyond the Lupine Valley Ranch were to find another position as a cook. Still, it was a rather personal question. She ought to be open in return. "I want to get to know you better."

His eyes widened. Then he turned away to stare into the distance.

He was quiet so long, she didn't think he was going to answer. She swallowed a sigh. How was she to help him if she didn't fully understand him?

Then he spoke, eyes still fixed on the horizon ahead. "Father died. Mother and I couldn't keep up with the work on our own. The bank foreclosed."

More silence.

"I'm sorry. Did he die in the war?"

"No." Gideon's Adams apple bobbed. "He was too old to fight."

"Then how—"

"He was killed shortly after I—I came home."

She gasped. "Murdered?"

He shook his head, his jaw muscle flexing. "He was trampled by a bull."

"How awful. I'm so sorry." She squeezed her eyes against the mental images his words created. "Your mother must miss him. Is she still in Texas? Did she remarry?"

"She died last year. Never remarried."

Gideon spoke of their deaths as though they'd occurred weeks ago, not years. There had to be more to the story than he was sharing, but she couldn't bring herself to press him further.

"Perhaps while we're in town, you might inquire whether there are any local ranchers looking to sell out."

He gazed at her with a raised brow. "Why would I do that?"

"Well, you've got to start over somewhere. Why not here?"

"What makes you think I want another ranch?"

"Don't you want to use all the skills your parents taught you?"

He turned away. "Who do you think taught me to cook?"

191

"Your mother, of course, but what about your ranching skills? You must have so much experience that could—"

"I'm not a rancher. Not anymore." He nudged his horse to a trot, ending their conversation.

∾

*G*ideon made sure not to overwork the horses while also keeping as much of a distance between himself and Biddie as reasonable. He wanted no more of the types of questions she'd asked earlier. His past was the past, and there was no changing it, so there was no point discussing it. And he certainly had no interest in discussing the confined future he'd laid out for himself.

After Mother's death, he'd considered moving to a city where there were no cattle, corrals, or anything else to remind him of his failure. But he'd visited a few cities during the war. They were noisy and made him feel hemmed in. He couldn't imagine spending the rest of his life in such a place. Work as a ranch cook would keep him out of the corrals but still give him the wide-open spaces and natural beauty he craved. When he wasn't stuck in a kitchen. That had been the plan, at least.

Somehow, he'd let those women rope him into splitting rock, digging trenches, and building walls. The constant fear of dropping one of those heavy stones on their delicate feet or accidentally knocking one of them into the firepit haunted him. Yet he couldn't bring himself to leave them on their own. And there was no chance Virginia would allow another man to come help them. It seemed a miracle she hadn't kicked him off the ranch after the tantrum she'd thrown over Biddie's baking lessons.

Whatever Virginia had said to Biddie after he'd left them at the spring seemed to have healed the rift her temper had caused between them. But she still wouldn't let Biddie teach

Gideon any more about baking. Which, if he was honest with himself, was probably the wisest decision Virginia had made since his arrival.

He spotted Luman Gaskill chatting with two men outside his store. Nearby, two wagons sat loaded with supplies, a woman on each bench and a child or two in each wagon bed. What was unusual were the weapons each woman gripped as they scanned their surroundings. Even one of the older boys in the wagon bed held a rifle. The men seemed nervous, too, glancing over their shoulders as they spoke. They'd stared hard at Gideon and Biddie until Luman said something—likely recognizing them and setting the others at ease with the information.

Gideon reined his horse to a stop and dismounted. "Afternoon." He tipped his hat. "Everything all right?" He tipped his chin toward the armed women and boy.

The younger of the two men scowled. "Bandits attacked a homestead in the foothills north of here. Killed the husband. Rap—"

His friend elbowed him in the ribs. "There are ladies present."

The younger man's freckled face flushed as he glanced at Biddie, who'd come to stand beside Gideon. "Sorry, Miss. They, uh...it was a terrible tragedy."

The older man nodded. "I heard they'd cleared out a stage station a few days before that. The manager survived, but he's hurt real bad."

Gideon joined the men in scanning the land around them. "Where are they now?"

Luman's expression turned grim. "Not sure. The women on that homestead said the vermin rode east when they finally left."

Biddie gasped. "East?" Her wide eyes found Gideon's. "Ginny and Lucy."

Luman raised his hands as if to calm her. "It could be they started west and then turned north or south when they were out of sight. No real way of knowing."

Biddie continued to stare at Gideon. "We should head back."

Much as he wanted to protect her reputation by staying in town that night, he shared her concern. At the same time, he didn't want to risk encountering the bandits on the trail. He looked to the men. "How long ago was the attack?"

"Started yesterday afternoon, but the varmints didn't leave till morning."

Gideon frowned. "Depending on the direction they took, there's a chance we could encounter them on our way back to the ranch."

"That's true any time we come to town, isn't it?" She gripped his forearm. "At least we know to be on guard. Ginny and Lucy will have no clue."

"Your sister is always on guard."

"*If* she's back from fetching Patty." Her fingers dug into his muscle. "Gideon, what if Lucy is still alone?"

Much as he hated it, there was no good solution. "Fine. Let's leave your goods with Luman, feed and water the horses, then head back." He faced the store owner. "Oh, and we'll need to purchase more ammunition."

Biddie paused. "More?" They'd already purchased what seemed like a year's worth the last time they'd been in town. Not that she had any idea how many bullets ranchers usually shot in a year, but surely, they couldn't need more.

Neither of the men acknowledged her question.

Luman nodded and turned to the store. "I'll get it ready for you."

Gideon looked at her again. "If we ride hard, we should make it to the ranch not long after sunrise."

CHAPTER 21

*G*ideon cocked his rifle, took aim, and fired. The round clay target he'd been aiming at shattered. Pieces scattered across the ground surrounding the dirt slope he'd chosen for their shooting lessons. He'd been careful to select a section with no close rocks. Not an easy thing in this boulder-speckled valley. But it meant less risk of a bullet bouncing the wrong way if they missed their target. And the women were missing most of their shots.

He'd made thirty clay targets from the same stuff they'd been using for their mortar, but with less water, and had formed the mixture into fist-sized balls with a dent in the middle for something better to aim at. In hindsight, that dent had been overly optimistic. It was late morning, and they'd been practicing for a little over an hour. This was the third time he'd shot at a target himself. At the rate they were going, if he didn't shoot any more, they'd still have twenty-seven targets to work with tomorrow.

Not that they could spend all day tomorrow practicing their shooting as they were today. Virginia hadn't protested their plans once she'd learned of the latest attack, but she couldn't finish the corrals and barn by herself.

Patty, Legend, and the rest of the horses might now be secured within the first corral they'd completed—hopefully, putting an end to Patty's unapproved adventures—but Virginia was dead set on being ready for a small herd of cattle by the fall. That meant they needed to complete at least three more corrals in just a few weeks. So today would have to do for getting Biddie and Lucy as close as possible to being able to defend themselves.

At least there'd been no sign of the bandits on Gideon's and Biddie's ride home, nor since their arrival back at the ranch.

To his right, Biddie lifted his pistol from where he'd set it on an upturned crate. She balanced his weapon on her flat palm. "This is much heavier than it looks." The muzzle swung in his direction.

He snatched it away from her. "Don't forget what I told you. Always treat these as if they're loaded and—"

"Don't aim at anything I don't intend to shoot." She offered an apologetic smile. "Sorry, I know. I promise, I was listening. I was just distracted by the surprise."

He frowned. This was exactly why he'd been so reluctant to train them to shoot. But learning about the latest bandit attack yesterday had left him little choice. "If this ranch is ever attacked, there's going to be plenty of distractions. You've got to learn to focus. I saw men killed in the war by fellow soldiers who'd lost their focus." His instructions came out harsher than he'd intended, so he softened his tone. He didn't want to hurt her, but she needed to understand the seriousness of using such a weapon. "You can't take a bullet back."

Her smile fell. "You're right. I'll do better."

A few feet to his left, Lucy leveled her rifle at the target he'd assigned her. "Am I holding it right?"

He considered the placement of her hands. The knuckles of

her fingers were almost white. "Loosen your grip just a bit. You don't need to strangle the thing. That's going to make you pull off target."

She did as he instructed.

He checked that Biddie was behind him and the shooting area was clear, then turned back to Lucy. "Now, pull the lever to load and cock the rifle. Then make sure your sights are lined up, take a deep breath, and as you let it out, squeeze the trigger."

A second later, dirt burst from the ground just left and above the target she'd been aiming at.

She lowered her rifle with a grin. "I almost hit it that time."

He nodded. "You're getting better." She might even the hit the target before the sun set.

Biddie clapped. "Good job, Lucy." Her blue gaze sobered as she turned to him. "Is it my turn?"

"Yes." Once more, he talked her through the process of loading and aiming her weapon. When she pulled the lever, she lifted her barrel. "Move it down. You're aiming too high now."

She lowered the gun more than she needed to. "Like this?"

"No, a little higher."

She moved the barrel back to where it had been before.

He suppressed a groan and stepped behind her. He placed his hands over hers and adjusted the rifle. "There. Now, are your sights lined up?"

"I think so. That metal point at the front needs to be lined up with this notch at the back, right? Like this?"

Without thinking, he moved his head to get a look at her sights, and his cheek brushed hers. He released her, jumping back like a flame had burned him. Which is almost what the contact had felt like.

She turned to look at him. "Gideon?"

He glanced at her long enough to be sure her barrel was

pointed at the ground and nowhere near her feet. It was. He turned away. "Just a second." He needed a stick. He found one and used its tip to draw in the dirt. "This is the notch at the back." He drew a little triangle between the first two. "This is how the front sight should fit. The top of that point should be level with the back piece and centered in the notch. If that's what you're seeing, then your aim is good."

"Oh." Biddie turned back to the target and took aim again. After a moment, she declared, "I think I'm ready."

Again, he checked that the direction she was firing was clear, then told her to go ahead.

Biddie's clay target exploded, and she began jumping up and down. "I did it. I did it."

He snagged the rifle from her grip and set in on the crate with the barrel pointed away from any possible harm. She'd been keeping it aimed at the ground, but all that jumping made him nervous. With the gun safely settled, he turned to her. "Good work. Now think back. What did you do differently this time?"

Her face scrunched in adorable contemplation. "I think I squeezed the trigger more slowly...and I aimed a bit lower than that dent you told us to aim at."

He grinned at her. "Perfect. Since your shots have been going high, aiming lower was a good way to account for that."

She laughed. "It was your idea."

"But you listened and figured out how to apply it." He lifted her rifle and pointed at Lucy's. "Now, both of you load up and try again."

Both women complied, and even though he didn't take another shot, by the time the sun set, there were only twenty targets left. Now, if their would-be attackers remained perfectly still, there was at least a chance the women might be able to defend themselves.

~

OCTOBER 27, 1873
LUPINE VALLEY RANCH
EASTERN SAN DIEGO COUNTY, CALIFORNIA

*B*iddie sank to the floor beside her work table, exhausted. Alone in the cabin, she sat in the dirt and longed for a chair. There'd been no time to make one, no wood for making one even if they'd had the time, and no room on the horses for hauling home ready-made chairs during their previous trips to town. So there she sat. Too exhausted to continue standing. Too stubborn to crawl into bed.

It'd been weeks since she last baked, and tomorrow they were going to town to restock their supplies. Gideon and Ginny were outside checking that the animals and their gear would be ready for the trip. Lucy was taking their clothes from the line. Her friend had refused to go to town in the filthy clothes they'd been working in all week and insisted on washing everyone's laundry that day. Not that anyone had argued. Biddie was pretty sure even Ginny was tired of constantly being covered in dirt.

Meanwhile, Biddie had been sent inside to pack food for each of them so they could make an early start the next morning and not need to stop for their noon meal. But now she'd finished that task. Which meant if she wanted to take more baked goods for Mr. Gaskill to sell, this was her last chance to make them. Whatever she made needed to be quick and easy. Assuming she could convince her legs to prop her up again.

Every morning for weeks, she, Lucy, and Gideon had helped Virginia build the corral walls. It was almost the end of October, but the days were still long and hot. When the sun reached its highest point each day, they retreated to the shade cloth they'd set up near their shooting range. Biddie and Lucy would eat a hasty lunch, then practice shooting their rifles for an hour. Afterward, they'd return to building walls.

Biddie and Lucy now hit more clay targets than they missed, and the corrals were finished at last. But by the end of each day, Biddie was so exhausted, she had no energy left for baking. This evening was no different. But if she didn't find the strength somehow, she'd have nothing to offer at the store. Would Mr. Gaskill even want more of her goods to sell? What if what she'd brought him before hadn't sold and sat on the shelf until it spoiled? Or worse, what if customers hadn't liked her food and complained?

Maybe she should stay at the ranch instead of Lucy. It would make Ginny happy.

She hadn't liked the idea of Biddie and Gideon making another trip to town alone, but they'd all agreed Patty couldn't go without milking and Lucy couldn't be left alone. Since Gideon and Ginny were the best shots, it didn't make sense for them both to stay home or both ride to town. Gideon insisted on going to town since traveling was more dangerous than remaining at home where they at least had the new house to take cover in. Lucy had been the one to point out that Biddie needed to go so she could learn how well her baked goods had sold and be sure their account at the store was updated accordingly. Ginny had argued a bit, but even she'd seen the logic in the plan. That didn't mean she liked it.

Yes, if Biddie stayed home, Ginny would be much happier. Biddie could even help her sister dig the footing for the barn they were building next.

As though understanding and disapproving of her thoughts, Biddie's calf muscle seized. "Ow!" Her eyes pressed shut against the pain, and she held her breath, willing the muscle to relax.

Heavy boot steps thudded into the room. "What's wrong? Where does it hurt?"

She opened her eyes and found Gideon kneeling beside her. She pointed to where her skirts hid the offending muscle. "Muscle spasm."

"Oh." He stared at her skirt, his hands hovering in midair. "My...uh...my mother used to get those. I'd massage her, but—"

The pain intensified, traveling down to include the arch of her foot as well. "Ahh." Desperate, Biddie pulled the fabric up to her knee. "Please. Help."

Tentatively, he wrapped his fingers around the muscle just below her knee and gently squeezed.

The relief was minor but better than nothing at all. She forced her thanks out on a whisper.

He worked his way down to the top of her boot and back up to where he'd started. Slowly, the pain was lessening.

"That's helping." She bent, her movement causing her skirts to shift as she hastily removed her boot. "Can you do my foot? It's cramping too." Part of her was mortified that she'd voiced such a bold request—particularly while knowing how vile her stockings were after a long day working outside. But the bigger part of her just wanted the pain to end and didn't care about anything else.

When she leaned back, she noticed Gideon's hands were covered by her skirt where they massaged her calf. He pulled them out and reached for her foot—just as Lucy entered with an armload of laundry.

Lucy's mouth fell open. "What in the world?"

Gideon immediately released Biddie.

"No. Don't stop." Biddie pointed at her foot. "That was working."

Hands in the air, Gideon looked uncertainly between her and Lucy.

Biddie huffed. "My muscles are spasming horribly, and

Gideon is making them stop. Nothing to be scandalized over. We aren't in the city. Out here, people do what's practical. Now." She looked at Gideon and pointed at her foot again. "Please."

"No, wait." Lucy dropped her laundry on the table and knelt beside Biddie. She nudged Gideon out of the way and took Biddie's foot in her own hands. They weren't nearly as strong. "I can manage it."

Without a word, Gideon fled the cabin.

Lucy kept massaging as she leaned close and whispered. "For heaven's sake, Biddie. We may not be in San Francisco, but it still isn't proper for an unmarried man to fondle the limb of an unmarried woman."

"He wasn't *fondling* my limb. He was rendering medical aid. Surely, you see the difference."

Lucy's lips pinched. "Perhaps, but did you even consider that the two of you were alone in this cabin?"

"I didn't choose the timing. It just happened, and he was the only one around. He said it helped his mother, so—"

"How do you think your sister would have responded if she'd walked in on the scene I just did?"

Biddie clamped her mouth shut. She hated to admit it, but Lucy had a point. Ginny might have shot first and asked questions later. And now that the pain was subsiding, the reality of the liberties she'd allowed Gideon—no, begged Gideon to take —began to settle in. As did the smell emanating from her stockinged feet. She hid her face in her hands. What had she been thinking? There was absolutely no way she could ever face Gideon again.

She looked at her friend. "You need to go to town instead of me."

CHAPTER 22

*G*ideon nudged Legend into another trot as they crested a small rise in the desert floor. He cast a glance over his shoulder at Biddie. The trail was more than wide enough for her to ride beside him as she'd done during their previous trip, but she remained behind.

She'd barely met his gaze since he fled the cabin the night before. Yet somehow, without exchanging more than a handful of words, he and Biddie had managed to load up and ride away from Lupine Valley Ranch well before sunrise.

Just the two of them.

Alone.

Again.

And Lucy had cheerily waved them goodbye. Which made absolutely no sense.

Not that he planned to take advantage of their situation. Mother had raised him better. Besides, even if he and God weren't on speaking terms, there seemed no reason to go irritating the Creator of the universe by willfully dismissing yet another of his Ten Commandments. Bad enough were the sins he'd already committed.

But Lucy couldn't know that for certain. And after what she'd witnessed the night before, it stood to reason she'd object to the two of them riding off alone together. In fact, he'd half expected her to come out of the house this morning, ready to go in Biddie's place. Or in the very least, he'd thought she would stand in the yard trying to convince Biddie not to go, right up until the last minute. But she hadn't protested their plans at all. She hadn't even told Virginia about what she'd seen.

He had to admit, he was grateful for that last part. Worthless or not, he wasn't quite ready for his life to be over. He wasn't sure why. It wasn't as though he held any great hope or plans for his future. But still. He'd just as soon go on living for now. Something Virginia would likely have tried to alter if she'd learned his hands were up her sister's skirts.

He swallowed. Put like that, his actions sounded much worse than they were. The thought had him tugging at his collar and checking his back trail. He sure hoped Lucy didn't change her mind about telling Virginia.

~

*B*iddie continued avoiding Gideon's gaze as he held the door for her and she entered the store. She'd spent the entire ride tense, waiting for him to ask what had possessed her to make such a brazen demand of him. She wasn't about to give him the chance to ask now that they'd arrived.

In hindsight, she realized she'd interrupted his suggestion that someone else should massage her the way he used to massage his mother. Worse, Biddie had all but ordered him to perform the intimate action himself. Clearly, the pain had stolen her senses. It was the only explanation, but the thought of trying to explain herself to him was more than she could bear.

Why, oh why, did Lucy refuse to go in Biddie's place this morning?

Biddie had waited until Ginny was out on guard duty before pleading her case, but the effort had been wasted. Lucy was immovable. She firmly stated that she had no desire to visit town and was confident Biddie had learned her lesson. Nothing Biddie said would convince her friend to go. Maybe she thought the humiliation was Biddie's due punishment.

Luman was at the counter helping another customer. He spotted her and waved. "Miss Davidson, I'm so glad to see you. I was just telling Schmidt that I didn't know when you'd be back with more of those delicious little cakes."

The white-haired man across from Luman turned with a shy smile. "Them cakes were mighty tasty, Miss. I'd be right pleased if you brought some more to sell." He glanced hopefully at the sack Gideon had insisted on carrying inside for her.

Gideon set the bag on the counter.

Biddie beamed at Mr. Schmidt. "That's so kind of you to say. I'm afraid I didn't have time to make cakes, but I did bring several rolls." She opened the bag to reveal the golden rounds. "There are a dozen potato rolls and half a dozen herb rolls of my own recipe."

The man's eyes lit as though he'd spotted gold. "I'll take 'em all."

"Now, Schmidt, I have other customers that have been asking after Miss Davidson's baking. Old Man Pearson's come in every other day asking if I'd gotten more yet. What'll I tell him and the others if I sell them all to you?"

"Tell 'em I was here first and offered a penny more'n what you were asking last time." Schmidt reached for the open bag, but Luman beat him to it.

The store owner held the bag behind his back. "I'll sell you half what she's brought and not any more. But it'll cost you double."

Gideon took Biddie's arm and guided her away as the two continued haggling. Dazed by the unexpected pleasure of such a positive response from Luman's customers, Biddie didn't object.

Once in the opposite corner, Gideon released a chuckle. "Listening to those two, you'd think those were gold nuggets instead of bread."

She pulled free of his grip on her elbow and finally met his gaze. "You don't think my baking deserves such excitement?"

He didn't look away, and something she couldn't identify passed between them. "I think they're arguing over the golden eggs"—he cupped her cheek—"when I've got the goose who made them."

Her breath caught. "You do?"

Dropping his hand and his gaze, he cleared his throat. "Well, um...of course. All of us at the ranch do. Virginia, Lucy, and me. You don't charge any of us for what you make." He waggled his brows and jerked a thumb over his shoulder. "But those poor saps have to pay."

Biddie sighed. "Oh, right." Of course, that was what he'd meant. It had been foolish of her to imagine something more intimate in his look.

The arguing at the front of the store seemed to have stopped, drawing her gaze. Mr. Schmidt plunked a large pile of coins on the counter, and Luman handed him the entire bag of rolls. The store owner grinned as he scooped the money from the counter. He caught her watching and waved her over.

Separating a portion of the coins, he held them out. "Here you are. Your portion of the sale."

She lifted a hand to accept the payment and gasped at the large sum. She stared at Luman, who was grinning like a cat who'd swallowed the canary. "All of this for a few rolls?" Guilt pricked at her conscience. This was more than she'd charged for her fancy cakes back in San Francisco. "It's too much." She started toward the door. She needed to find Mr. Schmidt and return some of his money.

Luman beat her to the door and stopped in her path. "Where are you going?"

"He can't possibly eat all of those before they go bad."

Luman frowned. "Never underestimate a hard-working rancher's appetite."

Biddie hesitated. It was true Gideon had eaten more than she'd thought possible many times. "It's still too much money."

The store owner's brows pinched. "Did he look unhappy to you?"

She pictured Schmidt's gleeful expression as he'd strode through the door, bag in hand. "No."

"That's because I don't cheat my customers."

Oh dear. Had she implied that? "I'm sorry. Of course you don't. I just...I was surprised, I guess."

"Apology accepted." His smile returned, and he went back to the counter. He opened his ledger and turned it so it faced her. "Here you'll see where I've credited your portion of the previous sales against what you owe me for the supplies you ordered." He pointed at a number that had Biddie swallowing another gasp.

She set the coins he'd just given her on the counter. "Add these to the account as well."

"Happy to." He swept the coins into his register and made a note on their account. The amount left them with a marginal credit. "Now." He rubbed his hands together. "How soon can you bring me more? I wasn't lying about Old Man Pearson and my other customers wanting more of your baking."

Biddie looked at Gideon but he just shrugged. She looked back at Luman. "I'm not certain. I'll need to speak with my sister, but I might be able to come again next week." Biddie silently prayed her sister wouldn't mind Biddie making the trip again so soon or the extra hours she would need to spend baking.

"I'll let my customers know. Now, what can I get for you today?"

It didn't take long to gather the supplies they needed. Luman held them in the store until the next morning, when Gideon loaded their purchases onto the packhorse they'd brought along.

As they rode out of town just after dawn, Biddie considered the surprising amount of money she'd earned. Was it possible such success could continue? If so, there was every reason to believe she could run a successful business out here in the desert. The notion was shocking.

She studied the golden land speckled with shades of olive green, yellows, oranges, and even a bit of red. The desert had a beauty all its own that was perhaps not immediately apparent, but took some settling into. Rather like a new shoe. At first, the dust and heat had chafed her. Now, she felt comfortable and at home in this wide-open landscape with blue skies that seemed to stretch on forever.

Here, silence was normal. Noise was the exception. And there was something soothing in the soft clip-clop of the horses' hooves, the quiet whoosh of desert grasses in the gentle breeze, and the occasional scuttle of frightened lizards through dried weeds. Must she return to the familiar but crowded city, where she had to crane her neck to find clear sky and there wasn't a quiet corner to be found?

Of course she did. Finding success as a baker here, in the middle of nowhere, wouldn't restore the social status Father and Mother sacrificed all those years ago to raise her.

But did social status truly matter? It had seemed so vital in San Francisco—the key to opening doors of opportunity and financial security. Yet no one out here seemed to give the subject a moment's thought.

Ahead of her, Gideon's shoulders swayed with the movement of his horse. He certainly didn't care about society. What did he think of this land? Was it possible he'd make a home here?

~

*T*hat cursed, blurry *C* was back in Gideon's vision. He blinked hard, trying to rid himself of the problem, but it refused to go away. He bit back a growl. He couldn't have another headache. Not now. He and Biddie had another three hours of riding to reach Lupine Valley Ranch.

"What's that?" Biddie's voice had him twisting in his saddle.

He followed her pointing finger to a cloud of dust a mile or two south of them and traveling up the narrow valley toward them. The only thing out here that could make that much dust and move that quickly was a group of large animals. Horses or cattle, most likely. But why were they running? And who was with them? Animals like those usually came with men. He squinted, trying to force his eyes to focus on the darker shapes coming into sight among the clouds of dirt. It didn't work. Worse, the effort started the pain in his head.

He closed his eyes.

All right. If he couldn't see who was riding toward them, the safest choice was to avoid being seen until he could determine the type of men they were.

He opened his eyes and winced at the brightness of the afternoon sun. Forcing his lids to stay open, he searched past the blurry line in his vision for something large enough to hide not only him and Biddie, but their horses as well.

"What are you looking for?"

"We need to hide."

"There." She pointed to a large bush.

"That won't hide the horses." The pain in his head was quickly growing. He searched his memory of the trail ahead. "There's a turn just a little ways farther, then a big pile of rocks near the peak of that hill. We'll have to push the horses hard to make it before that group reaches us, but I think they can handle it." He nudged Legend into a canter, pulling the packhorse behind them.

Biddie passed him on the trail.

He glanced back and could now make out three figures riding horses with what looked like more behind. He still couldn't tell who the men were, but he couldn't think of any good reason for a group of men to be riding that hard. They didn't seem to have noticed him and Biddie yet. He turned back, putting all his focus on reaching the next bend and getting out of sight.

Biddie made it to the bend first, but he wasn't far behind.

Rather than continue on the trail, the smart woman made a sharp right turn. She slowed her horse and guided it into a gap between the boulders he'd remembered. The space was no more than four feet wide, but it was plenty long. They slipped all the animals in without any trouble.

Both horses and riders breathed heavily as they stood, waiting. Gideon's head pounded so hard, he was afraid his brain would escape his skull. His attention was torn between taking deep, long breaths and listening for the oncoming riders. Had the group spotted him and Biddie?

The thunder of pounding hooves grew louder. Raucous men's voices joined with what seemed like jubilant shouts and noises meant to hurry a herd of animals. The uproar grew so loud, Gideon feared the men had turned onto the trail and were headed east instead of continuing north along the canyon as he'd hoped they would. His vision blurred as specks of light burst in his sight. His stomach churned.

The clamor of the other riders began to fade. The surrounding rocks must have played tricks on his ears to make him think they'd turned. If only the drumming against his skull would fade as well.

Biddie whispered, "I think they're leaving."

Gingerly, he nodded. But he didn't speak until he could no longer hear the pounding hooves. "Let's go." He guided Legend backward out of the gap. Thankfully, the packhorse was smart enough to understand what was expected. If Gideon had needed to dismount and lead the animal out, he might not have able to remount. As it was, it would take a miracle for them to make it to the ranch before the pain in his head forced him from the saddle. He hoped the riders kept heading north and found no reason to turn east.

CHAPTER 23

*I*t was a close thing, but Gideon made it back to the ranch just after sunset. Biddie immediately warned Ginny of the potential bandit danger, and the three women began planning how to defend the ranch. He should help them.

He slid from his horse, and the thud of his boots hitting the ground sent pain through his head. His vision blurred and narrowed. He fought back the blackness and stumbled toward the boulder cave. Too tired and miserable to bother with his bedroll, he collapsed onto the hard dirt floor, threw an arm over his eyes, and fell asleep.

"Biddie! Lucy! Get your rifles, quick." Virginia's shout jarred Gideon awake

He found his belt holster propped against the rock wall beside him and strapped it on as he charged outside. Though his pain was gone, the bright afternoon sunlight nearly blinded him. He squinted, trying to locate the trouble.

Virginia had taken a position behind their wheelbarrow. Biddie and Lucy knelt behind the partially formed walls of the new barn. He followed the aim of their weapons and spotted three men on horseback. They'd clearly been following the trail leading into the valley, but they'd stopped at the ridge and seemed to be waiting for permission to continue. Smart men.

Virginia shouted, "State your business"

"My name is Karl Hofman." His words were thickened by a German accent. "Luman Gaskill said you were looking to buy some cattle. I have come to make you an offer."

Virginia kept her voice low enough their visitors could not hear her. "I want to talk to these men, but keep your rifles ready and stay out of sight until I say otherwise."

Biddie and Lucy whispered their agreement.

Gideon held silent. He'd decide his own course of action once he got a better look at these men.

Virginia raised her voice again. "Keep your hands away from your weapons and come on down, nice and easy."

Within a few minutes, it was clear the men had come for the reason they'd claimed. It seemed Mr. Hofmann was brother to the man who'd been murdered when his homestead and family were attacked. He'd come to take the widow and her daughter back to his home north of Los Angeles but had no interest in what remained of the deceased man's cattle. He was a blacksmith, not a rancher.

The price he offered Virginia was high. Maybe he thought to take advantage of a single young female, but Virginia was no fool. She negotiated a fair price and made it dependent on the condition of the animals. Hofmann was in a hurry to return home, so it was agreed Virginia would travel to inspect the cattle the following day. The men were invited to set up camp in the valley with the understanding Gideon would be standing watch all night.

He didn't like it. Not one part of this situation boded well in Gideon's mind. His gut told him these men were no danger, but he'd grown too used to being the only man on the ranch and had listened to too many of Virginia's dire warnings for the presence of these strangers not to chafe. Worse still, Virginia was actually going through with bringing a new herd to the ranch.

As Hofmann and his men set up camp several yards away, Biddie and Lucy helped Gideon prepare the evening meal. They were full of excitement and chattered about their plans for the trip.

Biddie diced onions to add to the soup Gideon was making. "I'm glad I baked extra rolls this morning. We'll need them for the journey tomorrow."

Lucy retrieved their dishes from the crate. "I hope they've brought their own bowls and silverware, or we'll need to take turns eating." She set their four bowls on the flat-topped stone they used for serving. "Do you think Clyve will be able to come milk Patty while we're gone?"

Biddie plopped the onion into the soup pot. "He did offer his help last time he was here. If he can't spare the time, I'm sure he'll instruct one of his hands to do so."

Gideon added broth to the pot. "I'm more than capable of milking the cow."

"What do you mean? We can't bring her with us." Biddie reached for the carrots.

He thrust a stick into the hot coals, adjusting the heat below the pot. "Which is why I'm staying here."

Both women froze. Biddie turned her wide eyes on him. "But we'll need your help with the cattle."

"I told you, I'm a cook, not a cowhand or a vaquero." Why was his decision so hard for her to accept? Why was she always pushing him to do more?

Lucy gaped. "You can't expect us to drive a herd of cattle across the desert on our own. You're the one with experience."

Virginia strode over to them. "Of course he does. I told you men are unreliable."

"What if there's a stampede?" Lucy's fingers covered her mouth.

Virginia snorted. "There are only thirty head. We'll let them run, then round them up."

Biddie planted her hands on her hips. "What if the bandits come back?"

He used the excuse of grabbing the pot lid to turn away. "If you think it's so dangerous, don't go."

"Ginny can't drive thirty cattle by herself."

"So pay Hofmann's men to drive them here, or better yet, don't buy the cattle at all." He slammed the lid onto the pot.

Virginia's nostrils flared. "I need cattle, and this is a good deal."

"You *need* to get rid of this fool notion that a single woman can run her own ranch in a territory overrun by outlaws." He yanked the hat from his head and thrust it to the west. "Hofmann's sister-in-law has been helping her husband run his ranch for over twenty years, but even she has the good sense to get out now that her husband can't protect her. Follow her example and sell this place. Start over somewhere new. Maybe give San Francisco a try. Your sister will be there. Who knows? You might even like the city. Some people do."

Virginia stepped forward until she was within inches of him. "You may have given up on your dreams, but I refuse to give up on mine."

Gideon looked away from the accusation of cowardice in her gaze. She couldn't understand, and she was too stubborn to listen. He pressed his lips against more pointless argument.

Virginia pivoted and began pacing in front of the fire.

Lucy rubbed her hands with her apron, her brows knit. "Didn't Mr. Hofmann already say the men with him had jobs lined up and couldn't help drive the cattle?"

Biddie nodded. "He did. If Gideon is staying here, maybe we can convince Clyve to help us with the herd."

Virginia crossed her arms. "We're better off not relying on any man. We'll just have to make do ourselves."

"But Lucy and I don't know anything about driving cattle."

Gideon shook his head. "Rowland's got his own ranch to run. How long do you plan on being gone?"

"I'll want at least a day to inspect the herd and ready them for driving." Virginia squinted at the sky. "With the time it will take to get there and back, I expect we'll be gone about four days.

Gideon jerked up the brim of his hat. "He's not going to want to leave his ranch for that long."

"It can't hurt to ask. We have to ride past his place, anyway. Don't we?"

Had they even considered how it would look for three young women to travel alone with an unmarried man of marriageable age? He swallowed the protest, too aware of it's hypocrisy. Still he didn't like the notion. Not one bit.

∼

OCTOBER 30TH, 1873
EASTERN SAN DIEGO COUNTY, CALIFORNIA

*B*iddie led her horse in the zig-zag pattern Ginny had taught her. The cows in front of her continued their lumbering pace across the chaparral and into the desert. Thankfully, the bandanna she wore over most of her face prevented most of the dust from entering her nose and mouth.

"That's it, Miss Davidson." Clyve called encouragement from his position to the left of the herd. "Just keep moving behind them like that, nice and slow." Not only had he been more than willing to help them, his father, Matthew, had insisted on lending a hand. Plus, they'd brought two of their vaqueros and three trained dogs along to help with the drive.

Ginny had been more trouble to convince. She'd only agreed to having the Rowlands along after Clyve suggested he claim a small percentage of the cattle for himself as payment. Later, as they rode toward Hofmann's place, she'd told Biddie, "Always know what a man wants when he offers help. It's always something. Better to know the cost up front."

Biddie had asked Ginny what she thought Gideon wanted for helping at the ranch.

Ginny didn't hesitate. "Some place to hide. That man is running from something, sure as the sun rises in the east."

Her sister's insight had shocked Biddie, considering how little she'd conversed with Gideon beyond what was needed to get the work done. Gideon was running from something—his past. Biddie had come to the conclusion he'd done something he regretted and didn't know how to forgive himself for it.

His adamant refusal to help them with this dangerous drive, when he'd done everything in his power to protect them until now, had her wondering whether whatever had happened was in some way connected to working with cattle. He'd mentioned his father had been killed by a bull. She didn't see how Gideon could feel guilty about an accident, but if he did, that would certainly explain his reluctance to pursue owning his own ranch again.

"Hold up, Miss Arlidge." Clyve's call interrupted Biddie's thoughts. "Let the dogs do their job."

Lucy, who'd been about to follow a wandering cow, reined to a stop at the sound of her name.

One of Clyve's dogs hurried after the creature and directed it back to the slowly moving herd.

Lucy smiled at Clyve. "That's very impressive. Does it take long to train them?"

Clyve moved his horse closer to Lucy's, and the two spoke in voices too quiet for Biddie to hear from the back of the herd. To her right, Ginny guided her horse forward to prompt a stalled cow into moving again. Then she pulled back to rejoin Biddie. "How are you liking your first cattle drive?"

"It's not as chaotic as I'd imagined." She nodded to where Matthew and one of the vaqueros kept the herd from turning down the canyon opening they were passing. "I'm glad we have help. I can't imagine trying to do this without the Rowlands and their men. Even their dogs are a blessing."

"Preston had a dog. His name was Scruff."

"Did he take the dog with him?"

"Oliver killed him."

Biddie gasped. She wanted to ask how Pa could do such a thing, but she'd witnessed the fury of his temper.

"That's why Preston left. Well, part of the reason." Ginny prodded another cow forward. "Preston loved that dog. He'd raised him from a pup and taught him a bunch of silly tricks like roll over and play dead. Problem was, Scruff loved Preston too. He was always getting in the way when Oliver took after Preston."

Biddie watched the Rowlands' dog corral another cow as Ginny continued.

"One night, Oliver started waving his pistol around, threatening to kill me. Preston shoved him out of the shack we were living in, and they wrestled over the gun. Scruff joined the fight and took a chunk out of Oliver's arm. Preston got the gun, but not before Oliver got a shot off. The poor dog fell down dead. Preston aimed that gun at Oliver and would've pulled the trigger if I hadn't gotten in the way. I couldn't stand for Preston to hang because of Oliver. But while I got Preston to see reason, Oliver started shouting that he'd kill him. So I told Preston to run and never come back."

"He left you alone with Pa?"

"He wanted me to come with him, but I refused."

"Why?"

"I knew if we both left, Oliver would come after us." Ginny's eyes narrowed. "What're those two talking about?"

Biddie followed Ginny's look to where Clyve was leaning almost out of his saddle to say something to Lucy. Her friend glanced back, and the look had Biddie nudging her horse around the herd toward her friend. "I'll be back in a minute."

Ginny raised her voice. "Hey, Clyve, you falling asleep in the saddle?"

He twisted to look at Ginny with a raised brow. "'Course not."

"Then what are you doing letting those two go off?"

Clyve finally seemed to notice the cows sneaking into the brush on his left. He said something to Lucy, then turned his horse to retrieve the strays.

Biddie reined in to ride beside Lucy. "Everything all right? Should I regret asking Clyve to help us?"

Lucy's cheeks were flushed. "No, it's nothing that terrible. I just...well, I'm not sure how to handle a man like Clyve. He's different than the men who pursued me back in San Francisco."

Biddie's heart sank at the idea her friend might marry Clyve and not return with her to San Francisco. She'd always imagined the two of them would go through life together, marriage or no. But she tried not to let any trepidation show in her expression. "What makes you think he's pursuing you?"

Lucy chuckled. "He asked to court me."

Biddie couldn't stop her mouth from dropping open. "So soon?"

Lucy shrugged. "He knows we don't plan to stay long and said he didn't want to miss his opportunity."

"But he asked Ginny to marry him barely three months ago."

Lucy looked away and ran her fingers through her mount's

mane. "That was different. He only made that offer because his pa convinced him it made good sense. It was a business proposition."

"But he claims to have real feelings for you? After only three encounters?"

Lucy huffed. "Is it so hard to believe a successful man could have feelings for me?"

"Of course not. I'm only concerned by the speed. You barely know him."

"I didn't claim to be in love with him."

"But you like him."

Lucy lifted one shoulder. "Maybe. As you said, I barely know him."

"Yet you're considering allowing him to court you."

"It's not a proposal of marriage. And how else am I to get to know the man?"

Biddie sighed. "I wish Father were here. He'd know how to advise you."

"Oh, I forgot to ask. Were there any new letters waiting when you went to town?"

"Several, though still nothing from Preston. Father's written every week of his progress. He holds out hope that the doctor will let him travel sooner than the four-month prediction. He says he's grateful for the letters I've sent when I've gone to town but that the wait for each delivery is too long and leaves him in agony of worry."

Lucy gave her a knowing look. "He's still asking you to return?"

Biddie nodded. "If I thought he truly needed me, you know I'd go. But"—she twisted to look back at Ginny, now riding the tail of the herd alongside one of the Rowlands' vaqueros—"How can I leave Ginny? You know she'll kick Gideon out if we leave, and then she'd be all alone." She turned back to Lucy. "I'd never be able to sleep at night."

Lucy nodded, her expression sympathetic. "But you can't stay here forever, and your sister swears she'll never marry, nor hire any hands."

"I know." They'd reached a rise in the land, and Biddie stared out over the wide desert floor. *Preston, where are you?*

CHAPTER 24

$\mathcal{G}$ ideon ignored the rising pain pressing against the inside of his skull. He'd told the women he'd have the barn finished by the time they returned with the cattle, and he'd do it if it killed him. He couldn't bear the look of disappointment in Biddie's eyes again. He'd expected her to be angry over his refusal to join the cattle drive, to push and plead until he gave in. Not that he would have. Instead, she'd gone silent and stared at him with those big blue eyes that seemed to see into his soul.

He lifted another rock onto the final wall of the barn. He would *not* let her down again. At least, not in regard to this barn. What did it matter if he worked until the pain blinded him? The only toes around to be smashed were his own. He could live with a few broken toes. So on he worked.

By the time the sun set, he'd capped the last row of stones with a final bed of mortar. He stepped back to admire his work. Unfortunately, the world tilted, and he lost his stomach instead. No matter. The walls were finished. All that was left was the roof. He could add that tomorrow. In fact, if he worked quickly enough, he might even have time to add walls for the three stalls the women wanted inside.

Having the lumber close at hand would make the work go faster in the morning. So he wiped the spittle from his mouth and shuffled, half-blind, to the stack of beams he'd already notched for the rafters. He grabbed the end of one and dragged it toward the house. Then he moved another. And another. On the third trip, the ground beneath him gave way and he toppled to the ground, the rafter beam landing with a soft thud.

Maybe he'd better go to bed and finish moving the wood in the morning. Yes. That was a good plan. Now, he just needed the energy to move himself.

He lifted his cheek off the ground. Immediately, his stomach surged. He rolled onto his side to avoid soiling his clothes. It took several minutes for the heaving to stop.

When it did, it took still more time for him to find the energy to budge. Finally, he found it and planted his hands on the ground beneath his chest. With a mighty heave, he made it onto his knees. And that would have to do.

Like a sad dog, he crawled to the rock house, too done in to reach his own bedroll in the cave. Once inside, hoisting himself onto one of the women's bed frames required more than he had left. So, graceful as a sagging sack of flour, he sank to the ground once more and let the blackness take him.

~

*S*moke.

Gideon's nose twitched and his eyes flew open. Smoke filled the little rock house. He blinked against the stinging, searching the haze for a fire. Not one flame met his sight. Then he noticed something odd. Rather than drifting out the open door, the gray billows seemed to be drifting *in*. As was an eerie, flickering light.

Gideon surged to his feet and ran outside.

A great pyre of flames engulfed the side of the new barn, lighting up the yard beneath a moonless sky. That couldn't be right. The barn was built of stone. The whole reason Virginia had insisted on using the heavy material was to avoid such fires. He rubbed his eyes. The flames were still there, lapping up toward the open roof.

The roof. His gaze shot to the bottom of the flames. The rafters. Like a terrible nightmare, Gideon remembered pulling the expensive beams closer to the barn. He followed the trail of fire and ash to the firepit. He'd dragged the last beam through the hot coals left over from his supper. Then dropped it there when pain overtook him.

He covered his face. What a fool he was. When would he learn, he was no longer a real man. He couldn't do real men's work. Every time he tried, it ended in disaster. At least this time, no one had gotten hurt.

Patty's distressed mooing brought his hands down. The cow was tied to a stake not far from the burning barn. He needed to move her away from the harsh smoke. But first, he needed to put out the flames creeping onto the dry weeds near the barn. It was bad enough the barn rafters would need to be replaced. If the fire spread, it could reach the house.

Gideon threw last night's wash water onto the flames. It sizzled and vanished in a cloud of steam, barely slowing the flames. He ducked inside to grab a bucket, then sprinted for the spring as though the flames of hell were at his heels.

CHAPTER 25

*A*fter three nights spent on a thin bedroll in a tiny tent shared with Ginny and Lucy, Biddie couldn't wait to sleep in a real bed again. In San Francisco, she slept on a down-filled mattress supported by the ornately carved bedframe her cousin had built for her—a pleasure she'd taken for granted before coming to see her sister. The two simple wood frames and thinly stuffed tick mattresses they'd bought for Ginny's new home weren't nearly as comfortable, but compared to the ground, they seemed like luxury itself.

She squinted at the line of cattle ahead of her. They'd almost reached the top of the mountain. She resisted the urge to ride ahead and into the valley. Had Gideon heard the steady rumble of the cattle approaching? Did he know they were nearly back to the ranch? She prayed he hadn't suffered another one of his migraines while they were gone.

"Smoke!" One of Clyve's vaqueros shouted from the front of the line. "I smell smoke. There's been a fire."

Ginny shot forward on her mount, racing toward the ridge.

The cattle's mooing increased along with their speed.

Biddie held her horse back from following Ginny's and

made soothing noises the way the vaqueros had taught her to calm the cows.

Clyve left Lucy and joined Biddie at the rear. "That's it. You're doing great. Just stay steady. I'm going to ride up and make sure none of them try to break for it." His tone was as calm as her mother's at an afternoon tea, but his expression said he'd like to throttle her sister for taking off like that.

She was careful to keep her own voice equally calm. "What do you think happened? Is it bad? Could they see Gideon?" What if he'd been hurt while they were away?

Please, Lord, let him be safe.

"Not sure. I couldn't see anything from my position. Right now, I've got to make sure we keep these animals calm." He urged his mount to one side of the lumbering column and kept to a pace only a hair faster than what the cattle were doing. All the time, he kept up a chatter of soothing nonsense aimed at the cattle.

After several long seconds, she could tell it was working. The cattle were calming.

If only she knew whether Gideon was well. Then perhaps her own heart would return to its normal rhythm. As it was, it took every ounce of her self-control not to beg Clyve to take her place so she could ride ahead and discover the truth for herself. Instead, she kept her horse in its zig-zag pattern, steadily urging the herd along.

Eventually, Clyve rode ahead and positioned his horse at the top of the valley, watching the cattle file past and begin their descent. He turned in the saddle and caught her eye. He nodded. Did that mean Gideon was well?

Couldn't these stupid cows move any faster?

Though it seemed an eternity, reaching the top took less than twenty minutes. The sight that met her eyes stole her breath. Scorch marks disfigured the western wall of the barn. Charred weeds and remnants of ash stretched out on either side like death's fingers. One blackened trail led straight toward the house but seemed to stop before reaching Ginny's new home. The structure appeared free of damage.

More importantly, Gideon stood in front of the house. The pressure on her chest eased. His head was bent but he appeared unharmed. Still, she longed to draw closer and check for any wounds. By the time they'd settled the cattle in the valley and filled the troughs with water, Gideon was busy preparing a meal for them all.

As she approached the cook fire in front of the house, it was on the tip of her tongue to ask what had happened, but he avoided her gaze. She surveyed the others who were relaxing nearby as they waited for their meal and pressed her lips together. Asking now would embarrass him.

Gideon ladled stew into bowls. Despite the heat, he wore long sleeves and a pair of gloves. At least his face and neck appeared unharmed. She caught her bottom lip with her teeth. He didn't usually wear his leather gloves while preparing their meals. Was he hiding injuries?

No one spoke to him aside from an expression of thanks when he handed them their food. No one need ask him what had happened, as Ginny had been ranting off and on since their arrival. It seemed Gideon had suffered one of his migraines which somehow had led to the barn rafters catching fire.

Ginny caught Biddie's eye. "I told you we should have used willow poles instead of buying that expensive lumber. Now look at it. Nothing but ashes."

Biddie cringed inwardly. There was no way they could purchase new lumber. She understood her sister's frustration at owing money for something she couldn't use. But Ginny said nothing of the heroic effort it must have taken Gideon to put out the flames, and judging by the amount of blackened earth, it had been an overwhelming task for one man alone. Yet the house stood unmarred by the flames that had consumed the barn.

"We're going to have to tear down that wall." Ginny glared at the scorched west side of the barn. "The mortar hadn't fully set, and now it's dry and cracking. It'll take days to repair and even longer to gather the willow poles we'll need to replace the rafters."

"It could have been much worse." Biddie pointed to the unharmed house. "He saved your home."

"It wouldn't have needed saving if he hadn't started the fire in the first place."

Biddie opened her mouth to defend Gideon further, but he finally spoke.

"Virginia's right. I started the fire. Putting it out is nothing to be proud of."

"It *is* something to be proud of. You risked your life to save everything we've worked so hard to build."

"It doesn't matter—"

"It does matter." Biddie stepped over and seized his wrist. He winced and a hiss escaped his lips as she yanked the gloves free.

Murmurs of surprise and pity came from the group at the sight of the ugly blisters and red swollen skin covering his hands.

She moved her grip to his elbow, watching carefully for any sign that he was wounded there as well. He didn't flinch at her touch. Hopefully, that meant his injuries didn't extend much beyond his wrists. She glared at Ginny. "Did you even stop to consider what it cost him to save your home?"

Every bit of anger fell from her sister's face. Ginny set her food aside and came closer to stare at Gideon's hands. "These should have a liniment and bandages." Her glare returned as she looked up at Gideon. "Why haven't you taken care of yourself?"

Gideon shrugged.

Ginny went into the house and returned with the needed supplies. She pointed to a nearby rock. "Sit."

Gideon sat with his back to the rest of the group.

Ginny's ministrations were surprisingly gentle as she bathed, oiled, and wrapped his hands. Though Biddie could tell it still pained him, Gideon held himself rigid, neither wincing, nor releasing any sounds of discomfort.

Ginny stood as she collected her supplies. "You need to change the dressing every day and keep those wounds away from heat until they've fully healed."

Gideon scowled as he stood. "I'll do my best."

Ginny crossed her arms. "That means no cooking."

He spoke through clenched teeth. "That's my job."

"Not anymore." Biddie stepped closer, keeping her voice low. It couldn't be easy for him with all these witnesses. "I can handle the cooking until you're well."

He shook his head. "I'm not working the cattle. I can't—"

Ginny heaved a sigh. "No one's asking you to work the cattle. Nor can you rebuild the barn with your hands in that condition."

He raised his bandaged fingers. "Then I'm completely useless."

"If you take care of yourself, you'll be fine in a week or two except for maybe some scars. If you don't, you'll catch an infection. Then one of us will have to stop work and tend you to keep your sorry hide alive."

~

*G*ideon sat on a rock watching the women work with Clyve and his men across the valley. It had been bad enough not being able to help the women repair the barn walls this past week. Now, Silas Gaskill had completed the new branding iron Virginia ordered. Clyve had arrived this morning with the new brand and four men to help with the rebranding. And Gideon's hands still weren't healed enough to help.

Not that he wanted to. His goal of staying as far away from cattle as possible was unchanged. If anything, the fire had reinforced it. But it grated that he didn't have a choice. He couldn't even cook a meal for the women to enjoy after their long hours of hard work. Biddie had to do that. And she'd done such a fine job of it, he'd begun wondering why he was still here.

He ought to just pack his things, saddle Legend, and hit the trail. The women were decent shots now, and it was clear Clyve was smitten with Lucy. He'd be keeping an eye out for the women of this ranch. Gideon simply wasn't needed anymore.

He ought to move on before he caused another accident.

Biddie turned at that moment and caught him watching. She grinned and waved at him, then started in his direction. Great. She was coming to check on him again, the same way she did Pepper's kittens. Well, that wasn't quite true. She didn't pet his head and tell him how adorable he was. Lucky cats.

She came to a stop in front of him. "How are you feeling?"

It was the same thing she asked every time she came to talk to him. He gave the same answer. "I'm fine. How are you?"

As usual, she ignored him and reached for his hands. "Let me see your bandages."

Feeling like a child, he hid them behind his back. "I said, 'I'm fine.' Nothing's changed since you swapped the bandages this morning."

After that first time, Biddie had taken over the job of tending his wounds. Enduring the feel of her touch and the intimate closeness necessitated by her nursing had been torture, knowing now more than ever that he could never have her. Biddie was talented, brave, and stronger than he'd initially given her credit for, in addition to being beautiful. She deserved a husband who was whole and capable of giving her everything she dreamed of. Thankfully, the constant pain of his injuries served as a reminder to control his emotions. That, and her ever-watchful big sister.

She planted her hands on her hips. "Fine. I've got to get supper started." She marched toward the firepit and stirred the embers before adding more tinder and kindling. In less than a minute, she had the fire burning again and retrieved the bucket they used to collect spring water for cooking.

One of Clyve's vaqueros ran toward her. "I can fetch the water for you, Señorita."

Gideon leapt to his feet. "I'll do it." If he hadn't been so busy feeling sorry for himself, he'd have offered sooner.

Biddie looked at him aghast. "No, Gideon, you'll hurt your hands."

"They're almost healed and don't even hurt anymore." He flexed his bandaged fingers to reinforce the lie. If she had any idea how much the movement cost him, she'd turn him down flat. "Let me do it. It's my job." He stepped forward, reaching for the bucket.

She clutched it to her chest. "No." The look in her eyes told him his actions hadn't fooled her. Somehow she knew he was still in pain. She turned to the vaquero. "Thank you for your kind offer, but I can carry it myself."

The young Californio glared at Gideon before returning to help with the cattle.

Gideon watched Biddie disappear into the bushes around the spring, feeling the loss as acutely as a goodbye. As soon as his hands were healed well enough to hold the reins and shoot his pistol, it would be.

CHAPTER 26

*B*iddie dropped another fistful of dried grasses onto their row of cabbage. Two rows over, Gideon dumped an armful of dried grass onto their row of lettuce. On her other side, Ginny set traps for the rabbit that had gotten into the garden early that morning and eaten most of their carrot crop.

Lucy arrived with another wheelbarrow filled with more grass. Biddie crossed to the wheelbarrow and was scooping another armful when Clyve rode into the valley. After the branding, he'd asked permission to come back in two days and visit with Lucy.

Lucy glanced between the unfinished rows and Clyve. "I was hoping he wouldn't arrive until we'd finished with the garden."

"Don't worry about it." Biddie made a shooing motion. "Just go inside and freshen up. The rest of us can finish the garden."

Lucy hesitated another moment, then thanked Biddie and disappeared into the house.

Gideon helped Biddie carry grass and spread it over the rest of their leafy greens. A few minutes later, Clyve settled his horse in the corral and Lucy emerged from the house. She offered Clyve a shy smile, and the pair wandered toward the south end of the valley.

Gideon nodded at their backs. "Maybe I still don't know her that well, but she didn't seem that excited to see Clyve. I always imagined a woman would be excited when her beau came calling."

Biddie had no response. She shared Gideon's concern, but Lucy would not appreciate Biddie saying so to Gideon. Besides, her friend had had a number of admirers, but she'd never given any of the men in San Francisco a lick of encouragement. Yet Lucy had accepted Clyve's offer of courtship. That had to mean something, didn't it?

~

NOVEMBER 15, 1873
CAMPO, CALIFORNIA

*B*iddie stood outside the Gaskills' store, her fingers shaking as she held the letter. What was she to do?

Lucy noticed her distress. "What's wrong? Is it about The Home?"

"What?" Biddie's brow furrowed in confusion. Why would Lucy think something was wrong with the Davidson Home for Women and Children? "No, Mother says Mr. Green came to see her last week, asking about my return. It seems he was able to secure the funds he promised and has purchased the bakery. He plans to begin renovations next week."

Gideon untied Legend from the hitching post. "Isn't that good news?"

She looked at him. Did he want her to leave? Of course he did. He'd been trying to convince her to return to San Francisco since she'd arrived. Although why it still mattered to him, she couldn't understand. The day his hands were fully healed, he'd announced his plans to leave as soon as the barn was complete.

Tomorrow, they would cut and collect the last of the willow branches they needed for the barn's roof. In two days' time, the structure would be complete and Gideon would be gone.

She swallowed her disappointment and turned to Lucy. "Preston still hasn't arrived or sent word. How can I leave knowing Ginny will be alone again?"

Gideon stepped closer. "The ranch is your sister's dream, and I admire your loyalty to her, but what about your own dreams? Do they not matter?"

"'Greater love hath no man than this, that a man lay down his life for his friends.' Right, Lucy?"

Her friend toed the dirt. "Are you sure that verse applies here? What about the talents God has gifted you? If God called you to open a bakery, would He really expect you to ignore that calling for the sake of your stubborn sister?"

Biddie opened her mouth and closed it again. Of course she'd prayed about the bakery. In many ways, it seemed as if she'd been praying about it her entire life. But had God truly *called* her to open the bakery? She wasn't sure. Yet if she didn't go through with opening the bakery, how would she ever repay Mother and Father for all they'd done for her?

❧

The next morning, Biddie awoke with dread. Today was her last chance to convince Gideon not to give up on his dreams. How was she to do that while pondering sacrificing her own? For several minutes, she lay in bed listening to Lucy's soft snores beside her. Then she admitted refusing to start the day wouldn't keep Gideon from leaving, and she wouldn't find the answers she sought staring at the ceiling.

As she dressed, she considered her sister's sleeping form. Ginny had come a long way since Biddie's arrival. She hadn't even feigned a protest when Gideon offered to stand guard last night. Was there any hope she'd reconsider hiring more men to help on the ranch? If Biddie did return to San Francisco, she'd sleep better at night knowing her sister wasn't alone.

Not wanting to wake Ginny or Lucy, Biddie picked up her shoes and tiptoed outside. She pulled the door closed with an almost-silent click and turned, expecting to see Gideon preparing breakfast. Instead, he sat atop Legend on a nearby slope, one finger pointing and wagging in the direction of the cattle, as if he were counting.

She hurried to join him. "Is everything all right?"

"Shh." He continued counting, his lips moving silently. Then he ran his hand down his face. "There are five missing."

"What do you mean, 'missing'?"

"I mean, I caught a coyote trying to sneak into the herd and scared it off. The ruckus caused some of the cattle to scatter. I thought I caught them all before any made it out of the valley, but now there are five missing."

"There can't be." Biddie counted the cattle herself and found he was correct. Her shoulders slumped. "We'd better get Ginny."

She turned to fetch her sister, but Gideon jumped down and caught her shoulder. "Wait. Let me ride to the top of the valley, see if I can spot them. I don't want to worry her if we don't need to."

She nibbled her lip. "I don't know..."

His brown eyes pleaded with her. "Just give me five minutes. Ten at the most. If I haven't brought them back by then, we'll tell her."

"Fine." She marched in the direction of the horse corral. "But I'm coming with you."

"No."

She pivoted toward the house. "Then I'll get Ginny and she can go with you."

He stepped around her. "After all your talk about me buying my own ranch, you don't trust me to round up a few cattle?"

She pressed her palm against his clenched jaw. "Of course, I do. But you've said many times, cattle are dangerous. Not to mention all the dangers this wilderness holds. It's just good sense not to go wandering off on your own."

His eyes searched hers, and when he spoke, his voice was soft. "You really mean that, don't you? You still trust me, even after the fire."

"That wasn't your fault."

He opened his mouth, clearly ready to argue, but a mooing cow drew his attention. "Come on. It's getting late." He took her hand from his face and led her toward the horse corral. "Your sister will be waking up any minute. If we want to have those cattle back before she notices they're missing, we'd better get going."

inding the missing cattle was harder than Gideon had expected. Frightened cattle should leave plenty of track to follow. But if there was a trail of hoof marks leading out of the valley, Gideon couldn't find it after ten minutes of searching. He'd head out and see if the critters could be seen from the ridge.

Biddie followed him.

Having her along made as much sense as taking Mother's fine china on a cattle drive. He should have let her get Ginny. Except the selfish part of him wanted to keep her close for what little time he had left. And his pride couldn't admit he'd botched his duties again.

He couldn't even blame the pain for the missing cattle. His head had been clear as a summer sky since the night of the fire. Even so, he'd failed.

He led Legend along the valley's rim, scanning the slopes below. He needed to find these missing cattle and leave.

"Look." Biddie pointed to a broken shrub branch. On the ground beside it ran a trail of hoof marks.

Gideon turned Legend in that direction. "Let's go." He

searched the hillside below but saw no sign of the cattle. How had they traveled so far, so quickly?

The prints led to the foot of the mountain where they disappeared at the edge of a wide, flat stretch of rock. They picked up again heading north. Many times, Gideon lost the trail and wasted precious seconds searching to find it again.

Gideon reined to a stop. Something was wrong. He and Biddie had traveled more than seven miles from the base of the mountain.

Biddie came up beside him. "Did we lose it again?"

"No, but it's impossible the cattle could have traveled so far in such a short time."

Biddie looked down at the clear hoof prints driven into the sand of the wash they were crossing, then looked back at him. "Are you saying these tracks are from before the attack on the ranch? Before we arrived? It doesn't seem possible they'd still be here all these months later."

"It's not."

"Then how—"

"I don't know. But something isn't right." He pointed to the clear outline of a horseshoe in the hard-packed sand. "I thought I'd seen horse prints farther back but dismissed it as a trick of my imagination and not being familiar with this area. But there's no doubt now."

"Are you saying someone stole our cattle?"

"It looks that way, but what I can't understand is how. I couldn't have missed rustlers coming into the valley and herding off five head in the middle of the night."

"Unless you fell asleep."

"I didn't. I was awake all night."

"So...?"

"I didn't do a head count until the coyote showed up. It's possible the cattle were missing before I finished the evening meal and took over watch."

"Are you suggesting my sister missed seeing a group of rustlers stealing her cattle in broad daylight?"

"Of course not, but she was alone all day. Maybe she left to use the outhouse or tend to some other matter. I don't know, but—"

"The soap."

"What soap?"

"I told Ginny I was planning to buy more soap at the store. She said it was a waste of money, that she's always made her own soap from the roots of a yucca plant. She claimed an Indian woman taught her how and that she could make more soap in less time than it would take us to get back from town." Biddie laughed and shook her head. "Sure enough, she'd made enough soap to last all three of us a month." Biddie's wide eyes turned to him. "She might have left the valley to collect the roots she needed."

Gideon scratched the back of his neck as a throb kicked to life in his head. "I had an odd feeling we were being watched as we left for town, but I looked around and didn't see anybody. So I ignored it. Now, though, it makes sense." He studied the bumps and dips of the desert mountainside on his right. Then he searched the shadows cast by scattered shrubs and dry gullies stretching across the desert floor. There was no sign that anyone was watching them now. "If someone *had* been watching, they might have known Virginia was alone at the ranch. They could have waited until she left to make their move." The throb grew to a generalized ache.

Beside him, Biddie shuddered. "Do you really think someone was watching us?"

"It's the only thing that makes sense. It was always a risk leaving her alone. I'm just glad these thieves seem to have no interest in confrontation." He wheeled his horse around. "We should head back. If I'm right and we're dealing with rustlers, it'd be foolish to confront them on our own." Especially if his pain grew worse.

Biddie turned her mount to head south, and he nudged Legend into a canter. Gideon wanted to punch himself for letting his pride overrule his better judgment and exposing Biddie to danger. If this pain messed with his vision, he wouldn't be able to shoot with any accuracy. He'd be next to useless if the rustlers attacked them. Biddie would be on her own. He leaned low, urging Legend into a gallop.

~

*B*iddie started to spur her mount after Gideon but froze when the sound of cattle lowing reached her ears. She opened her mouth to call after Gideon. But what if the rustlers were still around?

She stared hard at Gideon's shoulders. *Look back.*

He didn't look back.

She turned toward the crevasse the sound had come from. One cow emerged to stand at the end of what appeared to be a narrow gorge.

She checked her surroundings again. Surely, rustlers wouldn't let a cow roam free. Could Gideon have been wrong?

She guided her horse toward the cow, murmuring softly to keep the creature calm. As she drew closer, she could see farther into the gap between wrinkles in the mountainside. There were more cows behind the first. The space was so narrow, they were all bunched together and she couldn't get a clear count. She checked once more for any sign of people. Assured she was alone with the cows, she urged her mount into the middle of the group. She began to count, but thundering hooves distracted her.

"Biddie, where are you?" Gideon's shout and rapid approach agitated the cows.

She didn't dare call back for fear of upsetting them further. Instead, she began to work her way out of their midst and toward the opening of the gorge. One of the cows proved stubborn and wouldn't let her pass.

Before she could escape the herd, Gideon shouted again. This time, his voice came from above. He must have ridden up the mountainside for a better view. Small rocks tumbled down the backside of the gorge.

The cow in front of her bolted for the opening. The others stampeded in her wake. They jostled past Biddie.

Her horse reared.

Biddie lost her balance. She nearly fell from the saddle, but her wrist tangled in the reins. The last cow brushed past her, leaving her alone in the gorge.

"Biddie!"

Hanging half sideways from her saddle, Biddie looked up.

More rocks skittered down the mountainside as Gideon half ran, half slid down the steep slope. "Hang on. I'm coming."

She finally got one boot into a stirrup and heaved herself back into the saddle, relieving the pressure on her wrist.

Gideon reached for her waist.

"No, wait." She gingerly unwrapped the leather strap from where it was twisted around her right wrist. Then she nodded.

Gideon lifted her from the saddle and set her on the ground. He wrapped his arms around her, crushing her against his chest.

Pain burned from her wrist up into her shoulder, forcing a cry from her lips.

Immediately, he released her and stepped back. "Where does it hurt?"

"My arm." She gingerly ran the fingers of her left hand from her right wrist to her shoulder. "My wrist got caught in the reins." She tugged her sleeve toward her elbow, revealing the nasty red burn marks left by the leather.

Gideon pivoted and kicked a large clump of dirt hard enough to break it and send pieces flying more than a dozen feet away. He turned back to face her, a mix of anger and regret pouring from his eyes. "We've got to get you back. Do you think you can still ride?"

"Yes, but what about the cattle?"

"Forget the cattle. I never should have brought you out here. It was a fool thing to do. I could have gotten you killed." His hand circled her waist, and he lifted her into the saddle. He started back up the slope to where Legend waited.

She reached for the reins, but the movement made her flinch. She pressed her aching wrist against her stomach and grasped the reins in her left hand. "Gideon, wait. This wasn't your fault. I should have told you when I saw that cow instead of coming after it alone."

He continued stomping up the mountain. "*I* should have realized you weren't behind me sooner. I was so worried my headache would get worse, I wasn't paying attention to anything else. This is exactly why I'm leaving tomorrow."

Something broke inside her. "But I don't want you to leave. I want you to stay with us, with me." It was true. In that moment, she knew she loved him. She still didn't know how their lives could ever work together, but there had to be a way. Because the thought of spending her life without him felt too empty.

He froze with one boot in the stirrup and a hand on his saddle horn. His head and shoulders drooped, his back still facing her. "You don't want me. You need a real man, not one so broken he can't keep you safe."

CHAPTER 28

*G*ideon was careful not to get too far ahead of Biddie
but set a pace back to the ranch that kept her from
airing the argument he'd glimpsed in her expression
as he mounted up.

Virginia spotted them long before they reached the valley
and rode to meet them. If looks could kill, he'd have been
tarred, feathered, lit on fire, dragged behind a horse, strung up
on a tree, and shot for good measure. "Where in tarnation have
you been?" She drew her pistol and aimed it at his chest. "Give
me one good reason I shouldn't shoot you."

"I can't." She should shoot him for the danger he'd put
Biddie in.

"Ginny, put your gun away. Nothing happened. I'm fine."
Biddie reined to a stop on his left.

"If you're fine, why are you babying your right hand?"

"There was an accident, and my wrist's a bit sore, that's all."
Biddie's tone was firm. "It's nothing to worry about, and it isn't
his fault."

Gideon's jaw tightened. "Yes, it is."

Virginia narrowed her eyes at him. "What kind of accident?"

Biddie spoke at the same time he did.

"It doesn't matter."

"A stampede."

Virginia's gun lowered as her gaze shot to Biddie. "And only your wrist is hurt? You're sure you're not hurt anywhere else?"

"I'm sure."

Virginia looked back to Gideon. "What do you mean, 'a stampede'?"

Biddie answered for him. "We were searching for the cows that went missing. We thought we could find them and bring them back before you noticed and started worrying, but they'd gone much farther than we expected. So we started to think maybe rustlers had them, but then I found them. I was trying to count and make sure they were all there when they startled and took off. But again, I'm fine."

Virginia's voice grew deadly quiet, her gaze still locked on Gideon's. "Let me be sure I understand this right. Some of my cattle went missing and instead of waking me, you took my baby sister to hunt rustlers and got her caught in a stampede."

Gideon nodded. It was close enough.

"No." Biddie thrust her arms in the air. "It wasn't his fault. I—"

Virginia leveled her gun on him again. "Pack your things and get off my land."

"No!" Biddie shouted, but he and Virginia both ignored her.

"Let me help round up your missing cattle. Then I'll go."

"I can round them up myself."

He adjusted his hat. "Of course you can. But it'll take you longer, and Biddie and Lucy will be alone at the ranch the whole time you're gone. Plus, if I'm right about rustlers stealing those cattle in the first place, you might run into more trouble than you can handle on your own."

"And I'm supposed to trust you to watch my back?"

"No, you're supposed to stay at the ranch to keep watch over Biddie and Lucy. I'll go after the cattle alone, like I should have in the first place."

～

*T*he next afternoon, Biddie paced in front of the house as Ginny cleaned her pistol. Before coming to the ranch, Biddie'd had no idea the weapons could be disassembled. Nor had she known guns required regular cleaning. She nodded toward the rifle leaning against the rock beside Ginny. "Are you going to clean that next?"

Ginny shook her head. "I cleaned it while you were gone to town."

Biddie searched the valley's rim again. "Still no sign of Gideon. He's been gone for hours. What if there's been trouble?"

Ginny ran her cloth along the barrel of her pistol. "You heard him. It was his choice to go alone. Besides, I'm sure he's fine. You said yourself there weren't any rustlers in the gorge where you found the cattle. I haven't heard of any thieves who steal livestock just to abandon the critters."

"Maybe they heard us coming and ran off."

"If that were so, you'd have seen their dust trail." Ginny stuffed the cloth into her pocket. "And what's more, anyone that cowardly isn't likely to start shooting."

Biddy stopped and scowled at her sister. "Then why isn't he back?"

"There's no telling how far those cows ran." Ginny began calmly reassembling her pistol. "I don't expect he'll be back much before sundown. If then."

Biddie rubbed at the bandage encasing her sore wrist. "You don't think he'll stay out past dark, do you?"

Ginny shrugged. "Could do."

Biddie looked to where Lucy was hanging clothes on the line. Biddie had offered to help with the laundry, but Lucy insisted Biddie rest her sprained wrist. Ginny had agreed, leaving Biddie with little to do but pace and wait for Gideon's return.

She went inside to check on Pepper and her kittens. It was amazing how quickly the little fur balls had grown. They'd outgrown their crate and now scampered freely around the cellar and the house. She had to be careful what foods she left out. The tiny bundles of energy were constantly playing when they weren't eating or sleeping and hadn't yet learned the rules of the house.

She searched the room for the five tiny kittens. She spotted two near the top of the cellar stairs, another peeking from beneath Ginny's bed, and a fourth swinging its tiny paw at the hem of Biddie's shawl, which hung from a peg in the wall. The fifth kitten had the claws of all four paws sunk into the knitted fabric and was climbing quickly.

"Oh, you naughty boy." She rushed to pluck the daring adventurer from her garment before he ripped a hole or fell onto the hard dirt floor. She nuzzled her nose against the top of his head. "What am I going to do with you?"

She gathered all the kittens and moved them back to the cellar.

Poor Pepper's nap was interrupted by tiny hungry mouths, but at least eating kept the little stinkers busy while Biddie moved her shawl to her trunk and checked the house for anything else she should hide from the kittens. Eventually satisfied that she'd tucked away as much as she could, she returned outside.

She scanned the valley. Still no sign of Gideon. A pair of white drawers waving on the clothesline caught her eye. Perhaps there was one reason to be glad of his delay. Wait.

"Where's Lucy?" Her friend no longer stood among the clothes fluttering in the breeze.

Ginny looked up. "She was there a moment ago. Maybe she went to the spring for more water."

Biddie started in that direction. Perhaps Lucy would have some ideas for convincing Gideon not to leave and Ginny to let him stay.

But Lucy wasn't at the spring, nor was she at the house when Biddie returned.

Ginny waved toward the south end of the valley. "She wanders off that way sometimes. Told me she just likes to amble with her thoughts."

Odd. She couldn't recall Lucy ever enjoying walks back home, but then wandering alone in San Francisco wasn't advisable. Especially for a single young woman.

Biddie headed south until she heard a faint scratching noise coming from behind a large juniper bush. Only then did she remember her friend's excitement over discovering the hidden mine. Was it possible Lucy had been coming here despite Ginny's clear orders to stay out?

Biddie pressed the scratchy branches away and stepped toward the entrance of the tunnel. Sure enough, the scratching was coming from inside and the candle that had been stabbed into the rock wall was missing.

Flickering light illuminated Lucy kneeling at the back as she chipped at something with her chisel and hammer.

Biddie planted one hand on her hip. "Ginny will be furious if she catches you in here."

Lucy startled so hard, the hammer missed her chisel and smashed into her fingers. "Ow!" She popped the injured appendages into her mouth.

Biddie rushed forward. "I'm sorry. I didn't mean for you to get hurt." She knelt beside her friend. "Let me see. Is it bad?"

Lucy withdrew her fingers and wiped them across her skirt

before holding them up with a sheepish expression. "Just bruised."

Biddie relaxed. "What are you thinking, being in here? Ginny was very clear, she didn't want any of us coming into this mine."

"I know, but look." Lucy lifted a bucket and angled it to catch the candlelight.

The metal container was nearly half full, and most of the contents glittered with a tint of the cinnamon red she'd seen in the crystals Lucy had found before. "Are those all gems?"

"Yes, and this is what I've found with only a few hours of digging spread over the months we've been here. But look." She removed the candle from its holder and moved it slowly along the wall. Several places caught the light and shone with dull red. "There's so much. Can you imagine what this is worth?"

Biddie stared at the seemingly buried treasure. If these stones were worth anything close to rubies, they could pay for so many of the improvements desperately needed back home. She caught herself reaching toward the wall and jerked her hand away. "This isn't ours."

"Well, it isn't *mine*." Lucy tipped her head. "But you're a sort of investor in the ranch now. That gives you a say in what goes on here, doesn't it? If you persuaded Ginny to let me spend more time digging, I bet we'd uncover more than what she owes Mr. Davidson for the loan and maybe even—"

"What makes you think she'll listen to me? It's Father's investment saving her ranch, not mine." The memory of how angry Ginny had been when she'd found them in here the first time made Biddie grasp Lucy's shoulder. "We should go." She scooped up the candle.

"Yes, but he wouldn't have risked his money on this place if it weren't for you. You know how hard he's been working to get enough to pay for the new addition."

Biddie winced. Mother and Father had been discussing the

need for a new addition to The Home for over a year. The extra space would allow them to house six additional women and twelve more children. It would also give room for a desperately needed third classroom. Those plans had been further delayed when Father agreed to help Ginny.

Lucy continued arguing as Biddie propelled them out of the tunnel. "You've talked Ginny into plenty of things since we got here. Just look at Gideon. She wasn't—"

"Gideon's leaving." Biddie stopped at the end of the tunnel to replace the candle holder in the wall and blow out its flame.

"Tomorrow, I know, but that isn't the point."

"No, today. Or tonight." She clapped both hands over her face and shook her head. "I don't know. But I told him I loved him and he's leaving, anyway."

"You what?"

Biddie peeked through her fingers. "Told him I loved him."

"When? Why?" Lucy gaped at her. "I mean, I knew you cared for him, but love? And you *told* him?"

Biddie dropped her hands with a heavy sigh. "Well, not exactly. But I asked him to stay. With *me*. That's practically the same thing."

"What did he say?"

"That I needed a real man. As if he isn't one. As if I'm not a grown woman who knows what she wants."

Lucy peered at her. "And you're sure you want him? What about the bakery? Gideon doesn't strike me as a man who'd be happy living in the city."

"Well, it doesn't matter now, does it? He doesn't love me."

"You don't know that."

"Why else would he still be planning to leave?"

"It sounds to me like Gideon doesn't love himself. That's got nothing to do with whether or not he loves you."

Part of what Lucy said fit with what Biddie had come to

understand about Gideon. He couldn't see his own value. But did he love her? "I don't know. He's never declared himself—"

"Of course not. He doesn't think he's good enough for you."

Biddie shoved through the bush.

Lucy followed her. "Where are you going?"

"To find him and make him understand how wonderful he is."

Lucy grabbed her arm, drawing them both to a stop. "You can't do that."

"Why not?"

"Because something like that is between Gideon and God."

"Why can't I tell him all the things I love about him?"

"You can. But telling him why he matters isn't the same as making him believe it. Only God can change a heart."

Lucy was right. But Biddie had to at least try. She strode toward the house.

Please, Lord, help me find the right words to reach Gideon's heart.

CHAPTER 29

*G*ideon drove three cows into the valley shortly after sunset. He'd hoped to find all five and be on his way today, but the setting sun and his pounding head defeated him. As painful as it would be to spend any more time around Biddie after her request, he was trying to learn from his mistakes and not push his limits. He would get these animals secured in the corral and then duck into his tent. Hopefully, before Biddie spotted him. Once dawn came and it was possible to track the remaining two cows, he'd head out. There was no reason he need see again the look of hurt he'd put in those sky-blue eyes.

The silhouette of a woman sitting on the corral wall near the gate reminded him of a Bible verse. The verse said something about a man making his plans but God having different ideas. In spite of himself, his lips quirked with a small smile. Momma had often chuckled over God's sense of humor.

Biddie hopped down as Gideon approached. He braced himself for her pleas. Biddie could talk a camel into trying to swim the Gulf of Mexico. Not that it would take much to persuade him to stay if he weren't certain she'd be better off with someone else. The white bandage catching moonlight at her wrist was proof enough of that. No matter how the notion of her in another man's arms shredded his heart. He avoided her gaze. "How's your wrist?"

"It's fine. Barely even hurts. I'm really only wearing this because Ginny insisted."

Gideon said nothing. Ginny had many faults, but caring for her little sister wasn't one of them. He took comfort in knowing Ginny would do everything she could to keep Biddie safe after he'd gone.

She waited until the cows were in and the gate shut before she spoke again. "You couldn't find the other two?"

"That's it?" The question slipped out before he could stop it. "What do you mean?"

"Nothing. Forget it. I'll find the other two in the morning." He strode toward his tent.

She followed. "Can we please just talk?"

He flinched. "No." He reached for his tent flap.

"I'll be praying for you."

He ducked inside. She could pray all she wanted. Maybe God would listen to her. He certainly wasn't listening to Gideon.

~

*B*iddie lay awake all night going over in her mind every argument she could think of that might persuade Gideon to stay and give her a chance. No combination of words seemed good enough. So she prayed until early dawn filtered through the cracks around the door and shuttered window. Then she leaped from bed, threw on her shawl, and dashed outside to catch Gideon before he left.

She was too late.

Legend was gone, as was Gideon's tent. He couldn't have

found the last two cows already, could he? She ran with bare feet to the corral. She counted them twice to be sure. There were still two missing.

A dirty white bundle near the corral gate caught her eye as she turned away. Gideon's tent and his leather bag sat on the ground, a sure promise that he would return.

She studied the valley rim though it was too early to expect him. She almost missed the shadow of a man standing near a pile of boulders to the south. Her breath caught.

But it couldn't be Gideon. He'd be riding Legend, and he wouldn't stand up there staring down at her.

Biddie hurried toward the house and threw the door open. "Ginny, wake up. There's a strange man outside."

Ginny flew from her bed and was halfway to the door, rifle in hand, before Biddie finished speaking. Rather than go outside, Ginny shoved the door closed until only an inch of opening remained. She pressed her eye to the crack. "Where is he? Which direction?"

Biddie picked up her rifle and loaded it as she answered. "To the south, on the rim." Handling the heavy weapon increased the burning pain in her wrist, but she ignored it. And prayed the injury wouldn't affect her aim. Then she prayed shooting wouldn't be necessary. Blasting apart clay balls was one thing. Pulling the trigger on an actual person was something else entirely.

Silence reigned as Lucy joined Biddie in loading their guns.

Ginny continued staring outside. "Are you sure he was south? I don't see him."

Biddie pulled on her skirt and buttoned her blouse. "Yes, I'm sure."

Ginny shut the door and moved toward the keyhole window they'd built into the south wall. She slid aside the small wood piece covering the opening and peeked through.

Biddie stuffed her feet into boots and laced them up.

Lucy did the same.

By the time they were all dressed and armed, bright morning light was streaking through the gaps around the door and window.

Ginny closed the keyhole window. "I can't see a thing." She marched toward the door and threw it open but paused before stepping outside. "No shooting. No sign of smoke. That's good." She hung her hat on the end of her rifle and thrust it out the door.

Still nothing.

She drew the weapon back inside. "The two of you wait here while I take a look."

Ginny ran outside and Biddie followed her.

Ginny's head swiveled, her eyes searching the valley around them even as she whispered. "Can't you ever do as you're told?"

"Why should I leave my big sister to take all the risk?"

"Because I'm a better shot than you."

Which was a fair point. But it was too late now. Biddie glanced back and saw Lucy peeking from the doorway. At least one of them was safe.

Ginny crouched behind the rock they usually prepared meals on and waved for Biddie to get behind a nearby bush.

Once Biddie was out of sight, Ginny whispered, "Where, exactly, did you see him?"

Biddie leaned out far enough to point to the cluster of boulders where she'd seen the shadowed figure. He wasn't there. She searched everywhere but couldn't spot him.

"I think he's gone. If he ever was there." Ginny stood.

Biddie huffed. "He was."

Ginny moved toward the horse corral. "I'll mount up and do a circle, just to be sure."

Ginny returned by the time Biddie had breakfast warmed.

"Not only did I see no man, but there were no boot prints or any sign that a man had been anywhere near the rocks you pointed to."

Biddie handed Ginny a cup of coffee. "That doesn't make any sense. I'm sure I saw someone."

Lucy took a sip of her own coffee and winced. She still preferred tea, but Biddie had been so distracted she'd forgotten and served her friend the brown sludge Ginny insisted on. "Maybe the morning light played tricks on your eyes."

"Maybe." Biddie inspected every shadow around them. The man had seemed so real.

CHAPTER 30

*G*ideon drove the final two cows up the mountain to Lupine Valley Ranch. Before he'd left, he'd packed his belongings and left them by the corral gate. He planned to return the cows and make a hasty exit. More than eight hours in the saddle had given him plenty of time to reconsider those actions and know them for what they were—cowardly. He might be a broken man, but he was no coward. He needed to face Biddie and try one last time to convince her to return to the city, or at least to the ranch where her father was recovering from his injury.

This time, she wasn't waiting by the corral for him. Nor was she at the house.

Virginia came around the corner. "Did you find those cows?"

"I did. They're in the corral now."

"Good. Then you can be on your way."

He cleared his throat. "I was hoping to say goodbye to all of you."

Lucy rounded the barn toting a bucket of water and spotted him. "Oh, you're back. Did you find the cows?"

Virginia answered for him. "Yes, and now he's leaving."

Lucy's brow furrowed. "Without saying goodbye?"

Virginia waved a dismissive hand. "Goodbyes are a waste of time." She turned and strode toward the cattle corral.

Lucy scowled at Virginia's back. "Biddie doesn't think so."

Gideon took the bucket and dumped the water in the wash bin for Lucy. "Do you know where she is?"

Lucy jerked her chin toward the western valley rim. "Collecting tinder for the fire."

Gideon thanked her and collected his belongings. Then he mounted Legend and rode west.

He found Biddie sitting in a patch of dry grass, shredding a single blade, her eyes downcast. He dismounted and left Legend ground tied.

When he was close enough to speak, he pulled his hat off and swallowed against the lump in his throat. "Hello."

She jumped to her feet. "Oh, it's you."

He considered the rifle in her grip and cast a look about them. "You expecting someone else? There been trouble I don't know about?"

"No, I...I guess I'm a bit jittery since I didn't sleep much last night."

"Neither did I." He scuffed his boots against the dirt. "I'd sleep a whole lot better tonight if you'd agree to come to the city with me."

Her mouth fell open and hope lit her eyes. "I thought—"

She'd misunderstood. He raised his hat as if warding off the disappointment he was about to cause. "That is, if you'd allow me to *escort* you and Lucy to the safety of your father's protection."

"Oh." Her gaze dropped, and her posture wilted like a flower in the summer heat. "I thought, maybe..."

This had been a mistake. He crammed his hat back on his head. "I'm sorry. I'll go now." He turned toward Legend.

"Stop where you are, or I'll shoot," Virginia shouted.

Was she crazy? He spun to face her. "You're the one that—" He stopped talking when he realized she wasn't looking at him.

Instead, her gun was aimed south, at a man inching his way down the slope with his hands raised.

"Ah, Ginny, put the gun down. You know you ain't gonna shoot me."

Gideon gaped as Virginia dropped her weapon and sprinted for the newcomer with a squeal.

~

*B*iddie felt rooted to the ground beside Gideon. Could the tall, dark-haired man with his arms around Ginny really be her brother? He must be. Biddie couldn't imagine Ginny allowing any other man so close. For that matter, Biddie had never imagined Ginny being so excited to see anyone. Biddie could hardly believe what she was seeing now as the man who could only be Preston lifted Ginny off her feet and spun her around.

Ginny's laugh echoed through the valley.

Biddie wrapped her arms around her waist. Ginny hadn't hugged her since their arrival on the ranch, nor had she laughed so freely or appeared so happy.

Gideon nudged her. "Aren't you going to say hello? He's your brother, too, isn't he?"

She looked at him, and he seemed to read her insecurities.

"Your sister loves you too. She just has a harder time showing it. Likely, it's all those years you two spent apart. There isn't anything you can do about the time you've lost, so don't let it steal the time you have." He gave her another nudge.

She stepped forward, then turned. "You won't leave without saying goodbye, will you?"

He turned the brim of his hat in his hands, eyes fixed on the spinning garment. Then he glanced west. "I can wait another hour maybe, in case you and Lucy change your mind about leaving now that Virginia won't be alone."

Biddie hesitated. She *had* said she'd leave once Preston arrived to help Ginny. Not to mention, Mr. Green was clearly anxious for her return. She couldn't afford to lose him as an investor.

She looked back to where Ginny and Preston were busy laughing and talking as they walked toward the house. A full beard hid Preston's mouth, but happiness created wrinkles at the corners of his eyes. He wore strange clothes—his leather jacket, leather vest, and leather pants were all trimmed with long fringe. Even his bandanna had a trim of fringe. His black slouch hat and everything he wore looked new, aside from the coating of dust that covered him head to toe. The clothes, though odd, looked expensive. Had her brother become a wealthy man? She knew so little about his life since she'd last seen him. How could she leave without getting to know the man he'd become?

CHAPTER 31

*T*he scent of cinnamon and apples tempted Gideon as he mounted Legend. Part of him wanted to join in the celebration and enjoy the delicious meal Biddie was preparing. He had thought to assist Biddie with the heavier tasks of preparing the meal, but Preston beat him to it. She insisted she could manage the remaining work and held firm in her decision not to leave. Though Preston had been on the ranch less than an hour, he'd already proven himself a trustworthy man. The women would be in good hands with him.

Gideon was out of excuses to linger. It was time for him to go.

He nudged Legend up the trail. Biddie's laughter reached him as he crested the rim of the valley. He didn't look back.

~

*B*iddie's heart ached even as she laughed over Preston's recounting of the time a small boy had left his mother's lap and climbed onto the stage during one of his traveling shows. She left the others beside the empty firepit and went inside to check on the baking pie she'd made especially for Preston's return. The rehydrated apples wouldn't be as good as fresh, but it was the best she could do with their current supplies. Hopefully, her brother would enjoy the treat.

The pie was finished, so she pulled it from the oven and set it on the table.

Outside, Preston was telling another story. It was something about a knife-throwing act that had gone wrong and separated a woman's hat from its feather. Lucy was giggling. He had a knack for telling stories. She'd forgotten that about him. Perhaps that was why he had joined the traveling show. He was a born entertainer.

His joviality seemed a stark contrast to Ginny's dark moods.

Biddie stepped outside. Preston's eyes shot to hers, his hand reaching for the pistol at his waist. Then he smiled, moved his hand back to his lap, and continued his story.

Biddie frowned. He'd been jumpy since he arrived. Was it his new surroundings, or was he always so alert? His eyes never seemed to rest on anyone or anything for very long.

Her own gaze searched the darkness, though she knew she wouldn't find what she was looking for. She'd seen Gideon sneak away. It had taken everything in her not to follow him, not to try one last time to convince him to stay. Watching him ride out of the valley had felt like watching part of herself disappear into the night. But Lucy was right. Biddie had tried to tell Gideon of his many wonderful qualities, but he'd refused to listen. Instead, he had again tried to convince her to leave the ranch with Lucy and return to Father. But she couldn't leave yet, not without getting to know her big brother once more. She prayed two weeks would be enough time. She didn't dare press Mr. Green's patience any longer than that.

Ginny's voice brought Biddie back to the present. "So how'd you get here from Chicago?"

"I took the train to San Francisco and the steamer to San

Diego. Bought a horse there and started east. I stopped at the store in Campo and asked directions from the owner."

Ginny scowled. "Luman told a complete stranger how to find Lupine Valley Ranch?"

"No, ma'am. Not even after I showed him the letter you sent. It was lucky Clyve showed up and told me how to find you. Since it was late, I stayed at his place last night. Didn't want to scare you, showing up after midnight."

Lucy's eyes widened. "What was Clyve doing in town?"

Preston gave Lucy a speculative look. "He wouldn't say exactly. I had my suspicions it was something to do with a girl."

Ginny's brow furrowed. "How'd he even recognize you? You two ain't never met."

"He didn't." Preston smirked and patted the engraved leather holsters at his waist. "He recognized my new holsters. I had them special made last year and told him about them in my last letter."

Biddie took a closer look at the fancy leather work. Every bit of the dark-brown leather was covered in elaborate tooling, with three large stars drawing the eye toward the center of each holster. The belt was equally covered in decoration and clasped with a large silver buckle. "Did you also have the buckle made?"

Preston's grin widened as he looked down at the buckle. "No, that I won at a shooting contest in Indiana."

Lucy's lips scrunched. "But if you stayed at Clyve's place last night, why didn't he come with you?"

"He planned to, but one of his hands came in just as we were riding out this morning. They seemed concerned about some cows in a far pasture. He rode off to check it out."

Biddie crossed her arms. "It doesn't take all day to get here from Clyve's place. That was you I saw this morning in the shadows."

Preston's cheeks turned a bright red. "Yeah, sorry about that."

"I don't understand." Ginny shifted on the rock she was sitting on. "Why didn't you just come on in?"

The smile he'd been wearing since his arrival vanished. He wiped his palms across the top of his trousers, his eyes downcast. "I needed to be sure."

"Sure of what?"

Preston's gaze lifted to Ginny's. "That Oliver was really gone."

Something passed between Biddie's older siblings in the look they shared. Again, she was reminded of the many years they'd spent together without her.

~

*B*iddie joined Preston and Ginny at the gate to the cattle corral just after breakfast.

"I don't know much about cows, Ginny, but this looks like a fine herd to me."

Ginny leaned against the stone wall and shrugged. "It's a start. I'm not aiming for a large herd, but I'd like a few more than this. At the very least, I hope to buy a bull soon."

"There was a man at that store in town talking about selling his bull. Wish I'd known you were interested."

Ginny straightened. "You mean in Campo? What man? What was his name? How old was the bull?"

"Whoa. Whoa. Whoa. I didn't ask all that many questions. Like I said, I didn't know you were interested. I just heard the man say he was looking to sell his bull."

"Did you at least catch his name?"

"Let me think." Preston scratched at the stubble on his chin. "I think I heard the store owner call him 'Bartoli.'"

"Bartoli Morales?"

"I don't know. I just heard him say 'Bartoli.'"

"It has to be Bartoli Morales. That's the only Bartoli in the

263

area. Only one I've heard of, anyway." Ginny held her hand about shoulder height. "Was he about this tall, a bit wide, and with curly hair?"

"Yeah, I think so."

Ginny clapped. "It has to be him. He owns that big ranch northwest of the McCain place. He's got fine stock. How many others were in town and heard him talking about selling his bull?"

"Just me and Clyve, as far as I saw."

"Perfect. We've got to go." Ginny marched toward the horse corral.

Biddie chased after her. "Go? Where are you going?"

"To the Morales ranch. I've got to get there before anyone else learns he's looking to sell."

"Now? You're leaving right now?" Biddie skidded to a halt beside the gate as Ginny stormed through and retrieved her horse.

She led her horse toward the barn. "Not just me. Preston's got to come too. Morales won't sell to a woman, but he'll sell to Preston." Ginny lifted Preston's saddle and thrust it at his chest.

He caught the heavy leather. "What about Biddie and Lucy?"

Ginny paused and considered Biddie. "You'll have to keep a sharp eye out. Take turns sleeping while we're gone. Keep your rifle close. There shouldn't be any trouble, but you be ready just in case."

CHAPTER 32

"Time to get up." A boot nudged Gideon's backside none too gently.

He rolled over on the rocky ground and pried his eyes open. The pale pink of an early dawn silhouetted Clyve's head hovering above him. "Up."

Clyve gave a satisfied nod and strode on to kick the backside of the next sleeping man.

With a groan, Gideon pushed to a sitting position.

Last night, he'd found chaos in the Rowlands' yard when he'd arrived to say goodbye. A dozen cattle had gone missing from their herd. Clyve, his father, and their vaqueros were readying to pursue the rustlers. Gideon wanted no part in the chase, but when Clyve asked for help, Gideon couldn't refuse. Not after all the help the Rowlands had given Lupine Valley Ranch.

The small posse rode well into the night, following the rustlers' trail. Eventually, they'd made camp and set guards. Knowing he needed sleep, but too restless to lie down, Gideon volunteered for the first shift. By the time one of the vaqueros relieved him, the ache of his goodbye to Biddie had no longer been enough to keep him awake.

With the sun rising, the posse could again follow the trail and would set out soon. He rose to his feet, every muscle groaning with complaint. An ache started at the back of his head. Not good. He needed to make his excuses and continue to San Diego. Leaving was no way to repay Clyve for all he'd done to help the women, but better to go than put anyone in danger.

Clyve returned with a steaming mug.

Gideon accepted with gratitude. He took a sip, searching for the words to explain his decision. "Listen, Clyve, I'm sorry, but I've got to move on."

"What do you mean, 'move on'? Are you worried about the women? I thought Preston was with them."

"He is, which is why I'm leaving."

Clyve made a choking sound and swallowed hard before setting his mug aside. "Leaving? You mean for good? I thought you worked for Ginny."

"That's done. It's time I move on." Gideon couldn't meet Clyve's eyes. He downed the rest of his coffee in two big gulps and strode toward Legend.

Clyve was at his heels. "What about Biddie?"

"What about her?" Gideon cast Clyve a knowing look. "She and Lucy are staying at the ranch, if that's what you're worried about."

"No. I mean yes, but I thought you and Biddie—"

"No." Gideon turned and marched back to his bedroll. He rolled it, grabbed his hat, and marched back to Legend. He plopped his hat on his head and tied the roll to the saddle.

Clyve followed him. "So the two of you *don't* have an understanding?"

Gideon clenched his teeth. "No. We don't." He put his boot into the stirrup.

"What happened?" Clyve's hand landed on Gideon's shoulder, holding him in place.

"Nothing. It's just time for me to move on."

Clyve's father joined them "Something wrong?"

"Gideon says he's got to leave."

Matthew nodded. "Probably best not to leave those girls unprotected for so long."

Clyve shook his head. "They're fine. Ginny's brother, Preston, is with them. Besides, Gideon isn't heading to the ranch. He's heading out."

"Listen." Gideon ran his hand down his face. "I'm sorry to leave you in the middle of a search, but it's better if I go." He tried to shake off Clyve's grip and failed.

"That's a mighty strange thing to say." Matthew stroked his mustache with his thumb and forefinger.

Gideon sighed and lowered his boot to the ground. "It's strange that a man has someplace he needs to be?"

"No, but the way you said it, almost makes it sound like we'd be better off without you."

"That's because you would." Gideon's head pounded. "Everyone is better off without me." He pressed his lips tight. He hadn't meant to say that last part.

Clyve dropped his hold and stared at him as if he'd grown a second head. "Why would you say such a thing?"

"Because I'm broken. I'm a danger to everyone around me." The words broke free like a wild stallion busting through a fence. Forget his pride. What did it matter what these men thought of him? He needed to get out of here. If telling the truth made that happen faster, so be it. It wasn't like he'd ever see these men again. "Just let me go. You've got rustlers to catch." He turned toward Legend.

Matthew harrumphed. "The rustlers will keep. What's this about you being a danger?"

Clyve's brows drew together. "Haven't you been looking

after the women all these months? Didn't I hear you saved Biddie from a rattlesnake in Campo?"

"Yes, but you don't know how many times I've hurt her."

Clyve's eyes narrowed. "And how many times did you intend to hurt her?"

"None." Gideon glared at him. "I would never purposely hurt her or any woman."

"Exactly. And I bet she didn't want you to leave, did she?" Clyve smirked. "I've seen the way she looks at you."

Of course, Clyve had noticed what Gideon had been oblivious to. He'd been so busy battling his own feelings, Biddie's near-declaration after the stampede had come as a complete shock. He pinched his nose against the pain pulsing at the back of his eyes. "That doesn't matter."

"Of course, it matters. You can't tell me you don't care how she feels."

"I'm not who she thinks I am."

"Who's that?"

"A real man."

Matthew snorted. "You look pretty real to me."

"You don't understand." Gideon pressed the heel of his palm to the side of his head.

Clyve crossed his arms. "So help me understand."

Gideon sighed and looked around. They'd drawn the attention of every man in the group. Wonderful. "The war changed me. I'm not the man I once was."

One of the vaqueros stepped closer. "The war changed all of us." He raised a hand missing its thumb and forefinger.

"Yes, but you can still work. I can't see past here." Gideon held his hand up to show where his right peripheral vision stopped. "And I get headaches that mess with my vision and cloud my thoughts. The pain empties my stomach and knocks me on my back, sometimes for days at a time."

Mathew frowned. "So what? We've all got our problems."

"Have you burned down a barn?" Gideon resisted the urge to mount Legend and just ride away. These men would never understand. "I got my own father killed, and two days ago, I nearly killed Biddie. I can't predict when these pains come on, and I can't control them. I have no business on a ranch and even less pursuing a wife." He jammed his foot into the stirrup and threw himself into the saddle.

"Whoa, now." Matthew held up both hands, palms out. "Wait just a moment. If what you say is true, then sure, you need to make some changes. Maybe be a little more careful in certain situations. But these pains you're talking about aren't any reason to deny yourself a happy life."

"Biddie must know about these pains you have, right?" Clyve cocked a brow.

Gideon resisted the urge to roll his eyes. "Of course." As if he could have hidden his condition for as long as he'd been living at the ranch.

Clyve pointed at him. "And she still wants you to stay."

"She deserves a real man."

Clyve scratched his beard. "Why do you keep saying you aren't a real man?"

"Men are supposed to be strong." Gideon jerked his hat from his head and slapped it against his thigh. "That isn't me. Not anymore."

One of the other men watching scoffed. "Says who?"

Gideon shrugged. "It's in God's Word."

Clyve looked at his father. "Do you know any verse in the Bible that says a man is supposed to be strong?"

"'Course. It's in First Corinthians. Chapter sixteen, if I remember right." Matthew shifted his gaze to Gideon. "But that isn't about physical strength. It's about the strength of your faith and not being swayed by the lies of the devil. That old trickster will use the nastiness of this world to try to fool you into believing lies, like God doesn't care about you, or you aren't worthy of God's love. Sometimes he'll even try to convince you your sins are too great to be forgiven." He jabbed a finger toward Gideon. "But that's not what the Bible says. It says Jesus died for *everyone's* sins, no matter how bad. There isn't one person who ever lived whose sin was greater than God's love and forgiveness."

Gideon set his hat on his head and looked to where the sun crested a distant hill. He hadn't heard God or felt His presence since the war. The silence made sense after the unforgivable things Gideon had done. But what if Matthew was right? Was it possible God had forgiven him for the men he'd killed in the name of honor and country? "If I'm forgiven, why hasn't He answered any of my prayers?"

"You sure He hasn't answered? Just because He says *no* or maybe *wait*, doesn't mean He isn't listening or doesn't care." Matthew squinted at him. "In my years, I've learned that when it seems the good Lord isn't listening, more times than not, it's the other way around. If you doubt God's forgiveness, then it seems to me, you've been listening to the wrong voice. God's voice convicts us when we've done wrong, but it sounds like you've been living with a heap of shame clogging your ears." He glanced at the brightening sky. "Now, we've got to get moving, but when this is over, you and I are going to take a look at my Bible and see if we can't clear things up." The older man nodded as if the matter were settled and headed for his horse.

Clyve grinned at Gideon. "Guess that means you're sticking with us."

Gideon glared at him. How had a simple goodbye turned into a talk about God? "Even if God does forgive me, Biddie deserves a husband who can protect her—not put her in harm's way. She needs a real man."

Clyve's grin vanished. "Being a man isn't about what you *can't* do, it's about what you *choose* to do. Your head pains and whatever vision problems you have can't stop you from being a man. But running away from a good woman who loves you just as you are...well, I'm not sure about the Bible, but in my book, that makes you nothing more than a coward. Is that who you want to be?"

～

*I*nk dripped onto Biddie's paper. She set the pen down and quickly blotted the errant mark. The words just wouldn't come. She glared at the three crumpled papers already littering the table beside her. She needed to explain her delay to Mr. Green, but nothing she came up with seemed good enough to assuage any irritation he might be feeling. What if it was too late? What if he considered her absence a sign of irresponsibility or a lack of commitment to the bakery?

She shoved back the crate she'd been using as a chair and stood. She would take a break. She would go and see what Lucy was up to. Maybe when she came back, the right words would come to her.

She stepped out into the hot afternoon sun and glanced around. Lucy was not in the yard. Biddie checked the barn but Patty was alone. Lucy wasn't at the spring either. A sneaking suspicion led Biddie toward the hidden mine.

She wove her way through the shrubs and rocks littering the valley floor. What was she going to do if Mr. Green had decided not to invest in her bakery, after all? Did she even still want to run the bakery?

Had the desert heat baked her brain? Just months ago, such a doubt would have seemed impossible. She'd been planning this for years.

Her gaze turned west and found the rim of the valley. Had Gideon slept in Campo last night, or had he continued on and made camp at some point closer to San Diego? Did any part of him regret his decision to leave? Should she have tried harder to make him stay?

Lord, was I wrong to let him go? Will I ever see him again?

She had to go after him. Pivoting, she started toward the horse corral. Ginny wouldn't like Biddie leaving the ranch unprotected, but it wasn't as though Biddie and Lucy could fight off a bandit attack all on their own in any case. Should she bring Lucy with her? Who would milk Patty? Biddie's steps faltered. She was being foolish.

Movement just beyond the cattle corral caught her eye, and she froze.

The gate stood open and cattle were wandering out. How in the world had that happened? She lifted her skirts and jogged toward the opening.

The cattle seemed to be moving up the north side of the valley and disappearing over the ridge. How many had already escaped?

She ran faster. She had to get that gate closed.

She reached the corral and grasped the wooden crossbeam just as a hand clamped over her mouth. Her scream was no more than a whimper against the strong, callused fingers.

An arm came around her waist, cinching her against her captor's chest. He stank of cigarettes, sweat, and cow dung.

She jabbed her elbow into his stomach.

He laughed.

"Oh, this one's got spirit, boys." He lifted her off her feet and slung her over his shoulder. His comrades up the hill laughed and made lewd noises.

She sucked in a breath to scream but swallowed it instead. Who would hear her? Only Lucy was close enough. What could Lucy do against a gang of bandits? No, Biddie couldn't drag her friend into danger. Biddie was on her own.

She beat on his back and tried to kick, but he held her legs firm. If only she had her rifle. She had been so distracted by her attempts to write that infernal letter that she'd forgotten her weapon inside the house. That mistake was going to cost her dearly. She swallowed, trying not to think of what might come.

Where was Lucy? Biddie craned her neck to search her surroundings. Still no sign of Lucy. Good.

Another strange man came around the northeast corner of the house. "I can't find the other one. It's like she just disappeared."

Biddie spotted the butt of her captor's pistol at his side. She twisted and clawed at the leather holster. Her fingers curled around the handle of the pistol and yanked. The weapon came free. She almost dropped it and scrambled for a better grip.

"No." Her captor spun.

Biddie was flung sideways and slammed into a boulder. Blinding pain filled her head. The weapon slipped from her fingers as darkness filled her vision.

CHAPTER 33

Gideon slid from his horse in front of the Rowlands' home as the sun crept toward the horizon. The men had ridden all day but lost the rustlers' trail in a rocky stretch of the desert. They'd searched for two hours but couldn't determine which way the thieves had gone. Bone-weary and discouraged, the posse had given up the chase and returned to the ranch.

Gideon walked Legend to the trough. As the horse drank his fill, Gideon removed his tack and gave his faithful friend a thorough brushing. Once Legend was settled in a stall with hay and oats, Gideon shuffled toward the house where Matthew had promised a hearty meal.

Before he reached the door, men near the eastern edge of the yard began shouting for Clyve.

Gideon drew his pistol and dashed toward the commotion. In the direction the vaqueros were pointing, a flash of blue appeared amid the browns and greens of the desert. A woman. She staggered toward them, clearly attempting to run but too exhausted.

Gideon sprinted forward. "Lucy?"

"Help!" The petite brunette's cry was hoarse. Her cheeks bore dust-covered tear tracks.

"Get water," he yelled over his shoulder before turning back to Lucy. "Where are Biddie and Ginny? Where's Preston? What happened?"

Clyve raced toward them. He scooped up Lucy and started back to the house. "Are you hurt?"

"No." Lucy struggled to catch her breath. "Rustlers. They took her."

Gideon's chest tightened. "Took who?"

"Biddie. They hurt her. I saw them ride away. She wasn't fighting them, just hanging over his lap." Lucy's lower lip trembled, and new tears joined the streaks already marring the dust coating her face. "She was so still. I think she's..." She broke into full-body sobs, burying her face in Clyve's neck.

Clive turned sideways to pass through the front door. "Hush now. They wouldn't take her if she was dead."

Lucy lifted her chin. "You mean she's still alive?"

"For now." Clyve's gaze rose.

His grave expression made Gideon's blood run cold. His own cowardice had driven him to leave Biddie. And now she was in the hands of evil men.

~

*B*iddie's stomach surged into her throat. Her eyes flew open as her body heaved. The world was upside down. The ground rushed by above her. Plumes of dust and pebbles filled the air, making her cough. She was bounced and jostled, flopping around like a rag doll. She couldn't feel her arms. They hung past her ears.

Hung? Wait. Where was she?

She tried to move her arms to her waist, but they refused her commands. She tried wiggling her feet, but her legs were equally as numb. How could her body hurt so much and at the same time feel nothing?

Her cheek bounced against something rough. She tried to see what it was, but it was too close. Her eyes refused to focus on whatever it was.

She craned her neck to look up—or was it down? Hooves pounded the ground. She looked in the other direction. Was that a saddle cinch?

Saddle. Hooves. She was on a horse. Or rather, she was draped across the horse, on her stomach. How long had she been here? Judging by the pounding of her head and the numbness in her limbs, it had been a good long while. She needed to get off.

Something pressed against her back, holding her in place.

She tried again to command her arms to move. This time, they lifted several inches before flopping back down again. With all her might, she flung one arm toward her back. Her fingers collided with...

What *was* that?

A rough, callused hand clasped her wrist, wrenching her shoulder. "So you're finally awake. Good. We're almost there." Though his English was clear and confident, a Mexican accent thickened his voice.

The sound brought her memory back with a whoosh. The rustlers. She'd been kidnapped. She needed to escape. First though, she needed to get upright. She wouldn't get anywhere with her legs and arms the way they were.

Her face smashed into her captor's leg. That's what she'd been bumping into. Now that she understood her situation, she recognized the rough fabric of his trousers and the cool slap of the stirrup against her cheek.

"Please, let me sit up."

The man laughed. "Wait. We'll be there soon."

He'd said that before. But where was he taking her?

Already the urge to return to pain-free oblivion teased her senses. Darkness crowded the edges of her vision, but she fought it back. Wherever they were going, she needed to be alert. Weak as she was, no one else was here to help her. No one even knew where she was.

No, that wasn't true. God knew where she was and would help her. His Word promised never to forsake her. She let her eyes drift closed.

Please God, help me.

CHAPTER 34

Strong winds drove sand across the desert, stinging Gideon's face as he rode beside Clyve. Ahead of them, Matthew watched the ground for any signs that the tracks they followed were taking a turn.

After seeing Lucy safely settled with the Rowlands' cook, the weary group of men had immediately set out for Lupine Valley Ranch.

Finding the rustlers' trail was easy. The thieves had made no effort to hide their tracks. The prints led roughly northwest for two miles before turning east into a wide, sandy wash that led to a narrow gorge.

As the sun touched the horizon, dark clouds rushed in overhead. The gorge slithered its way through the mountains, a perfect spot for an ambush.

Matthew ordered the posse to split into two groups. Half rode along the north side of the gorge and the other half along the south side.

It was slow going. Gideon itched to urge Legend into a gallop. How far had the bandits taken Biddie? Was she still alive? If so, what were those varmints doing to her? The not knowing ate at him. But rushing forward would lead to a fool's death. He couldn't let his fears rule him.

By the time the trail turned north again, sunset had faded to twilight and the air hung thick with the promise of rain. The tracks continued over hills and through narrow valleys.

Finally, the posse emerged into a wide space between mountains and canyons.

Clyve checked his pistol and glanced at Gideon. "They call this the Badlands. It's known for hiding thieves, bandits, and every other kind of criminal. Good men don't venture here if they can help it."

Gideon looked over his shoulder. The men fidgeted in their saddles as sporadic sprinkles of warm rain dampened their clothes.

They passed between two large rocks and entered a canyon lined with tall sandstone cliffs. Layers of brick-red and gray rock, sliced with thin lines of white, ran along the walls closing in on them.

"I don't like this," Clyve muttered. "Feels like a trap."

Gideon kept his voice low as he searched the top of the canyon for any sign of movement. "Is there any way to get to the high ground?"

"Not without backtracking. And there are dozens of slot canyons through here. If we're up top when the tracks turn, we could find ourselves cut off. Getting around those cracks from the top could waste precious time."

It made sense, but blindly following the bandits' tracks felt like navigating the Battle of Gettysburg with his eyes closed.

Tense silence reigned as they followed the canyon through a series of sharp curves. The trail eventually opened into a broader plane where hard cliffs gave way to softer mounds. On either side, slopes of dried mud grew slick in the steady mist. Legend's hooves sank deep into the damp sand of the wide wash. Scattered, squat, brittle trees cast dark shadows in the deepening dusk.

Gideon gritted his teeth as the path narrowed and canyon walls rose and fell on both sides. His shoulders burned, and he forced himself to take a long, deep breath. He couldn't afford a headache now. Rain soaked his hat and dripped down his collar.

Every two-dozen feet or so, narrow finger canyons shot off from the one they followed. He kept a sharp eye on those openings for any sign of men lying in wait.

Matthew turned back. He brought his horse alongside Gideon and Clyve. "The tracks split up ahead. Best as I can tell, four of the riders continued with the cattle, but three of them went that way." He pointed to one of the narrow canyons heading west. It was walled with tall, steep slopes of slippery mud.

Clyve and several of the vaqueros let fly words Gideon's mother wouldn't have approved of.

Gideon glanced from Clyve to the canyon and back. "What's the problem?"

"These are mud canyons, and some lead to mud caves."

"So?"

Matthew sighed. "Riding through there in good weather is risky. With the rain, it's downright foolish. Water makes the mud unstable. I've heard tales of men swallowed up by this land and never seen again."

Legend flung his head, and Gideon realized he'd been holding the reins tight. He loosened his grip. "Can you tell which way they took Biddie?"

Matthew's mouth twisted to one side, and he scratched his head. "That's hard to say, but I'd wager they took her off away from the cattle where any screaming wouldn't startle the herd."

"Then she's in the mud canyon?"

"That'd be my guess."

Having heard all he needed to, Gideon rode around them and headed for the side trail.

"Wait." Clyve's father closed the distance. "Let me go first. I've got some experience here. You don't."

Gideon opened his mouth to protest, but the old man had already ridden ahead. This mess was Gideon's fault. He should be the one taking the most risk.

Clyve rode up next to him. "Don't worry about it. Pa's as stubborn as they come. There was no chance of him turning back. He just wanted to give his men a choice. He won't order anyone to their death, but he doesn't think twice about risking his own life to save someone else."

There was unmistakable pride and affection in Clyve's voice as he spoke of his father, reminding Gideon of his loss. But the familiar stab of guilt that came with thinking of his father was softened by his earlier conversation with the men. God had forgiven Gideon. He needed to forgive himself. Maybe when this was all over and Biddie was safe, he'd figure out how to do that.

As they entered the narrow canyon behind Matthew, Gideon moved ahead of Clyve and glanced back. Only two of the six vaqueros had chosen to follow them.

The group had traveled about twenty feet when they turned a corner and were forced to stop. The canyon was too narrow for the horses to continue.

Without a word, Clyve's father dismounted, and the rest of them did the same. The last man was left to guard the horses as the rest of them continued on foot.

Thick dribbles of mud slid down the steep sides of the narrow path they followed. Brown smears coated Gideon's clothes as he turned sideways to pass through an especially narrow space.

In several places large clumps formed odd bridges or over-hangs. Climbing them wasn't so bad, but twice they were forced to crawl beneath. He caught himself holding his breath until he reached the other side.

Matthew scrambled over another mound ahead of Gideon. Then he was gone.

Without warning and with barely a rumble, the ground beneath Matthew had given way.

"Dad!" Clyve knocked Gideon into the canyon wall as he plowed past.

Gideon clambered up the slick pile of mud behind Clyve. By the time he reached the opening, Clyve had his father's wrist and was hauling him out.

Matthew appeared unharmed, though he was missing his boots, which were stuck in the mud that had slid into the hole after him. The older man tried to stand but toppled into his son with a grunt.

Clyve caught his father around the waist. "What's hurt?"

"I think I twisted my ankle. Let me wrap it and I'll be fine."

Clyve helped his father down the slippery slope to the ground. "No way. This place is dangerous enough without an injury to contend with, and you just got real lucky. That hole could have been much deeper. I might not have been able to get you out, or worse, you could have been buried alive. Besides, you've lost your boots. Let's head back. We can camp out in the wider canyon tonight. We'll send one of the men to get you a new pair of boots, and try again when it's finished raining."

Gideon clamped his lips against a protest. He understood Clyve's concern, but there was no way Gideon would rest until Biddie was safe.

Matthew waved a dismissive hand. "I'm fine. I just need a wrap." He jerked away from Clyve's hold and took a step forward. His ankle held, but his clenched jaw gave away the pain he was in. He tried another step and swayed. He pressed one hand to the wall for support and the other to his mud-streaked forehead.

Gideon clasped the older man's shoulder. "Did you hit your head?"

Matthew rubbed his hand over his eyes and blinked hard several times—the whites showing bright in his muddy face. "I'm fine. Just need a second."

Gideon nodded to Clyve. "You take him."

Against Matthew's protest, Clyve slid an arm under his father's shoulders and began guiding him back the way they had come. The only vaquero still with them followed behind.

Gideon waited until the men had rounded a corner before turning in the opposite direction. The heavy rain and sliding mud had washed away any remaining prints—not that he'd have been able to see them now that night had fully settled in. Still, no paths or canyons had branched off from this narrow passageway. Biddie must be ahead.

Please, God, let her still be alive and help me reach her in time.

❧

*B*iddie studied the three bandits conferring near the opening of the cave. They were smeared with mud, spoke in low tones, and kept glancing the way they'd come. She couldn't make out their words and struggled to think past the pounding in her head.

Her merciless captor had left her upside down for the long ride through the mountains and gorges until the bandits who'd been watching their back-trail spotted a posse in pursuit. The leader then ordered the gang to split in two and yanked her from the saddle. He bound her wrists together and forced her to stumble ahead of him into a narrow mud canyon.

Had it not been for the narrow walls she'd used to brace herself, her swirling head and riotous stomach would've brought her to her knees. As it was, her slow pace earned her several jabs in the back with the man's pistol. He and the others exchanged lewd comments as they walked, describing what they'd do with her once the posse was off their trail. She tried to shut out the terrifying words and focus on putting one foot in front of the other. Then they'd shoved her into the cave.

She wasn't sure how long they'd been here, but the sky had turned dark and what started as a faint drizzle had become a steady downpour in the time it took her head and stomach to begin settling. A small stream of muddy water now coursed along the bottom of the canyon and pooled into the cave, soaking her skirts and stockings.

A fat drop smacked her cheek. She looked up. A thick glob of mud dripped onto her nose. She wiped it away. As she watched, several more drops dribbled from the ceiling of the cave. A rivulet of water streamed along a growing crack just to her right. The sections to either side bulged downward as if pressed by a heavy weight. What if the cave collapsed? How many tons of mud were suspended above her head?

She had to get out of here.

The bandits were still talking, their gazes fixed eastward down the canyon.

Slowly, she rose to her knees, then to her feet. Her bound hands and pounding head threatened her balance, but she managed to remain upright. Crouching low, she crept toward the exit. Every squelch of her boots in the wet mud made her wince. So long as the men kept talking, their voices might be enough to disguise the sounds of her movement, but if they turned...

She made it to the opening and faced west. With no idea where she was or which way to run for help, she might wind up lost in the desert with no food or water. But at least she'd be free of these men. And she wouldn't be buried alive.

She lurched forward.

Her boot slipped in the swiftly moving, inch-high water, and she tumbled forward. She threw her arms up to catch herself, but her bound wrists hampered her efforts. She managed to save her face, but her chest slammed onto the ground, driving the breath from her lungs.

When she could breathe again, she rose onto her elbows and glanced back.

Four pistol barrels were aimed straight at her.

The man who seemed to be their leader stepped forward and hauled her to her feet. "Chavarria, get me more rope." He dragged her back into the cave.

The leader jerked her down and reached for the hem of her skirt.

Panic squeezed her throat. She backpedaled until her back pressed against the cave wall.

He followed her with a sinister glare.

She kicked at his hands. "Leave me alone."

He snatched her ankles and held them with one huge hand. His other hand whipped out.

Pain stung her cheek and jaw, drawing tears to her eyes.

The short, muscular man with a small angular scar on his cheek and hard gray eyes brought the rope.

The leader, whose name she still didn't know, wrapped the cord tightly around her ankles.

One of the two men still guarding the entrance shouted, "I hear something."

The leader leapt to his feet, pistol drawn. "Arturo, you wait here." He rushed from the cave and crept eastward. Chavez and the other bandit followed him.

Arturo remained at the cave entrance. He watched his companions leave, then faced her with a grin that sent shivers down her back.

CHAPTER 35

The mud bridge collapsed beneath Gideon's boots. He plummeted to the ground, his head bouncing off the canyon wall as he went.

He lay still a moment, waiting for the air to return to his lungs. The pounding inside his head felt like a tiny bull trying to break free through his temples. He pressed the heels of his palms to his eyelids, pasting them with mud.

With a groan, he turned his hands over and tried using the backs of his fingers to remove the sludge. It didn't help.

Was there any part of his clothing not covered with mud? The inside of his shirt might be clean enough. He grabbed his collar and twisted so that the inside fabric faced outward. Craning his neck, he rubbed one eyelid and then the other. The job wasn't perfect, but he was finally clean enough to risk opening his eyes.

He found his hat and pulled it from the mud.

Something moved farther up the canyon.

Gideon flattened himself against the ground. He squinted through the pouring rain. A full moon occasionally slipped between the clouds, lighting his path, despite the tall walls of the canyon doing their best to block out the meager light.

He couldn't make out much. Just the dark silhouettes of two or more men making their way in his direction.

A flash of moonlight glinted off the barrel of the closest man's pistol.

Had they seen Gideon? He braced himself for the men to rush forward. Instead they continued creeping along the canyon.

Moving as slowly as he dared, he slithered backward on his stomach until he came to a small overhang. The ledge was barely a foot off the ground. He slid sideways, pressing himself against the slimy wall until he was sure the narrow mud shelf protected him from being spotted from above.

He drew his pistol and waited. His skull felt as if it would crack open from the building pressure and his stomach turned. He gritted his teeth. This was no time for a headache.

The bandits drew near.

He trained his sights on the man in front. Ignoring his pain in the past had ended in failure and tragedy, but this time, he had no choice. Biddie was counting on him.

God, for her sake, just this once, don't let me fail.

Four men passed by so close Gideon could have reached out and grabbed their legs.

One of them whispered, "What about the woman?"

"Tomás tied her up good. She ain't going nowhere," another hissed.

The man in front made an angry gesture, and the two fell silent.

Gideon held his breath and waited for them to round the next tight curve in the canyon. Then he slowly counted to thirty. When they didn't come back, he scooted out of his hiding place and rose to his feet.

He waited, gun at the ready.

Still, they didn't return.

If they made it to the end of the canyon, they'd find Clyve, Matthew, and the vaqueros, but the Rowland men were no fools. They'd have guards posted. Which meant they'd have advance notice of the bandits' approach.

Matthew might be injured, but he could still fire a gun, and Clyve plus the two vaqueros who'd followed them into the canyon would make any battle a more than even match. No need to worry about four well-armed men. Not when Biddie was out there somewhere, alone and defenseless.

Gideon pivoted to stare up the canyon in the direction the bandits had come from. He couldn't see anything moving. Where was Biddie?

～

*B*iddie rolled onto her hands and knees. With a shove, she made it to her feet just as Arturo entered the cave. The ropes around her ankles chafed through her stockings. She wobbled but managed to stay upright.

Arturo grinned. "You ain't going nowheres." He reached for her.

She hopped out of reach.

He easily caught up and snatched her bound wrists.

She jerked out of his hold and toppled into the cave wall.

He lunged for her.

She rolled away.

He was on top of her in a blink.

She twisted and shoved, trying to break free. He was too heavy.

Please, God, help me.

Arturo shifted, providing her with an opportunity. She kicked him hard between the legs.

He fell away from her with a howl.

She rolled onto her hands and knees, preparing to surge to her feet.

"You're going to pay for that." He grabbed her hair and thrust her to the ground at the back of the cave.

Her head smacked into the hardened mud. The throbbing in her skull doubled. She ignored the pain and sat up.

Arturo drew his gun and aimed at her.

She froze, not daring to breathe.

He flipped the pistol and brought the butt down on her head.

She screamed and her eyes slammed shut. Pain consumed her. She twisted to the side and retched into the mud. The world spun. Her body trembled. She collapsed to the ground, too weak to hold herself up. Tears spilled from the corners of her eyes as she took long, slow breaths.

A long time passed before the pain subsided enough for her to think clearly again. She couldn't give up. She had to escape.

She wiped her mouth with her sleeve and forced her eyes open. Pressure built in her throat, but she swallowed it down. She could do this.

Please, God, give me strength.

She pressed her palms against the muddy ground and rose until her back rested against the wall of the cave. The room wavered, and she closed her eyes, focusing on breathing slowly.

Where was Arturo?

Squinting, she searched the cave. He wasn't there. She looked through the entrance and spotted him at the mouth of the canyon. His back was to her as he watched for his comrades' return.

She tried to stand, but her legs gave out. As desperately as she wanted to leave, her body needed rest.

She watched Arturo, but he didn't seem to have noticed her movement. What sort of man chose the life of a bandit? Surely, not one with a happy story to tell. What had happened to him to turn him so evil? Had anyone ever shared the wonder of God's forgiveness and love with him? Mother always told the women who came to The Home that no sin was too great to be forgiven. Almost without thought, the words of Mother's favorite hymn emerged from Biddie's lips.

"'Amazing Grace, how sweet the sound, that saved a wretch like me...'"

~

ideon placed a hand against the canyon wall and focused on breathing. The pounding in his head was almost unbearable. The pain turned his stomach, threatening to up-heave the jerky he'd eaten in the saddle earlier that afternoon. He had no doubt that if it were daylight, his vision would be blurry. As it was, he could barely keep his eyes open. Still, he staggered on.

A scream ripped the air.

Biddie. They were hurting her.

He forced himself into a run.

Moments later, he tripped over a shin-high clump of mud and landed on his hands and knees in the inches of water now flowing along the canyon floor. His eyes closed. He didn't have time for this. He punched the ground. New pain spread through his knuckles and up his arm.

Nausea won the battle.

When his stomach was empty, he shoved to his feet and wiped his mouth with his sleeve. Battling the pain, he forced his eyelids open. They slammed shut. He tried again, but the effort caused him to heave, despite having nothing left to cast up. His legs trembled beneath him. He sagged against one wall of the narrow canyon.

This couldn't be happening. Not now. Biddie needed him. He would not give up.

Please, God, give me the strength I do not have.

Bracing himself against the canyon wall, he sloshed forward through the muddy water and up the canyon. With his eyes closed, he relied on the touch of his fingers and his sense of hearing to guide him. The wind traveling through the canyon brushed his cheeks. The pattering rain joined the faint gurgling of the water flowing past his boots. He slid his soles along the ground, wary of anything that might trip him again.

Long, agonizing minutes passed, and with each step, he begged God to take away his pain so that he could save Biddie.

Despite his prayers, the pounding in his head did not cease, nor did his stomach fully settle. But he did not fall. He kept going.

Until the wall stopped and he found himself grasping at air.

He sank to his knees before he fell entirely. Had he reached the end of the canyon?

He took three long breaths, then tried opening his eyes. He only managed a peek, but it was enough to tell him he'd reached a fork in the canyon.

Which way should he go?

He tried to reason it out, but his thoughts were growing murky. Ideas slipped by, too blurry for him to grab hold of. He yanked his hat off and gripped his hair. *Think, Gideon. Which way?*

The harder he tried to think, the more muddled his thoughts became.

Help me, God.

Then he heard something out of place. Was that a voice? The sound was like a murmur in the mud caves. Were the bandits talking?

He froze, focusing every ounce of his energy on that sound.

The faint noise wasn't speech. The pacing was more like a melody. Singing?

No. That didn't make sense. The bandits who'd passed him

had clearly been on alert. They wouldn't be singing. They'd be keeping watch. The noise had to be the wind playing tricks on him.

Except it didn't sound like the wind. It sounded like a woman's voice. But why would Biddie be singing? Surely, she was terrified. If she was singing, they must be forcing her. The notion that she was being forced to do anything made him want to punch something.

On the other hand, if she was singing, she was still alive. And there were much worse things they could be forcing her to do. Besides, the sound was an answer to his prayers. With a prayer of thanks, he followed the left split in the canyon, drawing closer to the murmur.

~

"*He* will my shield and portion be, as long as life endures.'" Biddie's throat tightened. Would her life endure this night? She wasn't ready to die. She had so much more to do, so much more to say. She'd only begun to heal the relationship with her sister and barely had a chance to speak with Preston. She wanted to see her parents again. She swallowed hard and closed her eyes.

Lord, please protect me. But if this night is to be my last, I thank You for the assurance of Your forgiveness and my place in heaven.

"'When we've been there ten thousand years—'"

"Ten thousand years is about how long you've been singing that song," Arturo shouted from the entrance. "If you're thinkin' to save my soul, you're too late. I done sold it years ago. So hush up." He spit in the dirt and turned back to watching the canyon.

A glob of mud the size of her palm fell from the ceiling of the cave. The once-narrow crack was now wide enough she could put her fingers into it if she chose. Water poured through the opening and puddled on the ground before trickling out through a fist-sized hole at the back of the cave. There, too, water dribbled in through a hairline crack that zig-zagged up from the top of the hole.

Chunks of mud broke free from this second crack, but instead of dribbling down with the water, they burst away from the wall as though struck by an unseen force.

What in the world?

She glanced at Arturo, but his attention was still fixed on the canyon. She turned back to the new crack just as more mud flakes flew off a hole that materialized at the top of the crack. Fingers emerged and tore the opening wider.

She gasped. Someone was trying to save her. It was the only explanation that made sense.

She glanced again at Arturo, but he paid her no mind. She turned back to the widening hole.

Gideon's face appeared, streaked with mud.

Her heart leapt to her throat. He'd come back for her. But how?

After a final glance at the oblivious bandit, she hobbled as quickly as she could to help Gideon dig through the mud.

As soon as the hole was large enough for her to fit through, Gideon reached for her.

She lifted her bound hands over his head to clasp his neck as his fingers gripped her waist.

"Hey!" Arturo drew his gun and started shooting as he ran toward the cave.

CHAPTER 36

*G*ideon yanked Biddie through the hole and thrust her behind him.

He drew his own gun and returned fire. He only got off two shots before the ceiling of the cave collapsed, blocking the hole he'd just pulled Biddie through. He listened, but no more shots rang out. No sound came from the other side of the mud at all.

He faced Biddie. "Are you alright?" He holstered his pistol and pulled his knife from its sheath.

"Yes." She held up her wrists, and he cut the rope binding them. "How did you find me?"

He sank to his knees and his vision narrowed. He waited for it to clear, then set her ankles free.

She knelt in front of him. "How did you even know I was in trouble?"

He clasped her shoulders and tried to make out her expression in the darkness. "Are you sure you're all right? They didn't hurt you? I heard you scream."

"Well, I do have many bumps and bruises, and my head hurts terribly, but I'll be all right."

"Then they didn't..." He hesitated, searching for a delicate way to express his concern. "They didn't hurt you in any *other* way?"

She cupped his cheek. "I promise you, I'm fine."

He pressed his forehead to hers. "Thank you, Lord." His head ached with the thunder of a thousand stampeding cattle, and his stomach swirled, though it had nothing left to give up. He desperately wanted to lie down and fall asleep, but they weren't safe yet.

The other bandits could return at any moment. Finding Biddie and Gideon in the canyon that ran behind the cave would be difficult but not impossible. "I need to get you out of here."

He took her hand and stood. Too fast. His head spun, and his vision narrowed to pinpricks of faded black. Sheer force of will kept him from passing out, but his knees refused to hold him. He sank to the ground.

"Gideon!" Biddie knelt before him. "What's wrong? Were you shot?" Her fingers probed his scalp, ran down his neck, and traced his arms. "Where are you hurt?" Her hands moved to his torso.

"I'm fine." He caught her wrists. "It's just another headache."

She winced at his touch and sucked air through her teeth.

He immediately released her. "I'm so sorry. I should have realized the ropes burned you. We need to get you back so we can treat your wounds."

"Can you walk? Where's your horse?"

❧

*B*iddie pressed her lips against a whimper. She was worn clean through. The butt of Arturo's pistol had left an egg-sized lump on her head that throbbed with every heartbeat. Her skin burned where the ropes had rubbed at her wrists and ankles. And it seemed every other part of her body had taken a beating during her long ride stretched across the bandit's horse.

In truth, she wanted nothing more than to sit down, have a good cry, and go to sleep. Right there on the desert floor. But she could not give in to the desire. If Gideon discovered how hurt she truly was, he'd do something foolish like try and carry her when he could barely remain upright himself.

Gideon stepped across a wide crack in the mud hills, then turned back to assist her. She accepted his hand and jumped across.

Rather than retrace their steps through the winding canyon and risk encountering the returning bandits, Gideon had led them up a steep slope to the top of the mud hills. He'd warned her the choice was risky, explaining how Clyve's father had been injured. Still, they both agreed they preferred the risk of a mudslide over an encounter with three or more armed bandits. Gideon was good with his pistol, but with his migraine he could barely see to walk. There was no way he could aim well. With Biddie unarmed they would be outnumbered.

At least the rain had moved on, allowing the full moon to light their way. Then again, being able to see their path also meant it was easier for others to spot Biddie and Gideon on these barren peaks. For that reason, they were taking a circuitous route to rejoin the posse.

Biddie studied the uneven ground, careful to step in Gideon's footprints. "Are you certain we're still headed the right direction?"

"I've been using the moon's position to guide us. We should be about halfway there." Gideon's foot caught and he stumbled forward. He teetered at the edge of another canyon.

She fisted the back of his shirt in both hands and yanked backward. Momentum carried them both to the ground. She couldn't stop her cry of pain as his back crashed into her bruised ribs.

He immediately rolled off of her and tried to raise up on one elbow but fell flat on the ground.

Lightning pain shot from the bump on her head and spread throughout her skull. Her chest spasmed and she fought for air.

"Are you—" His eyes slammed shut with a moan. Then his lips pressed tight and his cheeks bulged.

More than a minute passed before either of them said anything more. Finally, she said, "I'm all right, but what about you?"

"Fine." He'd pushed the word through gritted teeth. Clearly, the stubborn man was not fine.

She brushed a muddy lock of hair from her forehead and stared up at the stars. "Actually, I could use a rest. Can we just lie here for a few minutes?"

"Sure."

No sooner had the word left his mouth than distant gunfire shattered the stillness of the night.

They both bolted upright. "That's coming from the east. Isn't that where you said Clyve and the others were camping?"

Gideon tried to answer but was overcome with dry heaves.

She raised a trembling hand to rub his back.

The distant fighting continued.

She felt utterly helpless. Part of her wanted to run from the gunfire. The other part wanted to charge in and help the men who'd risked their lives to save her. But even if she could find the strength to run, she had no weapon to aid in the battle.

Lord, help me know what to do. As if in answer, she remembered a verse she'd been made to memorize as a child.

Yea, though I walk through the valley of the shadow of death, I will fear no evil; for thou art with me.

She might be unable to join the fight physically, but she could pray.

By the time Gideon had stopped heaving, the night was once again silent.

She said a final prayer for the well-being of the Rowlands and their men, then met Gideon's gaze. "What do you think happened?"

Gideon pressed two palms to the ground and shoved onto his knees. Slowly, he pulled one booted foot beneath him and stood. He wobbled a bit and she hurried to steady him. His bleary eyes met hers with a look of grim determination. "Only one way to find out."

CHAPTER 37

*G*ideon made it fifty feet before his body defeated his will. When he sank to the ground yet again, Biddie suggested they take a nap before continuing. He was too weak to argue.

After what seemed like a moment but had to have been hours, he awoke to the pale gray of a coming dawn. Something soft and warm rested on his chest.

Biddie.

Her golden locks, now coated in mud, were splayed across his chest. Her closeness created a longing in him never to let her go.

Still asleep, she snuggled deeper into the crook of his arm.

Without thinking, he tightened his hold on her, the desire to keep her close irresistible.

She gave a small jump and her head came up. Wide sky-blue eyes met his.

"Even covered in mud, you're the prettiest thing I've ever seen." He hadn't meant to voice his thoughts, but he couldn't regret them. Not when they brought such a beautiful smile to her face.

A blush covered her pale cheeks. Cheeks that he was just noticing were mottled with bruises. He wanted to beat the stuffing out of every single bandit.

Biddie's smile vanished. "What's wrong?"

"I thought you said you were all right?"

She pushed away from him and sat up. "I am. Mostly."

He sat up and pointed at her. "There's marks all over your face."

"I thought you just said I was pretty."

"You are. Don't change the subject."

"Shouldn't we get going?" She turned toward the rising sun, revealing a patch of dried blood matted in her hair. "Clyve and the others might need our help."

He caught her chin and gently turned her face toward his. "What happened to your head?"

"Arturo hit me with the butt of his pistol."

Gideon prayed that the man had been caught in the cave-in because if he were still alive, Gideon was going to kill him. A small voice warned that maybe that wasn't something he should be praying for, but he was too furious to pay it heed. "Does it hurt?"

"Not anymore."

Still holding her gaze, he lifted one brow.

"All right, it hurts a little. But nothing like last night. I'll be fine, I promise. But what about your headache?"

"It's gone." Which was a relief considering he had a bunch of bandits to hunt down. First, though, they needed to check on Clyve, Matthew, and the vaqueros. "Are you up for a long walk?" He stood and offered his hand.

She accepted his assistance with a nod. "Let's go."

∽

*B*iddie paced the yard in front of the stone house. "Where are they?"

Two long days had passed since she and Gideon had discovered Ginny tending two wounded vaqueros at the Rowlands' campsite. It seemed Preston and Ginny's timely arrival hours earlier set the bandits on the run. Preston, Clyve, Matthew and the unwounded vaqueros had given chase.

Biddie still didn't understand why Gideon had insisted on joining the pursuit. As he mounted Legend, he'd said something about ensuring justice, owing Clyve, and trusting God. Then he rode off in a cloud of dust before she could protest.

She and Ginny had delivered the injured men to the care of the Rowlands' cook and brought Lucy back to Lupine Valley Ranch.

Lucy exited the house. "You should be resting."

"How can I rest, not knowing if the men are dead or alive?" Biddie had slept through most of the first day but had woken this morning anxious for the men's return. Restless, she had bathed, changed into fresh clothes, and eaten as much as she could stomach. She and Lucy had even baked bread and set a stew to simmering, ready to welcome the posse.

Except the men still hadn't come back.

Biddie snatched her rifle from where it had been leaning against the house. "I'm going to stand guard with Ginny."

Lucy made a sound of exasperation but didn't try to stop her.

Biddie joined her sister on the valley's northern rim. "Any sign of them?"

"Not yet, but I'm sure they'll be back soon."

Biddie studied the rolling range of foothills hiding the desert's narrow canyons and sandy washes from their view. Here and there, a bird fluttered and shrubs bent with the wind, but there was no sign of human life. "You sound so confident."

Ginny smirked. "Because I am."

"Why?"

"Because Preston is with them. Our brother is the best shot in the country. If he gets those bandits in his sights, they're as good as dead."

Biddie shivered. Of course, the bandits needed to be stopped, and it was unlikely they could be arrested without a fight, but she didn't like the image of her brother shooting people. Which was admittedly nonsensical being that he fought in the war. She just hadn't given the idea much thought before.

Ginny pointed. "Here they come."

Biddie looked to where Ginny indicated. Several riders were making their way through the hills. The men's shoulders sagged, but Biddie's heart lifted at the sight of Gideon among them. Preston was there too.

She faced Ginny. "Make sure they come to the yard for supper. I'm going to check that everything is ready."

By the time the posse reached the yard in front of the stone house, Biddie had readied plates full of stew and slices of bread. The weary men gratefully accepted and found places about the yard to settle themselves and eat.

They had pursued the bandits for two days and twice caught sight of them, but never within rifle range. Eventually, the bandits seemed to vanish, and with the posse's supplies running low and energy even lower, the men were forced to turn back.

On the return, they'd retrieved Arturo's body from where it had been half buried by the collapsed cave. They'd wrapped his corpse in a blanket and strapped him to a horse so they could turn him in to the law.

Biddie served Matthew a second helping of stew. "I'm glad to see you looking so well. Gideon said you'd injured yourself in a fall."

Matthew waved a dismissive hand. "Ah, I've had worse injuries. Nothing to fret over."

One of the vaqueros jabbed his spoon at the dead body. "Do you think he's got a price on him?"

Clyve shrugged. "It's possible, but I don't recognize him from any of the posters I've seen. Do you?"

The men all shook their heads.

Ginny strode over to the body and lifted the blanket covering his face. Her expression hardened and she let the blanket fall again. "He's one of them that attacked the ranch and killed Oliver last spring."

Matthew's eyebrows rose. "Are you sure about that?"

Ginny checked the load in her rifle. "As sure as I am that this is my ranch."

Clyve whistled and a heavy silence settled over the group.

A few minutes later, Gideon set his plate aside and came to stand before Biddie. "Can I have a word in private?"

She tried to read his expression but couldn't guess what he was thinking. "Of course." She handed the almost-empty stew pot and ladle to Lucy.

He silently led her to the valley's rim before stopping to face her. "Do you know where we are?"

She could've answered that they were on Ginny's ranch, but she sensed he meant something more specific. She considered their surroundings. "Isn't this where I found you spying on us?"

He smiled, and her heart soared with hope as he took her hands. "It's also where I first held you in my arms. I knew there was something special about you from that very first moment."

She couldn't contain her chuckle. "Are you saying I have a talent for jabbing men in the ribs and kicking their shins?"

He joined in her laughter. "Not exactly. As much as I wanted you to go back to the city, I couldn't help admiring a woman brave enough to travel to an unknown land and risk her life to help her sister. And I still think it was a foolish thing to do, but—"

She tried to pull free of his hold, but he refused to let go.

His thumb brushed the back of her hand. "*But* I'm so grateful you chose to stay."

She stilled and searched his eyes for the truth. "You are?"

"It gave me a chance to see your kindness, generosity, and incredible perseverance. These past few months, you've worked harder than most men I know and rarely complained. Not to mention, your talent for baking delicious food."

Warmth filled her cheeks and spread down to her toes.

"But the thing I love most about you is your amazing ability to forgive and your determination to believe the best about people. You see past their flaws and encourage them to do better, be better." He tugged her closer. "You believed in me when I didn't believe in myself. You've seen me at my worst and still didn't give up hope. I thought God had given up on me, so I wanted to give up on myself. But you wouldn't let me."

She extracted one hand and placed it against his cheek. "God doesn't give up on us, and He hasn't given up on you."

He smiled. "I know that now." His expression sobered. "But my condition hasn't changed. I'm still not the man I once was. And you deserve someone who can take care of you, not someone you have to take care of."

She opened her mouth to protest, but he placed a finger against her lips.

"But if you'll do me the honor of becoming my wife, I'll do my best to make you happy and give you everything I have for the rest of my life."

In answer, she wrapped her arms around his neck and pressed her lips to his.

CHAPTER 38

*B*iddie nibbled her bottom lip as she rode up the oak-lined lane leading to Grand Valley Ranch. How would Father react to her engagement to a man he'd never met?

She glanced at Gideon riding on her left, and he offered a reassuring smile. Surely, Father would approve once he got to know Gideon. How could he not?

Riding at Biddie's right, Lucy exclaimed, "This place is as beautiful as you've always said it was."

Biddie's family had been invited to visit the Stevens's ranch a handful of times over the years. Upon her return home, Biddie had always struggled to describe for Lucy the beautiful serenity of the place. Words never seemed to do justice to the welcoming ranch with its two homes, white schoolhouse, and large barn surrounded by corrals, chaparral-covered hillsides, and seemingly endless fields dotted by sheep.

Biddie led them past the original adobe house to the large

white clapboard residence behind it. The structure had been expanded many times to accommodate the growing Stevens family, so that it was now twice the size of the original adobe home.

Gideon dismounted and came around to help her off her horse. Once she was on the ground, he moved to assist Lucy as well, but her quiet friend had already dismounted. He turned back to Biddie. "Are you ready?"

She forced a nod. As eager as she was to see Father again, so much depended on this introduction.

Gideon took her hand, and they ascended the stairs to the wide porch together.

Before they could knock, the door flung open and Mother rushed forward. "Biddie!" She wrapped her arms around Biddie and squeezed tight. Mother would be horrified to know how much the hug pained Biddie's bruised ribs, so she smothered her gasp of pain in Mother's shoulder.

Mother grasped Biddie's shoulders and leaned back to look at her. "What's happened to your face?"

"It's a long story. But what are you doing here? Who's looking after The Home?"

"Eliza and Daniel returned from Boston last week, and I decided I'd been separated from your father long enough. I arrived only yesterday." Mother turned toward Gideon and Lucy. "Lucy, it's good to see you looking well, if rather dusty. But who's this young man?"

Biddie glanced at Gideon. "Mother, allow me to introduce Mr. Gideon Swift. He's saved my life on more than one occasion, and with your and Father's permission, I plan to marry him."

Mother's face paled. "Saved your life? Marry him? What are you talking about?"

Father's voice called from inside. "For goodness' sake,

Cecilia, let them come in so that we may discuss matters together."

Mother stepped back and waved them in.

Father sat sideways on a settee in the center of the room, both legs stretched across the cushion. His right trouser leg had been cut short above the cast protecting his injury. With a wide grin, he lifted his arms toward Biddie.

She rushed forward to give him a hug. "How I've missed you. How are you feeling?"

He released her with a sigh. "Not half as much as I've missed and worried about you. And don't worry about this." He patted his cast. "The doctor says it can come off next week."

Mother's eyes narrowed. "So long as you behave yourself." She shook her head. "I'm glad you've come. He's been so worried about you, he's been threatening to try riding again."

Father lifted his chin. "As if you weren't just as worried."

"Of course, I was worried, but you reinjuring yourself wouldn't do anyone any good. In any case, she's here now." Mother gestured to the chairs arranged opposite the settee. "Why don't the three of you take a seat while I fetch us some tea?"

Gideon waited for Lucy and Biddie to be seated before taking his own seat beside Biddie.

Father eyed Gideon. "Of course, we must discuss this matter of you marrying our daughter, but first"—Father looked at Biddie —"I'd like to hear what's happened since your last letter. Judging by the yellowed bruising on your face, I'm not going to be pleased."

By the time Biddy had finished recounting recent events, everyone had finished their tea.

Father adjusted his glasses and studied Gideon. "It seems I owe you a debt of gratitude for keeping my daughter and her friend safe. However, I cannot say I am pleased that you proposed marriage without first seeking my approval."

Gideon shifted in his chair. "I understand. My only defense is that I love your daughter so much, I found the desire to make her my wife irresistible. However, I assure you that in every other way, I have behaved as a gentleman."

Mother leaned forward. "But Biddie, what about your bakery? You've been talking about it for years, and you were so excited when Mr. Green agreed to invest in your endeavor."

Father nodded, his eyes still on Gideon. "Didn't Biddie say you're a rancher? How does that work with the episodes Biddie has described? Not much ranch land available near San Francisco, and what there is demands a high price. How do you propose to care for my daughter? Where do you plan to live?"

Biddie looked at Gideon. He'd tried to broach the subject during their journey here, but she'd evaded his questions. She'd been afraid the discussion would end with the conclusion that there was no practical way for them to blend their lives. Her dreams lay in the city, his in the country. Still, her heart protested that there must be a way.

Gideon cleared his throat. "The headaches don't happen every day, and I've learned not to push myself when they're happening unless it's a life or death situation. Biddie and I haven't had a chance to discuss this, but I'm not quite confident enough to take on running my own ranch. I spoke to Ginny before we left, and she's agreed to keep me on as a hand for the time being. I'm hoping that I'll eventually find some land near Campo. Most of the land west of there has been claimed, but I've heard there are still a few good pieces to be had within a day's ride east of the Gaskill's' store. The settlement is just a speck compared to San Francisco, but the folks around there already have a fondness for Biddie's baking. And it will keep her close to Ginny and Preston, which I think is important to her."

Mother clasped her hands together. "That sounds like a wonderful plan."

Biddie gaped at them both. When had Gideon spoken with Ginny? And how could Mother think baking for a tiny country store was a wonderful idea? "But there are no wealthy investors in Campo."

Father's brow furrowed. "I thought you wrote in one of your letters that you were using your sister's oven to do your baking? If you're living on her ranch, can't you continue doing that?"

Gideon nodded. "I'm sure she will, and I'll buy whatever you need for our new home as soon as I can afford it."

Mother patted Father's shoulder. "Couldn't we gift them an oven as our wedding gift?"

"Money is a bit tight with most of our savings invested with Mr. Green and in your sister's ranch, but I'm sure we can figure something out."

Biddie barely heard Father's response as she stared at Mother. "But no one of any consequence will ever know about my baking if I only sell my goods through the Gaskill's' store."

It was Mother's turn to stare at Biddie in surprise. "Since when has social status meant a thing to you?"

Biddie frowned. "It doesn't, but you've always remarked on how many doors people with money and good social standing can open for a charity. I know you gave up your own standing with society to raise me. I'd hoped that establishing a sought-after bakery would allow me to return some of what you've lost."

Mother crossed the room to kneel before Biddie and place her hands on Biddie's cheeks. "My sweet Biddie. Is that what you thought? Taking you in cost me absolutely nothing I cared about. And I wouldn't trade having you as my daughter for all the money and social status in the world. You, your brother, and your father are my greatest blessings. Although I miss your mama terribly, I treasure the gift she gave, entrusting me with raising you. Biddie, you are a priceless gift. You owe us nothing. We are grateful to call you our daughter."

Tears shimmered in Mother's eyes, and streamed down Biddie's cheeks. She bent and hugged Mother. Father caught Biddie's eye and nodded his agreement with Mother's words. Biddie looked at Lucy and then Gideon. Love glowed in the eyes of everyone around her.

Biddie had hoped her baking and hard work would bring joy to her family. How foolish the thought now seemed. True joy came from true love, and true love couldn't be earned. It was a gift. One she planned to cherish for the rest of her life.

Did you enjoy this book? We hope so!
Would you take a quick minute to leave a review where you purchased the book?
It doesn't have to be long. Just a sentence or two telling what you liked about the story!

Receive a FREE ebook and get updates when new Wild Heart books release: https://wildheartbooks.org/newsletter

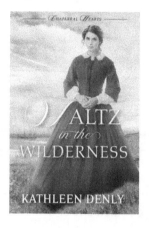

Book 2: Waltz in the Wilderness

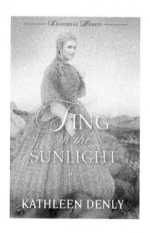

Book 2: Sing in the Sunlight

Book 3: Harmony on the Horizon

~

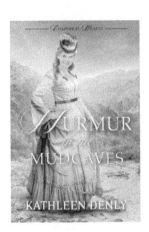

Book 4: Murmur in the Mud Caves

FROM THE AUTHOR

Dear Reader,

Thank you for reading this story. I hope you found Biddie and Gideon's journey entertaining, encouraging, and inspiring. Despite debilitating injuries that arose halfway through the writing of this novel, I had a lot of fun crafting the characters and adventures within these pages. The research was especially fun, because it included speaking with local historical experts and exploring the historically and geographically significant locations mentioned in this novel.

The wagon accident and the family who assisted the injured parties were inspired by a true event described on page 37 of *Memories of the Early Settlements, Dulzura, Potrero, and Campo* by Ella McCain. However, I used fictional names for those involved. The name of the mother, Arvilla Leach, came from the maiden name of one of the local historical experts I interviewed. (By the way, if you have the opportunity, I highly recommend a trip to the Gaskill Stone Store Museum in Campo, California, which is where I met and interviewed this delightful woman who has deep roots in the area's history.

Kathleen's Readers' Club members are able to view this interview in my KRC Freebie Library.)

The fledgling town of Campo and the surrounding region were described with as much historical accuracy as possible. The mountain valley that held my fictional Lupine Valley Ranch and the route the posse took in pursuit of the bandits were both inspired by actual locations. Though it seems odd that a dessert valley would provide the necessities for a successful cattle ranch, there were many cattle ranches which thrived in the region between Campo, California and what is known today as Jacumba Hot Springs. When this region was first settled by westerners, it was not as arid as it appears today. In fact, the area more closely resembled the chaparral biome seen today in areas west of this region. There was even an oak grove quickly harvested by settlers needing wood for their homes. However the majority of homes were built with imported wood, adobe bricks, and stone. Both the boulder cave and the stone house built on Lupine Valley Ranch are inspired by actual dwellings, historical and present.

Each detailed account of bandit attacks was inspired by the true historical events of 1873. The raid on Firebaugh's Ferry, for example, is a true attack carried out by the Tiburcio Vasquez gang—one of the most infamous in California's history. Members of this gang would go on to terrorize Central and Southern California for years. My fictional bandits are inspired by these notorious men.

Although, I found no evidence that the Vasquez gang ever ventured into the mud canyons or caves, criminals were known to frequent this area and the badlands south of it. My descriptions of these locations are based on my own explorations and research into their history.

I hope you've enjoyed learning more about the true history behind this fictional story. I'd love to share more history tidbits, books news, and giveaways with you via my Kathleen's Readers'

Club. You can sign up on my website at www.Kathleen-Denly.com.

And in case you're wondering, Lucy Arlidge and Preston Baker will continue their adventures in book six of my Chaparral Hearts series, *Shoot at the Sunset*.

Kathleen Denly

ABOUT THE AUTHOR

Kathleen Denly lives in sunny California with her loving husband, four young children, one dog, and eight cats. As a member of the adoption and foster community, children in need are a cause dear to her heart and she finds they make frequent appearances in her stories. When she isn't writing, researching, or caring for children, Kathleen spends her time reading, visiting historical sites, hiking, and crafting.

QUESTIONS FOR DISCUSSION

Gideon, Biddie, and Ginny, each struggle to understand their worth.

- What worldly things skewed each character's perception of their own value?
- What does the Bible say we should base our value on?
- How do you determine your worth?

Gideon's war wounds stole major parts of his identity.

- What roles do you consider part of your identity? (e.g. wife, mother, teacher, worship leader, etc.)
- If you woke up tomorrow unable to perform the tasks necessary for any of these roles, how do you think you might react?

Ginny struggles to accept help from anyone.

- Why do you think this is?

- Have you ever struggled to accept someone's help?
- Do you find it easier to be the giver or the receiver?
- Have you ever felt that someone was pressuring you to be someone other than yourself?

Biddie finds joy and purpose in her baking talents.

- Where do you find joy?
- What do you view as your purpose in life?
- What does the Bible say about these topics?

While working on the ranch, Biddie and Lucy take on challenges far outside their normal life experience, not to mention living in a place that is completely opposite to what they're used to.

- What do you think of how they handled that situation?
- Have you ever experienced such a drastic life change?
- What do you think of Ginny's demand that the others stay out of the mine? What do you think of Lucy's choice to disobey that command?
- Which scene caused the strongest emotional reaction in you?
- If you had to live in 1873 and must choose between living in San Francisco or the desert east of Campo, which would you pick and why? What do you see as the pros and cons to each location during that time period?

If you could have a conversation with just one character from this novel, who would you talk to?

Which part of this novel surprised you the most?

What do you think about the ending of this novel?

Which character did you relate to the most?

What most appeals to you about the book's cover?

Which of the Chaparral Hearts novels is your favorite and why?

Did you know that Kathleen Denly is available for live book club discussions? (No charge!) Email her for details at: WriteKathleenDenly@gmail.com.

Want more?

If you love historical romance, check out the other Wild Heart books!

Marisol ~ Spanish Rose by Elva Cobb Martin

Escaping to the New World is her only option...Rescuing her will wrap the chains of the Inquisition around his neck.

Marisol Valentin flees Spain after murdering the nobleman who molested her. She ends up for sale on the indentured servants' block at Charles Town harbor—dirty, angry, and with child. Her hopes are shattered, but she must find a refuge for herself and the child she carries. Can this new land offer her the grace, love, and security she craves? Or must she escape again to her only living relative in Cartagena?

Captain Ethan Becket, once a Charles Town minister, now sails the seas as a privateer, grieving his deceased wife. But when he takes captive a ship full of indentured servants, he's intrigued by the woman whose manners seem much more refined than the average Spanish serving girl. Perfect to become governess for his young son. But when he sets out on a quest to find his captured sister, said to be in Cartagena, little does he expect his new Spanish governess to stow away on his ship with her six-month-old son. Yet her offer of help to free his sister is too tempting to pass up. And her beauty, both inside and out, is too attractive for his heart to protect itself against—until he learns she is a wanted murderess.

As their paths intertwine on a journey filled with danger, intrigue, and romance, only love and the grace of God can overcome the past and ignite a new beginning for Marisol and Ethan.

~

Rocky Mountain Redemption by Lisa J. Flickinger

A Rocky Mountain logging camp may be just the place to find herself.

To escape the devastation caused by the breaking of her wedding engagement, Isabelle Franklin joins her aunt in the Rocky Mountains to feed a camp of lumberjacks cutting on the slopes of Cougar Ridge. If only she could out run the lingering nightmares.

Charles Bailey, camp foreman and Stony Creek's itinerant pastor, develops a reputation to match his new nickname — Preach. However, an inner battle ensues when the details of his rough history threaten to overcome the beliefs of his young faith.

Amid the hazards of camp life, the unlikely friendship growing between the two surprises Isabelle. She's drawn to Preach's brute strength and gentle nature as he leads the ragtag crew toiling for Pollitt's Lumber. But when the ghosts from her past return to haunt her, the choices she will make change the course of her life forever—and that of the man she's come to love.

∾

Lone Star Ranger by Renae Brumbaugh Green

Elizabeth Covington will get her man.

And she has just a week to prove her brother isn't the murderer Texas Ranger Rett Smith accuses him of being. She'll show the good-looking lawman he's wrong, even if it means setting out on a risky race across Texas to catch the real killer.

Rett doesn't want to convict an innocent man. But he can't let the Boston beauty sway his senses to set a guilty man free. When Elizabeth follows him on a dangerous trek, the Ranger vows to keep her safe. But who will protect him from the woman whose conviction and courage leave him doubting everything—even his heart?

CPSIA information can be obtained
at www.ICGtesting.com
Printed in the USA
JSHW012025220323
39340JS00009B/164